On the Edge of Memories

The Random Collection

Paul John Hausleben

Cover Photo, All Photos, and Cover Concept by Paul John Hausleben
Jigsaw Puzzle Design by Paul John Hausleben
Cover Model: Ms. Alejandra Lopez

Published by God Bless the Keg Publishing
Somewhere, U.S.A.

ISBN: 978-0-9906979-9-2

Dedication

To all the ghosts

Contents

Acknowledgements

Thank you, as always, to Harry M. Rogers Junior and to my family and friends. Thank you to Ms. Alejandra Lopez for enduring my incessant fiddling during the photo shoot for cover shot for this book. I would also like to thank those ghosts who continually haunt me with the inspiration that never seems to leave me alone. At times, you are a bit of a pain in my ass, but I guess without your haunts, then this life just would not be quite as much fun as it is. Someday, I will outrun all of your sorry asses and the words will stop writing. Someday.

"I write to occupy the empty house that I live in.
To chase away the ghosts who dwell in all the corners.
The ghosts who float everywhere I look.
That is why I write."

Paul John Hausleben

01 June 2017

In Memorial

Of

Paul William Hausleben

I can never thank you for everything that you taught and gave to me, but I can thank you for being my father. To me, in my mind, that sums it all up.

Paul John Hausleben

On the Edge of Memories

The Random Collection

The Revenge of the Ducks

Doctor Salami's Magic Elixir

Experience Counts

Under the Pomp and Splendor

The Great Beach Adventure

One White Duck Left on the Wall

No Boiler Required

I Write

Until the End of All Time

Preface from the Author

This collection of stories has a very appropriate title. Each one of them has parts and pieces of my own memories and experiences embedded within the story lines. The stories consist of random experiences of my own life from the edge of my own memories.

Short stories, novellas, and novelettes are my favorite type of story to write, and they are, in my opinion, where I thrive the best amongst the pages with my greatest inspiration.

This book, to date, is my most eclectic and unusual collection of stories. Some are romantic, some are religious, some are silly, some are hilarious, yet there remains a common thread between them. They are all from my own heart. I must say that composing and writing a collection of stories, without any central theme or specific subject, was certainly an enjoyable project.

When it all boils down, a little fun and being different, well now, that is the best part of life. I must say that so far, in my own life, it has treated me rather well.

I hope you enjoy reading this collection of stories as much as I have enjoyed the experience of writing them. Thank you for reading them.

Paul John Hausleben

01 June 2017

Prologue

I steal a quick glance at my wristwatch. Sometimes, I write with it on, but as of late, especially on the weekends, I do not wear it. I wore it tonight. I think that was a mistake because time means nothing when I am rolling in the flow with ideas. Eight o'clock, P.M. It is still Saturday night. It is early.

Good. I can finish this story.

It has been a long day. I began writing at about 5:00 A.M. this morning, but as I mentioned, time means nothing when the flow is rolling.

A quick pause.

Do I really want Julie to react in that manner? Pace the floor. Back and forth about ten or fifteen times. Pop the ear buds in and I can give a listen to a little E.L.O.

Jeff has the answer. Nice. A sip of beer. Time to sit back down and finish this story.

C'mon, Hausleben, get your brain in gear. A few words, a sputter, and then another roll of a few paragraphs. I sit back in my chair, fold my arms across my chest, and reread the last few paragraphs. A hint of a smile. It is coming together now.

Another quick glance at the watch and it is now 10:00 P.M.

Shit, this is just not going to work. No distractions allowed, and tracking time is a major distraction.

It is time to ditch the watch. As I said, time means nothing when you are in the flow.

Nothing at all.

The Revenge of the Ducks

It was a most unusual time for me to be thinking of summer vacations. It was cold, snowy, and the wind was whipping the snowdrifts outside our house and piling the snow up alongside the house in large drifts and piles. When I heard the wind blowing fiercely outside and the tinkle of snow and ice pellets tickling the windows; I stood up from my chair, parted the curtain and peered out into the weather. I sometimes wondered why my mind wandered so much and it amazed me at how often, such vastly different instances created a memory or two to flood my mind.

It was mid-January, and I was working rather unproductively on a Bible dissertation and opinion, in which a peer asked me to comment on, and write a few weeks earlier. There I was, working at my little desk in the office of our home, and now, I found myself staring out into a northern New Jersey snowstorm.

The essay was not going so well. My mind was restless and not focused on the subject that I needed to concentrate on this afternoon. In an effort to break up the work, I flipped on the radio in my office, and tuned the dial to a station that played some older progressive and classic rock that I enjoyed.

The radio announcer complained loudly of the weather, gave a quick synopsis of the weather predictions and then he commented of how he, "Could not wait for the summer!" He expressed his strong desire to head to his second home along the Jersey shore and spend his spare time there.

I loved the winter, and I loved the snow, and I certainly preferred the winter to summer heat and the wretched humidity. However, I could not help but chuckle at the radio announcer's comments. Suddenly, my mind became flooded with a memory of summer. As I looked out upon a beautifully incessant and relentless snowfall, I strangely found myself on the boardwalk at the New Jersey shore, on a family summer vacation of quite a few years earlier.

While recalling an incredibly hot and humid day on the Jersey shore and a memorable adventure on an amusement park ride, I mumbled under my breath the classic line that all stalwart Jersey shore dwellers can easily recite by memory, "Watch the tramcar, please! BEEP! BEEP! BEEP! Watch the tramcar, please! BEEP! BEEP! BEEP!"

"I want an ice cream cone with three scoops, dear Father!"

"Me, too! I want one of those cones that the ice cream goes up really high into the air and you lick it from the top down to the cone! Then you bite and chomp down the crunchy cone! Please, please, please!"

Our two children, Paul William Henson, and Heather Sarah Henson, both stood on the boardwalk at Whippywood Beach, New Jersey and nodded their heads in unison, until I thought perhaps, they would topple over from dizziness. They had inherited the nodding gene from the Hobnobber side of the family. Luckily, they had also inherited their extraordinarily good looks from their mother's side, and not from me. My lovely wife, Binky Hobnobber Henson, stood by them nodding her head slightly in agreement over the ice-cream cone request. Her long blonde hair flowed around her as she shook her head, and her smile was a mile wide. Her beauty was extraordinary, standing there in a pair of tight dungarees and a summer blouse, which showed off her fabulous figure and she attracted quite a few looks from passing men, jealous of my good fortune at having such a lovely woman for a wife. Now, what she saw in me, well, I never could actually figure out.

"Okay, I guess, I can go over there to that stand and get them there. . .." I trailed off my answer when I spotted all three of them, now shaking their heads in disagreement at my selection of the closest ice cream stand, which I currently pointed towards and I had selected.

"Not over there, eh?"

"No, of course not, dear Paul! Before we left home, I had researched into which ice cream would be the best for the children to consume on such a hot day. That horrible ice cream is loaded with air and excess sugar. *Everyone* knows that it will melt right away at this temperature and that brand of ice cream is poison to your inners! You will need to walk down the boardwalk just a little distance to the frozen orange custard cone stand. At least that ice cream cone has a solid frozen top, some fruit juice, some small quantities of nutritional value, and it will not melt right away," Binky explained to me, all the reasons that my logical, yet, random selections of ice cream cones from the ice cream stand that was about ten feet in front of us, was profoundly incorrect.

When she finished her explanation, as she often does, when she has conducted proper and in-depth research into a subject, she folded her arms across her chest, while fluffing her hair over her shoulders. Then, all three of them entered into another round of intense head nods, as the children agreed with their mother's recent research into the properties of ice cream cones on a hot summer day. Upon completion of the affirmative nodding, they all zoomed in for an intense stare and waited for my answer. Now, other people found my wife's incessant research and checking into every aspect of life (even ice cream cones) to be a bit unusual. However, I found it to be just one of the many reasons why I loved her so much!

Love is blind.

I proved over the years to be a glutton for punishment.

"You want me to go all the way down there on the other end of the boardwalk, to the Big Bob's frozen custard stand? For kinda, sorta, the same ice cream cones that I could buy ten feet away from us? I guess you and the kids are going to stay here?"

"That is indeed correct, dear number twenty-seven. Big Bob's is the best and we only consume the best ice cream. Besides, we need to organize the bathing bags, sand toys, and towels while you are gone. The children can dry off now too. We will spend the rest of the day here on the boardwalk before we return to the hotel. Frankly, I am a bit surprised that you would even consider that particular ice cream. You can see that no one is at that horrible ice cream stand for the same reasons!"

I turned, stared at the ice cream stand that I had first selected (let me emphasize the point that the stand that was only ten-feet away from us) and sure enough, there was no one in line, and a bored looking counter attendant stared out at the boardwalk dreaming of better days, or better ice cream. The counter attendant, in between checking out the women in bathing suits, played a game of solitaire in order to pass the time. No doubt, because of my logical choice, my new classification was that of an ice cream doofus.

"Well, mostly because it is right there in front of us and the temperature is almost one hundred. . .." My wife, of course, cut off my efforts at a meager and futile defense.

"Off you go! Here is some money. Two large size cones, twenty-seven! You could take the tramcar, dear Paul, but I know you enjoy the exercise. Thank you!" Binky smiled, promptly handed me a few dollar bills and went off dutifully in order to attend to the rather complex sand-toy organization.

I took the bills, stuffed them in my dungaree pocket, and off I went.

While wandering away, I heard Binky announce to the children, "Now, children, while your father is off on a mission for the proper ice cream cones, let's take out our beach trip checklists and double-check the toys and items. We need to load them according to the correct categories into the color-coded storage bags."

Beach trip checklists? Color-coded bags?

I moved quickly along the boardwalk, but the thought crossed my mind that not everyone had color-coded storage bags and checklists for beach adventures. No comment required. I knew better than to go there.

This entire holiday was more for the kiddies and my wife than it was for me. I was not much for ocean swimming, or even holidays at the beach. While my wife and children swam around in the surf, I sat on a beach towel, watching them enjoy the ocean. I sat there, my dark sunglasses on, my worn leather sandals on my feet, and I wore my favorite rock-and-roll tee shirt. I also wore a hippie's version of a bathing suit, also known as cut-off dungarees. Actually, when I was out there on the sand, it felt as if I was a hamburger cooking on a hot grille. Sand and surf were cool with me for about one hour, and after that, I was ready for an ice-cold beer and an air-conditioned hotel room. It was not my bag.

The Big Bob's frozen custard stand was all the way at the end of the boardwalk, and it was a bit of a hike. About four hundred miles away or thereabouts, give or take a few miles here and there. In the hot, blazing sun, on a one-hundred-degree day, for custard cones. Oh, well, correction required . . . *for frozen custard cones*. When there was an ice cream cone, stand ten or so feet in front of where we were currently standing.

That was usually the way it went for me. I was quite used to never being able to take the "easy" route, cheapest, or even the closest ice cream stand.

It was a Saturday in the first week of August, and the boardwalk here at Whippywood Beach overflowed with a hot, sweaty, and sunburned summer crowd.

"Watch the tramcar, please! Watch the tramcar, please! BEEP! BEEP! BEEP! Watch the tramcar, please! Watch the tramcar, please! BEEP! BEEP! BEEP!"

I heard the prerecorded message, and the loudspeaker of the boardwalk tramcar, bellowing the annoying and nonstop warning as the trackless train made its way up the boardwalk. Believe me, either you moved, put your head up and paid attention, or you faced the wrath of the famous yellow and blue monster known as the Whippywood and North Whippywood tramcar. It was serious as it rolled along!

I watched the huge crowd part wide open to allow the tramcar train to move through the crowd. I moved over to the side and watched as the tramcar floated by me and it had a full load on it of passengers, mostly women holding small babies, one immense man whose ass was the size of the State of Montana, and elderly folks who wore those big sunglasses that fit over the top of their prescription glasses.

I thought, while I watched the tramcar cruise by that spry, and in great shape folks, such as I am, walk! I may have retired from my career as a professional hockey player many years ago, but even in my new career as a Lutheran clergyman, I kept myself in good shape. I ate good meals, ran, worked out, and while I had gained a few pounds over the years, I remained within my comfortable playing weight.

I strolled along and in a very short order and time, I found myself on line to pick up two Big Bob's frozen custard cones.

Now, I was standing in a long, long line. I think that the

end of the line was on I-95 just past the Delaware tollbooth. It seemed as if Binky was indeed correct. No one in all of Whippywood Beach ever bought any other ice cream cones, except for Big Bob's frozen custard cones!

"Excuse me, long-haired, hippie freak, young man. Would you mind if I cut in front of you? My husband is rather impatient, and he is fuming that I had to have a Big Bob's frozen custard cone. Just because it was ten feet in front of where we were standing, he wanted me to buy one of those air-filled cheapo cones down at the other end of the boardwalk, but everyone knows that they melt right away on a hot day and are poison to your inners."

I turned around to see a nice, sweet, elderly woman with large sunglasses on and a hint of silver and blue in her hair smiling at me.

"Oh sure, sure, sure, please go right ahead," I happily agreed.

To fit in with the ice-cream expert crowd, and to use such common knowledge that I now was privy to, courtesy of my wife's research, I agreed with her ice-cream cone analysis.

"I agree. Those other cones are lousy. They melt so fast and turn your insides to mush. That is why there is no line at that stand."

She pushed me, rather abruptly now that; she no longer needed to be nice to me. She moved in front of me without saying thank you, while she mumbled, "Yeah, yeah, yeah, whatever there, ya long-haired hippie bum. Look, like ya stepped outta ya time machine and are lost from the 1970s. Hair blowing all around, need a damn shave, ya probably do not even have a job. Loser bum, milking the system. Ya most likely no shit from shinola, about ice cream cones. Up ya ass, get outta my way."

So much for the nice old woman with the gentle demeanor. She was correct about my hair. The other part, I refused to comment upon for now. So, what if I had long hair and I still wore my hair as long as I did back in the 1970s? As I stood there and watched the nice old woman elbow her way through another layer of the line, I thought, how perhaps; it was time to cut off all of this hair. It was funny how your mind could wander a bit, while waiting on the frozen custard ice-cream cone line, in the blazing heat and fiery sun.

"Excuse me there, lard ass, but why did you let that old, rude-ass bag of a washed-up prune chick go in front of you? Is she a relative or someone you know?" I turned around to see a heavyset, very sweaty man using his handkerchief to wipe drops of running sweat off his forehead while he was intently staring at me.

"Well, no, I do not know her. She just asked me. . .."

"So, with me standing here, weighing twenty-seven tons and sweating to death, a hippie bum like you has no sympathy for me? You only care about old ladies, not fat tubs of lard like me are? My ass is the size of Alaska and the sweat is running off the ends of it right now like a river. I could sweat to death here and die without granting my last wish, which is to have a Big Bob's frozen custard ice cream cone."

"I assure you, sir. I care about everyone, so go ahead in front of me."

The large man pushed by me and stood in front of me. He continued to emit huge drops of sweat that when they hit the boardwalk they echoed. I swore that they did. The large man did a lot of sweating. Trails of sweat dripped upon the boardwalk as he lumbered past me, and they lapped in huge puddles on my sandals.

"Say pal, ya gonna let the entire population of planet Earth push by ya, or are you going to stand your damn ground?" Now I had a middle-aged, short guy standing behind me, yelling out at me for letting the two people go ahead of us.

"No, that is, it! No one else is going to go ahead of me." I tried hard not to be offended by this gloomy guy and his attitude.

"Good, you look like a long-haired wimp! You would think that a guy as big as you are, would not be such a friggin' pansy la-la!"

All I wanted was to pick up two ice cream cones for my kids. Why, oh why, do I always have to run into such a collection of wackos and weirdos, when I try to perform the simplest tasks?

At first, I ignored him, and then I felt a little steam come out of my ears. I started to spin around and confront him, but then I remembered that I needed to turn the other cheek. In my heart, I wanted to mention the fact that I was a Lutheran minister, even if for nothing else, then just to watch his reaction.

I continued to ignore him.

Before I knew it, a tall, skinny chap with hair even longer than mine, who was wearing a ball cap on his head and had a tattoo of an ice cream cone on his neck, was shouting at me. When I woke up to reality, and stopped staring at the order sign displaying the multitude of sizes, numbers of ice cream dips, and TWO FLAVORS, I noticed the skinny chap's tee shirt. Emblazoned across the front of the tee shirt was a loudly printed, "Whadda Ya Want!!!???"

Very appropriate, I thought. This is New Jersey where customer service is optional and just a suggestion.

Through a wave of stutters and indecision, I squeaked out an order, "Two large cones please, ah, ah, ah, lemon, plus, one orange one too." I just randomly spit out the first order of flavors, which came into my mind.

"Ain't got no large size. Ya blind or just plain stupid? Look at the sign! I will help ya here because you are a cone doofus. These two cones, youse want triple dip with orange custard or zippy super-deluxe dip with lemon, there pal? C'mon, make a decision because the line stretches all the way to Asbury!"

Oh, no!

"Ah, ah, oh, well. . .."

"Geez, c'mon pal!"

The crowd was anxious and a bit testy. I was now in a bit of a pickle. I had forgotten to ask Binky which flavor the kiddies wanted! Why do things always have to be so confusing? Lemon or orange? I had no idea these stupid cones would come in two flavors. Whatever happened to chocolate and vanilla? That would be too easy. I made a split-second choice, based upon a testy crowd! My mind was spinning as the surrounding people shouted and cursed at me in a typical display of New Jersey unfriendliness.

In desperation, and since it was my favorite flavor, I shouted out, "Triple dip, lemon custard! Forget the orange one!"

"Really? Ain't made any of them in a long ass time."

Ignoring the frozen ice-cream custard guru's comments, I sat back and smiled at my spontaneous decision. I love lemon flavor! After all, they were my children, of course, our two, lovely little, kiddies would love lemon! I handed the skinny chap ten dollars, mumbled a bit at the ridiculous overpricing of these delicacies of frozen nothing, took my two cones, and made my way the four hundred miles down the boardwalk towards where Binky and our children were waiting.

I noticed drips of melting custard rolling off the edges of the cones, so I picked up the pace. I started a slow sprint with my head down to keep an eye on the dangerous manner in which the triple dips were wiggling precariously on top of the cones. One wrong move and they would topple over and flop to disaster.

Suddenly. . ..

"Watch the tramcar, please! Watch the tramcar, please! BEEP! BEEP! BEEP! Watch the tramcar, please! Watch the tramcar, please! BEEP! BEEP! BEEP!"

I jumped out of the way, narrowly escaped becoming hippie mush on the boardwalk, and somehow managed not to topple the twin peaks of my beloved custard cones.

"Get the hair out of your eyes, you hippie bum! Almost lost it all to the tramcar!" The driver of the tramcar waved her fist at me as she whizzed by.

Finally, I spotted the Holy Land, which in this case was a bench next to the rail on the sandy side of the boardwalk. Binky and the kiddies sat there patiently, waiting for my return. Covered in sweat, and with slightly dripping cones, I watched as the three of them jumped to their feet at the sight of the returning hero, smiles as wide as the beautiful ocean itself!

Then, I watched in horror as simultaneously, their joy at my triumphant entry faded into intense disappointment.

All together now. . ..

"LEMON? YOU ARE THE ONLY ONE WHO LIKES LEMON! WE SAID ORANGE!"

"You did? I don't actually recall any flavor. . .. "

Back I went, four hundred miles in the other direction. In the heat. The wretched heat. My suggestion for the gang to move to another bench closer to where the Big Bob's ice cream stand was met with strong opposition. The bench they had discovered was "special."

It was in the shade.

I did not really understand where the shade was, the nearest tree was in lower New York State, but I ended up in no position to argue any facts. While returning to the frozen custard ice cream stand, I tried to get my ten bucks worth. I licked lemon custard cones like a dog licks their favorite bone, while desperately fighting the odds of a blazing sun, angry New Jersey board walkers, and of course, what has now become my mortal enemy in life, that stupid ass, bloody tramcar!

"Watch the tramcar, please! Watch the tramcar, please! BEEP! BEEP! BEEP! Watch the tramcar, please! Watch the tramcar, please! BEEP! BEEP! BEEP!"

I refused to concede defeat and jump on that stupid tramcar. I did not care if my ass was dragging ten feet behind me. No way was I going to ride that evil monster because it now was a matter of principle and honor. The tramcar versus number twenty-seven. I was not going to give into the lure of an easy ride.

In a futile and crushing defeat, I ditched the remains of my ill-selected lemon cones into a trashcan and continued on my way. My long blonde hair was now all wet and stringy, I was soaked with sweat now to my very tippy toes, and red-faced, I was going to make it to the blasted Big Bob's ice cream cones stand, even if I met Jesus along the way.

I would buy him an ice cream cone and then we would talk.

I reached the Big Bob's frozen ice cream cone stand and stood in the rear of a line that was just a hairpin shorter than the previous line. Sure enough, some sweaty elderly man taps me on the shoulder and asks me, "Say hippie, do ya mind if I go in front of ya. I have a bad knee and my dog is blind and deaf and I am down to my. . .."

"NO!" I prayed under my breath for forgiveness, but there is only so much you can take.

"Geez, you do not have to get all nasty. I admit that I made the part up about my dog."

Two hours later, I hear the ice cream cone stand attendant's voice, "You must be hungry, hippie guy. Didn't you just buy some lemon cones?" The cone stand attendant asked me as he rubbed his cone tattoo.

"Yeah, yeah, yeah, please let me have the two triple dip orange cones there, chief."

"Ya was a dope and bought the wrong flavor, huh? Happens all the time. Most everyone knows that lemon cones are for old bags and kids don't like 'em. That will be ten more bucks."

At least he smiled a lot while hurling indirect and somewhat roundabout New Jersey shore insults.

Back I trotted, strategically evading the tramcar, shaking my fist in the face of danger, vowing to never bend or break and ride on that horrid tramcar! I was in prime physical condition! A little trek (or two, in one-hundred-degree heat) up and down the boardwalk to obtain my beloved children's frozen custard ice cream cones is fun! Ha! This is nothing to a solid father figure such as I am!

I trotted on, while balancing my custard cones in my hands, while not spilling a drop in the blazing heat of summer fun! Now, this was a summer vacation! Relaxing, enjoyable, and fun-filled! Binky and the children jumped to life at the sight of my, this time, correct flavor delivery.

"Oh, thank you, twenty-seven! The children and I have been waiting so patiently for you to return. I bet that the crowds were huge out on the boardwalk. Oh, my, you are sweating terribly."

Binky quickly moved into action, lovingly dabbing my forehead with a beach towel that my wife instantly produced from one of the color-coded bags gathered around her feet. Heather Sarah and Paul William jumped to their feet and nodded their heads fervently in agreement at my condition.

"We watched the tramcar go back and forth and wondered why you did not take it."

In a classic display of pride and minimization, I spouted off like a doofus, "Oh, it was nothing, dear Binky. I am not going to take that tramcar, it is not that far, and I still am in great shape. Here are your cones, kids. Enjoy!"

"Thank you, Father." Heather Sarah's smile was worth all the effort.

"Thank you!" Paul William shouted as he took the cone from my hand. The joy of summer, family time, and simple pleasures for your loving children. Wonderful memories.

"You are welcome, kids. What a great time!"

Paul William took one lick, and we all watched in horror as the frozen custard piled as high as the sky; wobbled, toppled, and over the railing . . . it all went. Upside down, it landed on the sandy beach below us with a sand deadened, "thud!"

"Bahhh! My custard cone! No fair! Now, I lost mine and Heather Sarah still has hers!"

I never knew the tramcar ride was so smooth and enjoyable. It glided along happily, magically weaving in and out of the crowd. I sat on the side of it, smiling, praising God and all the Major Prophets in scripture for this lovely day, watching the ocean lap on the sand in the distance. The breeze waved my long, golden locks of hair in the air.

"Watch the tramcar, please! Watch the tramcar, please! BEEP! BEEP! BEEP! Watch the tramcar, please! Watch the tramcar, please! BEEP! BEEP! BEEP!"

It was music to my ears, and the breeze while we moved along helped to dry my sweat-filled body.

"Back again, huh? Lemme guess . . . ya kid dropped the cone in the sand and cried his ass off."

I would classify Mrs. Binky Hobnobber Henson as one of the world's most fervent lovers of amusement park rides. She instantly could shift her usual prim and proper behavior into a thrill-seeking lover of flying in the air at breathtaking speeds, flipping upside down for hours until your eyeballs felt as if they would burst and your stomach left your body hours ago and other assorted teeth-chattering activities. The higher and more death defying the ride, the better, the more the ride twists and turns or flips and flops, then the happier Binky will be! In addition, just to put the icing on the thrill cake, Binky passed along the thrill-seeking gene to our two lovely children.

The kiddies not only received the thrill-seeking gene, but the research bug too. Along with the research bug, which includes drilling down and checking into the most minutiae details of every subject known to mankind, and some that even the world's greatest minds have not yet discovered, Binky also passed along the strange head-nodding genes.

It was just a small part of why I love them all!

After barely surviving the frozen custard ice cream episode and successfully ingesting seventy-seven bottles of water to help restore some bodily fluids that I had lost, we skipped happily to the amusement pier of Whippywood Beach. Before this glorious boardwalk adventure, I had not urinated in seventeen hours, but of course, now that I had replaced my bodily fluids, the excess made me a slave to the restroom.

Once we finally arrived at the amusement pier, my beautiful wife, and happy children pulled me onto every ride they could, while we twisted, spun, and flipped, in stomach turning delight, and passed the rest of the afternoon away in an acid refluxed induced haze. Now, it is not that I despise amusement rides that much; it is just not my favorite thing. I did not become sick to my stomach, or dizzy, but the constant spinning grew wearisome. Binky and the children were immune, and they loved every minute of it.

"We just love the speed, twenty-seven!" Binky would lean in and tell me as we zipped along some rickety wooden roller coaster track, while I pushed my eyeballs back into my head and adjusted my stomach.

This entire amusement incident reminded me of a time long ago. In fact, it was one of the first dates that Binky and

I ever went on. On that date, we journeyed with our best friends Harry and Rose to Seashore Heights and rode the amusement rides all afternoon. No, that is not quite correct because my best buddy, Harry M. Redmond Jr. managed to weasel out of going on the rides, under a sicky-wicky tummy complaint amongst other angles. You see, Harry was a tricky one. He had an ulterior motive, as he scampered off to watch, ogle, and gawk at young ladies who would lose their swimsuits on the nearby water slide.

That is, of course, another story for another time and place, but in looking back at that famous day, I was very thankful that the main attraction of that afternoon, a maniacal ride known as "The Flipper" no longer existed. In the interest of public safety, and amongst severe protests from the stomach antacid and coffin manufacturers, the federal government stepped in and outlawed the ride a few years ago.

Now, amusement park rides are not high on my hit parade, but as I mentioned before, I do not despise them. What I do despise, however, is the heat, humidity, and well, let me not pull any punches, and say the summer too.

Oh, yes, and sand. I despise sand.

Sand that has now infiltrated every single inch of my body, shoes, underwear, ears, nose, teeth, and hair. I think if I had a doctor take an x-ray, they would find sand inside of my bones.

The heat had turned up even a few more notches in the late afternoon and it lingered into the early evening. It surrounded us in a great cloud of moisture, which encapsulated us with a choking humidity that settled in and laughed at the meager attempts of an ocean breeze to move it away. Everyone's clothes stuck to their bodies as if they were glued to their skin. As the waves of humanity made their way along the boardwalk, people tugged at their pants, while pulling the drenched clothes out of their ass cracks, and they tugged at their armpits to pull sweat-soaked clothes out of remnants of long since failed deodorants.

After this long day of swimming, cooking on the beach under a blazing sun, spinning, flipping, stomach churning, and the maddening procurement exercise in search of frozen custard cones, my family, and I were both ready for a refreshing shower, a change into dry clothes, and a good meal.

It had been exhausting.

At least, I thought the family was ready for a shower, dry clothes, and a good meal.

Family excursions during summer vacations were such fun.

The sun was thankfully setting now. The boardwalk lights on the rides, food stands, and games flickered to life, casting a colorful glow all around, but the relentless heat and humidity remained. Despite my efforts to pull and steer the gang in the direction of the hotel, I found them strangely wandering off in another direction.

I shouted and pointed in vain, "Hey, gang! The hotel, food, showers, and dry clothes are this way!"

They ignored me and happily strolled along in the opposite direction. We wandered at the far end of the Whippywood Beach boardwalk and walked right into a water park of more "fun" amusement rides.

"Oh, dear Father! Look! Look! We want to go on the ducky ride!" Heather Sarah jumped up and down in excitement while she pointed towards a ride looming high above the rest of the water park. I lifted my sweat-soaked head, pushed the stringy mop of mush, formerly known as my hair out of the way, picked pieces of sand out of my ears, and stared at the ride.

"Mother, do you have, Fritzie? Please get Fritzie out of the red bag with the vertical blue stripes bag. That is the bag, which according to my checklist, has the stuffed toys in it. He wants to go on this cute, little, ducky ride too!"

Binky nodded, pulled her checklist out of her purse to confirm the color-code of the bag and upon confirmation of the information, my gorgeous wife, dug down in one of her forty-seven color-coded bags that she was carrying supplies and beach gear in, and pulled out Heather Sarah's beloved-stuffed doggie, "Fritzie." Binky packed Fritzie away for safekeeping during the beach adventures, but now was apparently the time for him to make a grand entrance to enjoy the cute, little, ducky ride.

"Father, that ride looks like such fun. Heather Sarah is right! We need to go on it!" Now, our son had joined in the chorus with his sister.

I tried to mount a futile defense and say what all fathers say after a day such as we had, "Don't you kiddies think you have done enough today? We could go back to the hotel, shower, change our clothes, pick the sand out of our teeth, and go out for a nice, big pizza pie!"

All fathers, in their hearts of hearts, know that it will never ever be enough with kids, never, ever!

Instantly, down-frowned mouths and pangs of severe disappointment appeared on their cute little faces. Long forgotten now, were all the other rides, body surfing in the ocean, building forts and sandcastles, running barefoot in the sand on the beach, picking up seashells, playing fifty games of chance, hot dogs with mustard, hamburgers, sodas, and popcorn, and those stupid, frozen custard cones. Not to mention that the bill for all of this fun in the sun had now reached the same level as the total economic budget for the country of Upper Zoolockia.

The old man was now a bum because he had not done a thing for them.

"Fritzie wants to go on the cute, little, ducky ride! You are always trying to take us back to the hotel too early, dear Father," Heather Sarah shouted as she shook the stuffed doggie in front of me.

Binky folded her arms across her mighty chest, dug her

left foot into the boardwalk and shook her finger at me as the scolding began, "Pastor Paul John Henson! Since when did you become such a stick in the mud and a killjoy for your children's dreams and wishes?" Binky walked over to me, while tying up her own long mop of sweaty hair in a futile and hapless effort to hide the fact that she had sweated away twenty pounds of water weight today. I knew of no defensive tactic known to humanity that would work when my lovely wife used my full name and prefaced my title of a pastor before it.

It was now officially hopeless!

My wife then shifted to a softer mode and approach, when she saw me picking sand particles out of my back teeth, and pulling my tee shirt out of my sweaty armpits, "Besides, this ride is a simple, little kiddies' ride. You just pedal the cute, little duckies around on the rail with pedals. It is relaxing, good exercise, and fun too, my dear, twenty-seven."

She then leaned in and whispered, "And do not forget that we have a double room. When the children are fast asleep, and we are cleaned up, we can enjoy some drinks, and well, you know . . . kind of pass the time. . .."

Binky stood by and tried to fluff her sweaty hair that she suddenly let loose, but realizing that her usual method of seduction was not going to work, she bagged that, and just posed, stuck out her very sweaty, but ample chest, and winked at me. The sweaty outline of her remarkable breasts told the true story. Still, she was awful hot. In more ways than one.

I looked up and studied the cute little ducky ride. It was a very high steel monorail, towering about thirty to forty feet above a water park. It turned and twisted through most of the park. The ride did seem simple enough, but it had to be at least forty miles long. The rail dipped a little here and there and had small inclines and twisty turns. The happy, little ducks rode on a monorail and you pedaled a cog gear that propelled you along the rail. Binky was correct, it seemed harmless enough, and I could see multitudes of sweaty, but happy families pedaling their brains out and laughing together as they sat in their cute, little duckies and happily propelled themselves along the monorail.

Our children were both staring at me and pleading with their eyes, and I looked between them and Binky, who was still holding her seductive pose. As sexy and beautiful as my wife was, she looked as if she was growing tired of waiting for my response. The heat was bloody intense. I could see the beads of sweat rolling down her face as she blinked and winked to keep the sweat from burning her eyes. It was hard to pose sexy and be alluring when you feel as if you are a hamburger on a charcoal grille.

"Twenty-seven, you have less than two seconds to take the children on this ride, and accept my offer, because I feel sweat rolling down the cheeks of my curvaceous backside, running down between my mountainous breasts, and spilling down into my socks. As much as I love you and find you incredibly sexy, you are about to be shut out of lovemaking time tonight!"

"Oh geez, as Uncle Harry would say, for the love of Pete! Let's go!"

I folded like a cheap camera.

The ride did seem harmless enough; we paid another exorbitant fee for the pleasure of pedaling ourselves on this long, long rail and climbed a tall set of steel stairs. Two very friendly and happy workers, one young man and a young lady, met us at the top of the staircase and the young gal greeted us loudly.

They were very sweaty too.

"Welcome to the cute, little, ducky cycle monorail! This is where human power is never underrated!" the young woman attendant smiled at us while she adjusted her shorts to wring some sweat out of them. She smiled widely as I stared at her and tried my best to smile back.

"Climb on in, kids, Mom, and Dad. It is quite simple and such fun. Let me show you. All you have to do is sit inside the duck, put your feet on the pedals, and start pedaling. Your plastic-molded and very realistic, duck will easily and rather happily go around on the monorail," the young man explained with his canned speech, while he waved his hand as if he was a game show host displaying the next prize.

There in front of us, sitting on the monorail, was a huge, white plastic duck wearing a sailor's hat. The duck had four seats to sit in, with four pairs of pedals for each seat. The duck had a large neck and molded plastic face, a little tail in the back, with an orange beak and stupid looking eyes. Oh, yes, he had a big smile on his beak.

"That's right, kiddies! Climb in the backseat of your duck and buckle the belt there on your lap. Now, please remember to stay safe. Never, ever, ever, no matter what the reason is, should you ever unlatch the belt or climb out of your duck!"

Binky hustled the children into the duck and they eagerly climbed in the backseat while I studied the contraption.

Binky waved them in while she said, "Come along, children. Remember, that we researched this ride before we left home. We even calculated, with complex algebraic equations that with your father's superior strength, from being a former professional athlete that we would not have to pedal very much, and your dear father would do most of the work."

My head whirled around—this had been a set up! My family planned on this stupid ducky ride the entire time! They snookered me!

The young man looked at me and shrugged his shoulders.

I guess he could not resist and he asked Binky, "You

research amusement park rides?"

The young ride attendant looked Binky up and down, obviously enjoying the view of her fabulous figure and gorgeous (but sweaty) beauty.

"Yes, yes, yes, of course, young man. It is fascinating! Don't you research them too?"

Binky, Paul William, and Heather Sarah, zoomed in for an intense stare while awaiting the young man's reply. He took a few steps back because the staring power overcame him. Oh, yes, the children had also inherited Binky's penchant for zooming close in when she is seeking an answer or a response to a question that she has asked.

I was quite used to it by now, but on our first date. . .. Another story down the road.

The overwhelmed young man finally managed a feeble, "Sure, sure, sure, especially rides here in Whippywood Beach. Now, let me, um, check your lap belts. Dad, I guess you are the lead driver or lead pedal guy. By the way, did you really play a professional sport?"

"Yeah, yeah, yeah, I was an ice hockey goalie, and I have a feeling that I am going to regret that fact in a very few minutes."

"Wow!" Hearing what I formerly did for a living was exciting to the young (sweaty) lady. "What do you do now, mister?"

I climbed in the duck, sat down, put my feet on the pedals, and buckled my lap belt.

"I am a Lutheran pastor and for some reason, I have a feeling that I am going to need to invoke some heavenly intervention very shortly."

The young lady smiled widely when she heard my occupation. She tugged at her sweaty shorts, which clung to her legs like vises, snapped her bra straps to relieve a gallon or two of sweat from her chest area and said, "Wow! You look more like a hippie than a minister."

After hearing that same comment too many times today,

I was not in the mood, and simply said, "Whatever."

With a disinterested wave in continuing comments of my hippie appearance, I started to pedal, and off our duck went, propelling along while cutting a path through the intense heat and humidity. I swore that the duck was sweating too.

"Heather Sarah and I cannot reach the pedals, dear Father," Paul William testified. Our son was tall for his age, but his legs did not quite reach the pedals. Heather Sarah was a year and a half or so younger than her brother was, and Heather was out of reach of the pedals too.

"Oh, that is not any trouble. I am pedaling along with your father and he is doing fine."

Binky fluffed her hair because I could tell she was proud of my ability to move us along the rail so easily. She was pedaling quite leisurely, but I could feel that she was providing some assistance when I eased up just a bit.

"So, this was a bit of a setup, Binky. You guys knew about the ducky ride, eh?"

Binky smiled at me but she did not answer. Instead, she strategically changed the subject as we rounded the first bend.

"Oh, look everyone! You can see the entire park from here. It looks so nice all lit up at night. Besides, it is cooling down a little too." I dabbed the sweat pouring out of every pore of my head and had to disagree with Binky's weather report.

"We love the cute, little ducky ride! Keep pedaling, dear Father!" Heather Sarah was shouting and waving from her backseat in the duck.

"Mother told us that the highest point in the ride is coming up. I remember from our research that we will be forty-two feet above the ground. We researched all of this a few weeks ago, dear Father!" Paul William was now spilling the beans on the inside scoop behind the ducky ride and rubbing salt into my sweaty wounds. Sure enough, there was a little sign on the side of the monorail happily telling you to: "Pedal harder, there is a little hill coming up!"

Joy, joy, joy.

I felt the instant resistance of the "little hill" and suddenly, I had to put a little more effort into the force that I was using to propel our duck. I saw Binky lean in a little harder. She breathed deeply, and she wiped her forehead as beads of more sweat popped out here and there. Now, my wife was very strong. At various times, Binky could perform feats of superhuman strength, mostly, when lifting suitcases that she packs for family holidays that contain one of every item in our house. My loyal wife also brings along a color-coded assortment of bags containing an entire department store full of first aid supplies, cosmetics, medicine for potential boo-boos, and of course, countless toys.

Sand toys. Stuffed animals. Board games.

Usually, my allowed luggage allotment consists of a small, cloth duffle bag, in which I can fit my Bible, a pack of gum, a stick of dry deodorant, and an extra pastor's collar.

"Pedal, Mother! Pedal, Father! This is so much fun!" Our happy little angels screamed from the backseat of our duck.

"Hooweee!" Heather Sarah screamed out. She certainly enjoyed the little ride down the other side of the hill. Binky and I quickly learned that the weight of the duck, forced the pedals to go around on their own as you went down the little hill, and you needed to take your foot off them, or you risked chattering your teeth or losing your feet in the pedals. The pedals spun around faster than Harry's head did while he was walking down a beach filled with ladies wearing swimsuits. I spotted Binky bouncing around in her duck seat as she tried to keep up with the pedals. Her large and sweaty breasts bounced under her shirt and she reached up to stop them from poking her eyes out while they were keeping time with the hop and skip of the pedals.

"Oh my, twenty-seven! This is a little tricky!" She called out as the pedals spun around and around at our feet. Another happy sign proclaiming another little hill, and suddenly, this leisurely pedaling was breaking out more mounds of sweat on my face, back, and neck. Despite the propaganda, they fed us at the beginning of the ride; this human power was not underrated! It was very real!

As we pedaled along, the rail flattened out, and when we were about at the farthest point from the starting line, I noticed a duck ahead of us that had stopped and it was not moving.

"Binky, that duck right there in front of us is not moving."

Binky nodded in agreement as she said, "I see that, twenty-seven. There are two people in the front of that duck. Maybe they just stopped to rest for a minute or two. Oh, dear, I hope they do not have a duck malfunction. I did not research what you would do in case that happened on the ride." I looked over at my wife but decided not to pursue that line of questioning.

As our duck approached, we realized that there were two people in the front of the stuck duck and they were two very, very, large people. In fact, the two-immense people barely fit inside the duck. They looked as if they were two mountains crammed into the cavity of the duck. They each resembled the size of the entire east coast of the United States.

Minus Vermont.

The two human duck propellers seemed to be in some kind of distress, or more accurately, they seemed to suffer from some kind of anguish. As we rode up behind them, they looked over at us and then pedaled a little. The duck moved about a foot and a little more when the two of them collapsed onto one another and they desperately held each other. Suddenly, the air filled with their screams and gasps.

"We cannot go on! Help us! Help us! We are going to have heart attacks!"

Binky and I looked at each other and I said, "I guess they are in some type of duck distress, dear Binky. I need to stand up and check it out."

I unlatched my lap belt, stood up, and looked over the neck and head of our duck.

I yelled out, "Are you two all right over there?" Considering they just told us they were going to have heart attacks, that seemed to be a stupid question.

Sure enough, there were two immense ladies sitting in the front of the duck. They wore bathing suits and looked as if they were stuffed sausages crammed inside of them. They filled the entire front of the duck and their girth spilled over the sides of the duck. Both ladies turned around, and I could see that they were dripping with sweat; they were gasping for air and holding onto each other in agony.

One of the mountains spoke, and she passionately explained their dilemma.

"We are so sorry. We have pedaled this stupid friggin' duck until our chests are going to explode. Our legs are like rubber bands and the damn sweat is rolling down our backs and the cracks of our asses and flooding the inside of the duck."

I heard Binky softly whisper, "Oh, my."

The two-ton tussies, then shouted in unison, "We cannot go another inch. Can you please help us?"

I did not know what to say. I never had to deal with a stuck duck on a monorail before, pedaled by two immense ladies.

"Those two tubby ladies used lots of bad words, dear Mother!" Heather Sarah correctly pointed out.

"It is okay, Heather Sarah. Your father will deal with it."

"Is it okay to use those words, Mother? I guess if your duck is stuck, then it is okay to use those bad words. If our duck is stuck, will we use those words to get going again? Or will you use the super bad word that begins with f that Uncle Harry always uses and rhymes with puck. As in a hockey puck?"

Binky stammered for a second or two as the line of questions by our daughter caught her by surprise.

"No, no, no, please, just wait a minute, Heather Sarah." Now cornered by our daughter's sharp mind, Binky stalled in her words while she undid her lap belt and stood up.

"The man in charge of the ride, said you should not unlatch your seat belts while on the cute, little, ducky ride, dear Mother," Paul William observed.

My wife lost her cool a bit and turned to our lovely children, wiped a wave of sweat from her face, tugged at her sweat-logged brassiere and said, "Okay, kids! Ya need to keep ya traps shut for just a minute! We need to think here!"

Our two lovely children immediately closed their mouths and nodded emphatically.

Binky then waved over our duck's head and neck and she cupped her hands around her mouth and offered a logical solution to the stuck duck situation, "It will be all right now, ladies! My handsome husband here is a former professional athlete and he will be able to push you with our duck. You see, he is now a Lutheran pastor and he will help you with prayers too. He is Pastor Paul John Henson of Reunion Lutheran Church in Hiberian, New Jersey. Just relax, and we will get our duck in back of yours, and push you the rest of the way in!"

"Oh, thank you! Thank you! God sent a savior to save us!" The two ladies held onto each other, panting, coughing, and gasping, while waving in the air at their perceived rescuers. When they could muster up enough air to speak between gasps, they called out to us, "We have been so lucky. God has also sent angels to save us!"

Despite the two-blimp's accurate Gospel testimony, I

found it hard to equate the biblical portion of this mission to my current earthly predicament. Besides, I could not exactly understand why Binky had to tell the two enormous duck riders all of that information, but something deep inside of me told me that I was going to need some prayers very shortly. I stood there studying my years of seminary and Bible training, for a prayer to use when saving gelatinous folks in stuck amusement park ducks, but my mind was blank.

Binky always provided people with so much extra information.

"You may have overestimated my strength, Binky. Those gals look as if they weigh a few bobs or two. We might be better off, if I jumped in their duck, and pedaled them to the end, and you pedaled this one."

Binky frowned at me and said, "Nonsense, twenty-seven. You are as strong as a bull. Despite your advancing age, you have actually increased muscle tone and strength now that you do not sweat off five to eight pounds per game, as you did during your hockey days. In addition, I am not allowing you to climb into a strange duck with people whom we do not know, and risk being in trouble for leaving our duck. You heard the instructions from the head ride attendant! He specifically instructed us never to climb out of your duck. It is a safety violation!"

"That's right, dear Father!" Heather Sarah corrected my direction and, of course, agreed with her mother.

Paul William added, "You might be arrested for breaking duck riding laws!"

Binky looked over at me and said, "I am very strong, too. Between you and me, we will rescue these unfortunate people. You can do it, twenty-seven! After all, you are the world famous, number twenty-seven!"

"Yeah, yeah, yeah, dear Father! You can do anything! Kick save and a beauty by Henson!" Paul William was encouraging me on from the backseat of the duck, by using some old cheers from my days as a hockey goalie.

It was not working.

"I used to be. Now, I am a wimp. Maybe they have a special tow duck, Binky. On the other hand, maybe I can tell them there are free hamburgers at the end of the ride to inspire them to pedal a bit. I am sure this is not the first time that a duck got stuck because two giant blimps could not. . .."

Binky was shaking her head, so I stopped in mid-plea.

I settled back into the duck and put my lap belt on. Very softly under my breath, I mumbled words in my second language of Welsh, while being extra careful to stay off Binky's radar. She knew the language now, too.

"What did you just say, Pastor Paul John Henson? That is not nice to call these ladies mean names. They might have medical conditions, which cause excessive weight gain. You are a pastor and need to save people. Might I remind you!" Binky stared at me.

"Nothing, dear, we are good. I did not say anything. I am up for the task."

I pedaled close, and we set our duck's nose into the tail of the duck in front of us. Actually, we did not set the nose of our duck into the tail of the duck in front of us. We set our duck's nose into a plastic molded ass-crack of the duck in front of us.

It was a disturbing scene.

We started to pedal and with extreme force, slowly, we started to move.

"Go, Father! Go, Mother!" The kiddies yelled in unison from the backseat. Binky was straining and pedaling with all of her might to help me. She was very strong, but most of her strength always seemed to be in her arms and upper body. Torrents of sweat immediately poured from every pore of our bodies.

I yelled out to the two ladies in front of us, "You guys pedal as much as you can too!"

"Oh, we are! We are!"

Somehow, I knew that was not the case. I could see over our duck's neck that the two tubbies were just sitting back, relaxing, with their feet off the spinning pedals while they enjoyed the view, while Binky and I pedaled our brains out.

"Oh no, Paul! A hill!" Binky screamed, as she pointed out the sign happily stating the approach to the last hill on the course.

"Paul William, please unbuckle your belt, jump in the front of the duck, and put your hands on your mother's feet and help her pedal.

"But, dear Father, the man in charge said for me to always keep my lap belt on."

"PAUL WILLIAM, GET YA ASS UP HERE! NOW!"

He immediately unlatched the belt and jumped up to help Binky. Paul William crouched down in the bottom of the duck, put his hands on his mother's feet and helped her push the pedals around and around with his hands.

"Dear Mother, dear Father is a pastor and I think he just said a bad word!" Heather Sarah commented and Binky just waved at her to indicate for her to be quiet.

Our daughter seemed satisfied that the situation required a bit of a harsher tone, but she was so much her mother's daughter.

Heather Sarah sat quietly for only a few moments, when she suddenly offered some advice, "Maybe we should use that bad word that the big lady said, if that is the word you use when your duck is stuck, Father."

"No, Heather Sarah, bad words when your duck is stuck is not the answer." I felt every muscle in my entire body screaming out, my legs were burning for relief, my mind was whirling in pain. It was worse than any hockey workout that I had ever performed. Sweat poured out of all three of us like a river. When I could focus my eyeballs and actually see in front of us, I could see the two tubs of lard, sitting back, now fully relaxed and enjoying the sights. Somehow, I thought that I would enact revenge on them.

I crossed myself multiple times for forgiveness and started to say a prayer just loud enough that the children and Binky could hear it. It must have been a prayer that I use quite often because my whole family started to pray along with me.

Heather Sarah held Fritzie in her hands, waved him in front of our eyes, and shouted, "Fritzie is helping too!"

Down below this torture track, I could hear my newfound enemy with the happy bellow of the incessant tramcar, "Watch the tramcar, please! Watch the tramcar, please! BEEP! BEEP! BEEP! Watch the tramcar, please! Watch the tramcar, please! BEEP! BEEP! BEEP!"

This was ridiculous! Heat, humidity, and stuck mechanical ducks forty feet in the air.

Binky's words echoed inside of my head, "Besides, this ride is a simple, little kiddies' ride. You just pedal the cute, little, duckies around on the rail with pedals. It is relaxing and fun too, my dear, twenty-seven."

As we rounded the final bend, and we were within fifty feet or so of the end of the track, I could see the two ride attendants running up along the maintenance walkway to help us. A line of stuck ducks a mile long was behind us. People were screaming and yelling for us to pedal faster, but not one of the loudmouthed idiots would push up behind us to assist us.

Plastic ducky ass crack to plastic ducky noses.

We stopped pedaling, and Binky, Paul William, and I gasped for air. The young man carefully moved one of the mountainous ladies to the back of the duck, and he took over on the pedals. I could see him straining and pushing as hard as he could to move the duck with the tremendous load inside. We finally reached the end and the three of us collapsed in each other's arms while gasping for air.

"Oh, my! Oh, my, twenty-seven! That was some

workout! I will not have to exercise for a month!" Binky held onto our son and me while Heather Sarah jumped from the backseat to embrace us.

"You saved them!" She screamed.

"Are youse guys, all, right? That must have been brutal. We wondered where everyone was. It was taking so long for the ducks to come in," the young lady was rambling on while checking on us.

I looked up to see the two ladies climb out of their duck, wave to us, and wobble over to our duck. God bless them, but they must have weighed five hundred pounds each. One of the sweat-filled ladies leaned over, while the other gal stood behind her, smiling.

The first lady said, "Oh bless you, pastor! Bless you and your wonderful family. I do apologize for cursing a bit in front of you and your family, but we were desperate!"

"Oh, it is all right. We understand. Just read a Bible verse tonight and all will be forgiven," I babbled some pastoral nonsense between gasps for air. I almost told them to read a diet book in addition to the Bible verse or two, but I held my thoughts. Instead, I made a blessing motion in the air and waved feebly towards them.

"Thank you!" The two ladies shouted in unison and they wandered off, the very pillars of the ride shaking with their every step.

I looked at the young man who was handing us all glasses of water and I said, "You know, chief, you better put a weight limit on this ride. Are you not the same guy who just said, all you have to do is sit inside the duck, put your feet on the pedals, and start pedaling? Your duck will happily go around on the monorail,"

"Well, yes, I am, sir. But, youse guys are all heroes! We have a rescue duck pull that we use for situations like this. We just did not know where you were, and it looked as if you were doing so well."

Ah hah! My redemption with my wife was now nearby!

A rescue duck and they did not know where we were. Well, that made no sense at all. Where did they think we had gone? Where the hell is the rescue duck? I was too exhausted to ask.

I looked at Binky, who gasped and tugged at her sweat-soaked brassiere once more to adjust her disheveled breasts, shrugged her shoulders and she said, "Sorry. I must have missed the rescue duck pull in my research, dear Paul."

We slowly climbed out of our duck and walked as if we had just finished a marathon race. Climbing down the stairs was total agony. Every step was a burner!

"We are taking the tramcar back to the hotel," was all I had to say. Binky with her forty-seven, color-coded bags, and the children followed me, as we slowly and agonizingly walked to the tramcar stop. A trail of sweat and sand dripped upon the boardwalk as we made our painful way to the tramcar stop.

We moved like slugs.

Sweaty, sandy, slugs.

"Watch the tramcar, please! Watch the tramcar, please! BEEP! BEEP! BEEP! Watch the tramcar, please! Watch the tramcar, please! BEEP! BEEP! BEEP!"

This was the longest day of my life. Back at the hotel, we all peeled our disgusting, sweat-soaked and sand-covered clothes off our bodies, and piled them into a laundry bag. We showered and cleaned the children up first, then tackled our issues. It took me fifteen minutes to unlace the laces on my canvas sneakers because they were so soaked with sweat. It took Binky and me both to combine our forces in order to tug them off my feet, and another ten minutes to peel my socks off my feet. Binky even suggested at one point that we just cut them off with a pair of scissors. We both excused ourselves, went into the bathroom and attempted to strip the rest of our clothes off our bodies. Binky carefully unwound my underwear from between my male parts and somehow, she preserved my manhood and our love life. Due to sweating and pedaling forty bijillion times, they were as if a spring had wound around my anatomy.

Binky even commented as she worked the sweaty mess from within my most private parts, "Oh my, twenty-seven, this might be the only time in our lives together, where I wished that you were not constructed as generously as what you are."

I did not comment.

I had to peel Binky's brassiere and underwear off her body. They were stuck like glue on her. Believe me when I tell you there was nothing romantic or sexy about this undressing. Instead, it was a matter of sheer survival. Finally, with great effort, I assisted Binky in peeling off her sweaty brassiere; her sweaty breasts and a pound of sand tumbled out of the cups while her glorious breasts screamed for air and relief. We climbed into the shower together and hosed off enough sweat to fill Lake Erie.

Binky swore off wearing bras. It would be at least two months before she could muster the courage to wear another one.

Thank goodness the hotel had a laundry service.

I would not want to be the chap who opened up that laundry bag in the morning.

After showers that felt heavenly and flossing the sand out of our teeth, we ordered pizza into our room and watched reruns of *Dinky the Orange Teddy Bear* on the television.

"Dear Paul, here, please have an ice-cold Big Boulder beer. I know those Dingleberries are way too sweet," Binky said as she smiled. My wife reached into the little refrigerator in our hotel room and handed me a beer. Binky skipped the usual question. After all these years, she knew the answer and she was too tired to waste the energy. The question remained of why the Dingleberries were even in the refrigerator to begin with. The hell with it. I would worry about it another time. I spun the top off the bottle and took a long swig.

I never tasted such a wonderful brew.

Within forty-two seconds, Binky and I fell sound asleep amongst the drone of the cool air rolling out of the front of the heavenly air-conditioner. So much for those seductive promises of romantic interludes.

The kiddies were thrilled as they stayed up watching cartoons on television, playing checkers and Warship until all hours of the night, while their exhausted parents recovered from the revenge of the ducks. I woke up a few times, when I heard Paul William complain that his sister was cheating and moving her warships around on the game board, but I was too exhausted to intervene.

I mumbled aloud, "Calm down, kids. Everyone cheats at Warship." I then drifted off into a blissful heavenly sleep of merriment. My mind was full of tramcars, frozen custard cones, and cute little pedal duckies.

The next day, Binky and I walked as if we were wooden soldiers. We moved so slowly that it took us four hours to make it from our hotel room to the lobby of the hotel. Our legs and back muscles were tighter than my old man's wallet. We stiffly sat through breakfast, and then went to the local pharmacy to buy heating pads and menthol heat rubbing ointment. We put any thoughts of romance on a back burner for a few days! Instead, we took turns rubbing ointment on the various painful areas of our aching bodies, and soaked in baths filled with bath salts. Our hotel room smelled like a menthol den of pain-relieving bliss. Instead of any additional sandy beach time, or boardwalk adventures, we retreated to our hotel room; we lazily slept the rest of our happy beach vacation away. We cranked the air conditioner temperature down and enjoyed an escape from sunburn, sand, heat, humidity, and pedal-powered ducks. Even the kiddies slept the day away. The entire holiday caught up with all of us!

I swear even in my dreams I could hear it, "Watch the tramcar, please! Watch the tramcar, please! BEEP! BEEP! BEEP! Watch the tramcar, please! Watch the tramcar, please! BEEP! BEEP! BEEP!"

Then my beautiful, sexy wife floated around above my head in my dreams seductively saying, "Besides, this ride is a simple, little kiddies ride. You just pedal the cute, little, duckies around on the rail with pedals. It is relaxing and fun too, my dear, twenty-seven."

I found myself sitting on the arm of the chair in my office, still staring out at the snowstorm. The wind blew hard and I could hear the impact of the snow hitting the glass windows of my office. I stood up and stretched. I felt the back of my legs. In my mind, I guess that I was just checking to be sure that my muscles were still not sore.

"Back to my essay," I mumbled aloud to myself.

Sitting back down at my desk, I realized that the ideas still would not come. I picked up the paper, and with my pen, crossed out the title of the essay with a big black letter, X, and instead replaced the title with, "Revenge of the Ducks." Just the thought of writing that story brought a smile to my face. The memories were so vivid!

What a great family holiday. Memories such as these we can never replace, and in a strange, painful sort of way, that holiday was very special. When summer comes, I just have to have a Big Bob's, triple dip, orange flavored, frozen custard. I am sure in one of my desk's drawers that I can find a grain of sand from that adventure. As a reminder of it, I still occasionally find sand in my old sneakers.

I wonder if those stupid ducks are still there?

You can be sure that I will first stake the ride out and see who climbs in the ducks ahead of me. Forgive me Lord, but no two-ton tubbies allowed. After all, it is just a cute, little, ducky ride.

"Watch the tramcar, please! Watch the tramcar, please! BEEP! BEEP! BEEP! Watch the tramcar, please! Watch the tramcar, please! BEEP! BEEP! BEEP!"

THE END

Dr. Salami's Magic Elixir

"Did you read the headlines on the front-page tonight, my dear? I see a plane had engine trouble, and the pilot had to land it on Route 23!"

"Huh? Yeah, yeah, yeah . . . so what? It is the biggest bunch of bullshit road in the history of the world. Ya know, it is Route 23. That ain't no big deal. All kinds of weird things happen on that road. A plane landing on it is perfectly normal."

"An airplane landing on the highway at rush hour is normal?" Our dear Mum asked.

The old man was now frustrated at my dear mum's efforts at making small talk before dinner. He pushed the newspaper down and away from his face, and looked over the top of the paper at Mum.

"Yeah, it is normal. Like I said, it is Route 23! Don't ya 'member last summer, when the circus wagon overturned and all kinds of zebras and big-ass elephants were running all over that stupid highway? I agree with the guys from the shop who ride that road every day. That road is full of ding-dongs, wackos, maniacs, and lunatic drivers that should have their licenses revoked."

The old man first looked at Mum, then he glanced at my sister, Dorothy and then me. He was waiting for our response.

We all shrugged our shoulders. I almost opened my mouth and made the comment that the guys from the shop seemed to have categorized themselves, but I decided that silence, in this case, was golden.

"Don't youse guys 'member the elephant story on the news, huh?" The old man was still staring at us. He seemed as if he did not want to let go of the elephant and zebra escape story.

Mum dove in to take one for the team, "Well, no honey, actually. . .."

The old man cut Mum off. His patience was nil tonight, in fact, his patience usually was nil most every night.

"You people can't 'member nuthin.' It was last year, one of the guys from the shop, saw the whole scene and they interviewed him live on the eyeball news update on channel seven. The big-ass elephant went nuts, chased some big lard ass guy who thought his ass was bigger than the elephant's ass was. He tried to corral him and the elephant trampled him like a pancake. The big dope ended up in the hospital. It was on the news. Soooo, a damn airplane landin' on that road, ain't nuthin."

Mum screwed her face up and said, "I think, I vaguely recall. . .."

"Say, when are we eatin'? Is it going to be sometime today, or in the near future?" The old man asked as he picked the newspaper back up and focused his attention back to the primary mission, which was the sports page, and news about his beloved New York Bugs baseball team.

"Ha! That bum, Billy "The Banjo" Hoppleburger is hurt again! I swear that bum is hurt every week. Oh well, it is early in the year yet, only May. Baseball, don't get serious 'till the all-star break. He got one hit in a World Series ten years ago, and he ain't done nuthin' since then. He is a bum! I bet he has a hangnail. He is the biggest pansy la-la, cupcake that evah played the game."

Mum served the old man a large helping of macaroni and cheese, with a side hamburger on a toasted bun, and in doing so, Mum cut the old man's rant and tirade short. Suddenly, Hoppleburger was a distant memory.

"That's nice. Here you go, my dear. This will make you forget guitar-playing Hoppleburger and all of his troubles."

Our English-born dear Mum never did understand the game, and she never correctly pronounced the names of the baseball players.

"Nah, nah, nah, the banjo . . . honey. Hoppleburger plays the banjo."

"Yes, dear. Do you want a Big Boulder beer or a Dingleberry tonight?" Mum stood in front of the open refrigerator and asked the question that I had heard more times than I could ever count.

The answer never changed.

"Big Boulder. Those Dingleberries are too sweet."

The age-old question remained. Why, oh why, did we even buy Dingleberry beer?

Dinnertime was always an adventure; however, the prelude to eating was usually more entertaining than the actual consumption of the meal was. Silence ensued once the meal was set down in front of us. Other than the occasional, "Please pass the pepper, or pass me a napkin," type of dialogue; it usually became remarkably quiet while we all ate.

In particular, the old man did not say much at all. His primary focus was in eating his meal as fast as he possibly could, and tonight was no exception!

The old man had a habit, which he claimed he adopted from his military days, of leaning over his plate and shoveling the food into his mouth as if it was his last meal on Earth. He told us that in the military, you never had more than a few minutes to eat.

The habit drove our grandfather crazy. "Gramps," as we called him, was Mum's father, and he lived in the apartment upstairs from us and he would usually join us for most meals. Gramps was out tonight with his other daughter, our Aunt Lois, so tonight we would not witness the usual humorous exchange between our very proper English Grandfather and the old man's unique eating display.

Tonight, the old man was in a fine dinner consumption form. He bent in closely over his plate and while keeping his mouth mere inches away from the plate, the old man, furiously shoveled in the macaroni and cheese, only taking an occasional break to come up for air, in order to take a sip of his Big Boulder beer, or to take a bite of the burger. A quick sip, a quick bite, a little gasp of air, and his head dove back down into his dinner plate, while heaping spoonful after spoonful of the macaroni and cheese into his mouth.

Even in the annals of many rather incredible, past displays of "speed eating," by the old man, tonight's adventure turned out to be epic in nature.

The old man swallowed the last scoop of the macaroni and cheese, a big gulp of hamburger, a swish of beer, he sat back, his eyeballs darting back and forth in his head, his chin full of a cheese residue, and some foam from the beer gathered in the corner of his mouth.

Mum admired the amazing performance, and she commented in her typical, gentle fashion, "My goodness, dear. I guess it was good, but you really should slow down a bit when you eat. Your poor stomach does not stand a chance even to digest the food. Ten minutes from now, you will need some of your Big Bob's Super, Whiz-Bang, Tummy, Fizzly Whizzly pills."

The old man leaned back, first a little smile, and then a wide smirk appeared on his face.

What is the saying? The path to a man's heart is through his stomach.

"Nah, nah, nah, ya been telling me that same bullshit for twenty years. I could digest a rock! In the Army, they called me, Iron Gut Henson! Let me have some more, will ya? A scoop or two more of that, there mac and cheese. Ya see, ya got to eat fast in the military on the chow lines because, they rush ya along."

My sister rolled her eyes as the old man, once more, glided into relating the tale of how he developed his bad habit of swallowing his food whole.

My sister Dorothy, being three years older than I was, had reached her archetypal teenage years. She now was firmly entrenched in the rebellious teen-age phase, where speaking to your parents required an intense effort and serious subjects. Therefore, she sighed and went back to chewing.

I tuned in to listen to the story for the bijillionth time, because somewhere deep in my heart, I knew that someday many years in the future, my heart would ache to hear our father tell this story just one more time.

Dinner finally ended, we broke up into cleaning up details, with my sister and me, helping Mum to clean the table and wash up the dishes. Automatic dishwashers did not exist in our household. Well, maybe they did. They called the dishwashers Dorothy and Paulie. As far as the automatic part goes. . ..

After clean up ended, my main mission would be to take out the garbage. If I ever forgot that mission, I always paid the price. The old man would place the garbage can in my bed. I would then not only have to take the garbage out to the main trashcan, I would have to change out my bed linens, the blankets and do the laundry too. The old man would even deduct money from my allowance, or dip into my savings and force me to pay for the laundry soap and water that I utilized, due to my error!

I did not forget too often. The old man had a very effective manner of teaching you never to neglect your duties.

The old man grabbed another Big Boulder beer, tucked the newspaper under his arm, put his coveted Bugs hat on his head, and headed for his easy chair. It was almost time for New York Bugs baseball! Hoppleburger or not, the games would go on!

Soon, our living room filled wall-to-wall, with the voices of Blabber Viscardi, Johnny Mclaughy, Ralph "The Rocket" Lenard and Bob McGee as the play-by-play announcers for the New York Bugs. The announcers were just as if they were old neighborhood friends.

We were just about finished with the kitchen duties, the garbage duty was behind me, and I was about to head to my bedroom to work on a report on world history for some annoying schoolwork assignment, when surprisingly, the old man appeared in the kitchen. It was a surprise, because as a general rule of thumb, once the game started, the old man would only leave his chair, and the television, for a bathroom call, which might be due to a slight over consumption of Big Boulder beer.

His usual war cries of, "Ya only rent beer, coffee and tea," would echo throughout the house, as he hustled off to the bathroom and then bolted back to the game, amidst the sounds of a toilet flushing as a backdrop.

This time was different.

The old man stood in the center of the kitchen. He was rubbing his stomach, his mouth turned up into a pug face, and his color looked a little on the greenish side.

Oh, oh!

Ole Iron Gut Henson was more as if he was Tissue Paper Tum-Tum Henson.

Mum instantly jumped into nurse mode, "What's wrong, dear? You look a little sick."

"Yeah, yeah, yeah, my gut is turning over and over. Do ya got any of those Big Bob's Super, Whiz-Bang, Tummy, Fizzly Whizzly pills? Ya know, the kind ya plop in the water and they fizz all over the damn glass."

"You really need to stop eating so. . .." Mum cut short the analysis that my sister and I also wanted to provide and we all bit our tongues in order to keep the words from emitting from our mouths. The glare from the old man warned all of us not to go there.

Instead, self-preservation kicked in. Mum deftly shifted her mouth gearshift and provided the requested location of the famous Big Bob's tum-tum cure-all.

"Of course, we have them. I buy a new pack every week for your stomach troubles. The lemon-lime flavor. You like them the best. In the top of the cupboard, over there, next to the cooker. Top, left side."

Mum bought Big Bob's magic pills by the caseload.

The old man nodded, and solemnly, he went over to the cupboard, grabbed the magic pills, took a glass, filled it with cold water and plopped the pills into the water. The soothing, gentle fizz told the old man that shortly, the fizzy cure would coat his stomach with happiness. Once the magic of the fizz died down, he gulped the tonic down. Since this was an adventure, which we had all experienced many times with the old man and a scene repeated many times, after many meals, we all knew what was coming next.

He stood there holding his glass while waiting for it to arrive. The coveted and highly anticipated "Belch of Relief," awaited.

A deep breath, a tummy rub, he leaned his head back and, and, and we waited. . ..

The old man said, "Now, I just got to belch out the fizzy stuff and I am fine."

Yes, same scene, but on this go around there was nothing! There was no arrival of the blessed Belch of Relief! The magic pills failed!

Another tummy rub, his head leaned back, and once again, nothing! A total misfire.

"Huh? A misfire! They did not work. Musta got a bad batch of Big Bob's Super, Whiz-Bang, Tummy, Fizzly Whizzly pills. Is the pack expired and the fizz all let out of 'em?"

The old man studied the box for an expiration date. Not

finding the answer for which he sought, he piped up with the obvious solution, "Let me try another shot. They musta forgot to put the fizzly in 'em."

Two more pills, into the water, fizz, swallow; head back, tummy rub . . . and nothing! Mum suggested that he go and lie down, of which the old man scowled at the mere suggestion of missing the Bugs game. Instead, he dispatched my sister to go check on the progress and report to him about what was occurring in the game.

"Dorothy, shake your little ass in there. Tell me what the score is, and who is up!"

My sister escaped the kitchen. She seemed happy to avoid the potential belch, which was looming eerily on the horizon.

Now, the old man looked for a deeper cause for his tummy woes. Anything other than his poor eating habits were fair game now. He already declared the magic pills to be a "bad batch," therefore, he required an alternate angle.

He looked at dear Mum and said, "Ya must have not cooked the macaroni and cheese enough. The cheese mix is erupting inside my gut with the macaroni cuz it was not cooked enuff. It can't be the burger because it was hard as a rock."

Oh, oh! I think I was going to exit stage left now.

Mum's face turned red. Steam blew out her ears and her eyeballs squinted down into anger mode. Mum put her hands on her hips; she shook her head at the mere suggestion that under-cooking the food was the source and culprit of the old man's tummy woes.

"We all ate the same thing. None of us have sick stomachs. I always cook our food well-done. I can't believe you would say that!" Mum was obviously angry.

That was true; most food that Mum cooked usually was so hot that it peeled the wallpaper off the kitchen walls when she removed it from the oven. I do recall one time when she melted a stainless-steel pot into a pile of molten steel. Under-cooking was definitely not the cause of the now controversial stomach woes of the old man.

As so often it occurs, in situations such as these, the truth finally comes out.

"If you would not swallow your food whole, and suck it down as if it is the last meal that you will ever eat, then your stomach would not be so upset!" The HMS Mum fired away with full Mum cannons and hit the USS Old Man broadside.

The old man was too green and too sick to his tum-tum in order to fight back. The USS Old Man turned belly up and sank.

He had played an impossible card with the under-cooking suggestion, there was no Belch of Relief on the horizon, and just to top off the disaster cake, Dorothy returned and reported that, "The other team was up at bat and they were now ahead two to nothing."

The old man put his head down and mumbled, "I hate them damn Minnysoder (Minnesota was an impossible word for a person from New Jersey to pronounce correctly) Retro-Rockets, they always beat the Bugs. I am gonna go to bed and listen to the game on the radio."

He put his head down and slowly wandered off to the bedroom. Now, Mum shifted gears and felt bad that the old man was this sick. For him to miss the game on television, even if the Retro-Rockets were winning, you knew he did not feel well.

"Come along, honey. I will warm-up the radio, tune in the game for you and tuck you into bed. You know, maybe tomorrow, you should make an appointment with Doctor Salami and have him look at your stomach. The Big Bob pills did not work."

I braced myself for the eruption. I thought, even in sick mode, the old man would not allow one of his foremost mortal enemies on Earth to go by unscathed.

The mere mention of Doc Salami's name, usually set the

old man off on a long tirade, laced with, "He is a rip-off, he is a bum, overpriced, crook, some jerk posing with a medical license that he bought at a department store" and many other adjectives of a colorful nature. Some of them were unrepeatable, and rather questionable, as the old man attempted to classify poor Doctor Salami. Ever since Doctor Salami moved into our neighborhood and became our family doctor, the old man and the good doctor waged a war of a love versus hate relationship.

To further the cause of friction between the two men, ever since I started playing the position of goaltender in street, roller and ice hockey, and due to the nature of the position and the game, I now almost constantly required medical aid and stitches for my various cuts and injuries.

The constant need for medical care had my father soundly pronounce Doctor Salami to be, "A con-artist, posing as a doctor! He charges me a buck a stitch to sew ya ass up, then a buck each to take out what he put in!"

The old man, in an amazing display of typical, New Jersey street deal-making had won a battle of bargaining, when he successfully negotiated the stitch removal price down to fifty cents per stitch, but that had done very little to elevate the old man's opinion of poor Doctor Salami.

About ten years ago, Dr. Salami moved into the old brick building right across the street from us. It had the obligatory second floor office and a treacherous wooden staircase, and the building smelled like mothballs.

One day, he came door-to-door introducing himself, asking folks to consider him for their family doctor. He was from Syria in the Middle East, and he was tall, round, and had a nice smile and dark mutton chop sideburns.

In reality, Doctor Salami was a nice guy. He always wore a stethoscope around his neck, and if he met you on the street or in the Foodworld food market, he would always stop to say hello, shake your hand, he would smile and say, (even if you knew him) "Hi, I am Dr. Salami" in his charming accent.

"Daddy, it's seven to nothing now!" Dorothy called out from the living room in keeping up with the old man's order to inform him of the Bugs' current dilemma.

The anticipated explosions at the mention of the good doctor's name and the score of the game, surprisingly, did not materialize. Instead, he offered a rather solemn and subdued description of Doctor Salami and his favorite baseball team.

The old man wandered off to bed, his head down, and his feet dragging along the floor, while speaking a barely audible, "Yeah, yeah, yeah, ya might be right. I might need to go and see that. Bum Salami. He is a bigger bum than Hoppleburger is. . .."

The old man's tricky stomach had won this battle, but the old man was not completely out of it. He still managed to speak out a mellowed, but still, hard-hitting analysis of Doc Salami and Hoppleburger.

Despite the adverse, tum-tum situation and the thrashing the Bugs were suffering from in this evening's game, we all knew that the old man would not be down for too long.

The old man would never allow a little green skin, a pug face, a sick stomach and a Bugs defeat; stop him from going to work. He had not missed a day of work in thirty-five years, and the next day was no exception to this rule. Off he went to work the next day, his lunch pail tucked proudly under his arm, and inside of the trusty pail was a stash of Big Bob's now disappointing pills. Off he went, still seeking the blessed Belch of Relief.

Late that afternoon, my sister and I arrived home from school and Mum announced that dinner would be a little late. The old man had arrived home from work and gone off to an appointment with Doctor Salami to have his stomach checked. As the late afternoon waned and turned into early evening, Mum, occasionally, would walk over to one of the front windows of our home, part the curtain, and glance over across Belmont Avenue, to see if there were any police cars responding to Doctor Salami's office.

Finally, the back door of our home burst open, our faithful fox terrier Skippy barked to signal the arrival of the old man, I heard the old man yell something to our sometimes, pet cat, Pussface, who was hanging out on the back porch and the door slammed shut. We all quickly responded to the kitchen to see how the old man made out.

He smiled ear-to-ear, and he seemed to be in good spirits. This, in itself, was a very unusual result for a visit to Doctor Salami's office.

"How did you make out, dear? Did Doctor Salami find anything?"

The old man had a bag tucked under his arm, and while still smiling, he pulled a large brown bottle out of the bag and placed it on the kitchen table. It was a large bottle, about the size of a glass milk bottle, and it had what appeared to be a gold-colored screw cap for a top.

The old man spouted off happily, "Yeah, yeah, yeah, I mean nah, nah, nah. He said I just got some kind of trapped gas or some kind of stomach bug. He gave me this here, tonic stuff that he mixed up in his office. He said it was an old remedy from where he is from. Ya know, the country where he is from. What is the name of it, Cereal? Or, whatever you people say."

I decided to prove my knowledge of geography, "Syria, Dad. He is from Syria."

"Yeah, yeah, yeah . . . that is what I said. Cereal."

It was now growing intriguing as to why the old man was so happy after a visit to the good doctor's office, and all of us sensed his strange euphoria. There was something more to this story, a doctor's visit, a bottle of medicine; it was all very strange behavior from the old man and not typical for him at all. As of yet, the old man had not even insulted Doctor Salami. Even Skippy sensed it and he crept into the kitchen and sat on the floor, looking up towards the old man for an explanation.

"Now, Paul, you seem to be very happy, especially after a visit to the doctor. What else did he say? Or did he just give you this bottle of medicine?" Mum asked, as she picked up the bottle and examined it. Before the old man could answer, she read the label aloud to all of us, "Doctor Salami's Magic Elixir."

"Awwww, yeah, yeah, yeah, he said, I ought to slow down when I eat. Slow down just a little, he says to me. Just a little, but this here goo in this bottle is the best part. I got that medicine for nothin'! The crook felt bad for ripping me off for all of these years and for having a medical license that he bought in the fishin' aisle at Crumbley's Department Store, so he gave me the bottle of stomach goo for free. A sample he called it."

Ah hah! Now it made sense! The source of the old man's euphoria now revealed. A free sample. That was almost as good as if Doctor Salami had given the old man a new stomach.

"What's for dinner? I am starved."

"Well, I made some homemade turkey soup. It has been on a low simmer since six o'clock this morning. I did not want you to eat a heavy meal. I did not know how your stomach would be."

"Six in the morning! Geez, it must be a damn volcano," the old man observed, while stirring the cavernous pot of molten soup, which was sitting on the oven burner. I prayed that we would not revisit the under or over cooking argument.

We all sat and enjoyed dinner. The old man sucked down about three full bowls of molten soup, a number of Big Boulder beers, and a few hundred crackers, all in record time.

With cracker crumbs lining his mouth, he wove intricate tales of bargaining and wrestling the magic elixir from Doc

Salami for free, then reluctantly admitted that he had to pay, "The bum, ten bucks for an office visit." Overall, when he tucked his newspaper under his arm, and fled for his easy chair to watch the Bugs final game versus the Retro-Rockets, all seemed well in the world.

The old man's stomach woes might be an ailment of the past.

Well, perhaps they might be.

We had just finished the dishes, and I had already taken the blessed garbage out to the trash cans. Pussface the cat, settled in for the night on the back porch, Skippy went to sleep on my bed, and the ball game seemed to be going well, since we did not hear any noises other than the occasional, normal obscenity hurled from the old man. It seemed as if it was going to be a normal evening.

Not that any night was actually "normal" in the Henson household.

Suddenly, the old man stood in the center of the kitchen. He was rubbing his stomach, his mouth turned up once again into a pug face, and his color looked a little on the greenish side.

Oh, oh! Here we go again!

Mum instantly jumped once again into nurse mode, "What's wrong, dear? You look sick once again! Is it your stomach again?"

"Yeah, yeah, yeah, my gut is turning over and over."

"Oh no. Here, let me get the special medicine from the cupboard. Sit down here and let me read the label to see how much to give you."

"The bum said to take two tablespoons of the goo," the old man already knew the dosage. We all watched intently as Mum unscrewed the top off Doctor Salami's Magic Elixir. She took a tablespoon and poured the tonic out onto the spoon. It was dark black, almost looking as if it were liquid tar. Even from a distance, it smelled as if it was mostly liquid tar.

"Open up now. One. . .."

We all cringed as Mum spooned the first shot down the old man's trap. "Here is another, two. . .."

The old man shook his head in anguish at the taste of the medicine, he mumbled a barely audible description of "This stuff tastes like damn motor oil," and then he finished the statement with something about, "Salami, being a pain-in-the-ass, rip-off, bum."

We all waited.

The old man stood up from the chair, Mum stood, poised with her trusty, tablespoon in hand. Skippy jumped off my bed and made a guest appearance. Pussface the cat meowed on the porch. We all stood in anxious anticipation.

A deep breath, a tummy rub, the old man leaned his head back and, and, and, from the deep recesses of the inner workings of the old man's tum-tum, it came bursting out. A sonic boom and a belch, heard around the world.

"BBBBBBUUUURRRRRRRRRRPPPPPPPPPPP!"

Geez! All the teacups in Mum's cupboards rattled, the front door to our house blew off the hinges, Gramps fell out of his chair in his apartment upstairs, a few Dingleberry beers rolled around in the refrigerator and exploded and dogs howled throughout the neighborhood. Skippy ran for his life. Pussface jumped out the back-porch window, and we all held onto the kitchen table as the floorboards in the old house at 182 Belmont Avenue shook, rattled and rolled.

I swore that I heard fire and police sirens going off in the background. It was indeed the greatest "Belch of Relief" ever recorded or heard in the history of mankind, and it echoed throughout the entire world.

The old man stood in the kitchen, smiling ear-to-ear. We, however, could have done without such a violent cure. Now mind you, we were all happy that the old man had found his magic cure, but admittedly, right now it was a bit of a rough cure to deal with. Once we all recovered from the sonic blast, and we checked the old man to make sure his mouth and his nose had not blown off his face, then we listened and observed.

"This stuff here is the greatest goo ever. Did ya hear that?"

"Ah yes, we did, dear. I think people in Australia heard it and are calling the police," Mum testified to the belch's power.

"I think that the number fourteen bus overturned out on Belmont Avenue," I offered my testimony.

"Salami has invented a magic cure here! The bum is a genius! I swear that I burped up a hot dog that I ate when I was ten years old!"

This was becoming even more graphic and a bit much for my sister.

"I am glad you feel better, Daddy," Dorothy said as she fled for the safety of her bedroom. My sister pulled the door to her bedroom closed behind her and she tore the mattress off her bed and stacked it against the door.

"Ole Iron Gut Henson has returned! I am back! Wait 'till I tell the guys from the shop. We can all have hot dogs all the way, with extra onions, over at Libby's Lunch for chowtime again, without spending the rest of the afternoon in the bathroom at the shop. There are only four toilet bowls in there, ya know."

Mum and I nodded our heads. It was nice to see the old man feeling so well again. We could do without some of his rather, graphic testimony, but it was nice that Ole Iron Gut Henson had made such an awe-inspiring comeback.

"Pack a tablespoon in my lunch pail and put that bottle of goo next to my pail, so that I can bring it to the shop tomorrow. Let me go see if Jim Beaver has those Retro-Rockets on the ropes now. If only that bum Hoppleburger would get his cupcake ass back off the disabled list!"

One day after school, a week or so later, I was sitting out on the front steps of our front porch at 182 Belmont

Avenue, watching the crazy world go by. I often sat here, sometimes by myself, or sometimes Gramps would join me and we would sit together. Sitting there on the front steps, we shared some special times. Sometimes, I would read a book, sometimes a magazine, or sometimes, I just watched the world go by.

I happened to look over towards Dr. Salami's office, and I noticed a line of people coming down the front steps from his second-floor office. It wound its way outside the front door, and continued down the sidewalk. There must have been fifty or sixty people waiting in line. Wow! Are that many people sick? It was now late May and the flu bug was long since passed, winter's grip and typical illnesses were gone now.

Spring had sprung, and summer loomed.

I looked up and spotted the old man's famous 1964 Putter Classic Model 200 car. Turning the corner and it hit the vehicle's threshold with a top speed of about twenty miles per hour. I could see the old man gun the gas pedal as he turned onto Belmont Avenue. A long line of cars followed behind him, with the drivers beeping their horns and shaking their fists at the slow speed of our beloved family car. The old man gripped the steering wheel in a death-grip and leaned into the car with a purpose. He looked as if he was standing on the gas pedal to squeeze every ounce of meager horsepower out of our old family vehicle.

Eventually, he pulled into the driveway, and looking down at my watch, I noticed that he was about a half an hour earlier than he usually would be for returning home from work.

The old man shut off the engine, and the car rattled to a dramatic stop. It had over four-hundred-thousand miles on it now. The car was not pretty, but it still ran. Well, the car sort of still ran.

The old man frantically jumped out from the car, he

slammed the door, ran over to me and shouted, "Quick! Get ya skinny ass over there and get in line, Paulie! The word on the street is that Doc Salami has a new batch of magic goo ready and he is gonna run out soon. I did not take lunch today so that I could get home earlier. Get ya ass over there and hold a spot while I go inside and get the dough from your mother. Go!"

I set my book aside on the steps, nodded my head, jumped up off the front steps, judged the traffic, sprinted across Belmont Avenue and moved into position in line. I had to do my part to preserve old Iron Gut Henson for posterity.

Standing on the line in front of me, there was a large assortment of people from throughout the old neighborhood. Old people, young people, construction workers, the realtor and the insurance guy from the office around the corner, and the daytime bartender from the Widow's Pub. It seemed as if the entire neighborhood was now waiting in line to buy a bottle of the now famous Doctor Salami's Magic Elixir!

I overheard the clatter of conversations while I stood there.

"My uncle took it for a month, he was as bald as a billiard ball, and now he has grown hair on his head!"

Another testimonial from the far end of the line, "Well, my son had this pain in his lower back for years. He had it ever since, a truck backed into him and squashed him like a grape, when he was working at the Paterson Bus Garage. Two bottles and he can now stand upright!"

I listened as some red-faced woman of about seventy years of age turned and whispered gently to the woman next to her, "Well, my Henry had the problem . . . you know . . . where *it* did not work. He had a limpy. Now, after three bottles of this, well, he can drill holes in the wall and he chases me around the house every night!"

Oh, my. It seems as if Doctor Salami has created a cure-all for much more than just winky-dinky, tum-tums!

The old man joined me in line. He was panting, his eyeballs were bugging out, and his ears were beet red, while he was eagerly holding six dollars in his hands.

"Did that bum Salami show up yet?"

"No, Dad. Not yet."

"That bum is raking in the dough on this stuff. Amazing. Wish I knew how to invent goo."

I looked around at the number of people standing in this line and most of us were dirt-poor people from this old neighborhood, and I had to agree with the old man. All of us were willingly digging around for a few extra dollars to purchase the magic tonic. It appeared as if Doc Salami had hit the big time.

We heard a murmur, and then a quiet calm of a hush come over the crowd, and standing tall above most people, I could see all the way to the front of the line. Right at the front door of his office, working the line one person at a time, I could now see that Doctor Salami had appeared. He had a young man with him, and they had boxes loaded upon a two-wheel hand truck. The young man followed along while Doctor Salami worked the crowd, selling his Magic Elixir to the eager world.

This was amazing. Soon, Doctor Salami would be world famous!

As each person received a bottle of the heavenly mixture, Doctor Salami would hand the person a bottle. He would smile and say, "Hello, I am Doctor Salami. Please, a limit of one bottle per person. That will be four dollars please."

When the old man overheard the transaction, he double-checked with me, "Did that bum just say four bucks and only one bottle per person!"

"He sure did, Dad. Yes."

"Holy shit, Paulie! That bum just raised the price, a buck a bottle and now, I can only get one bottle!"

"Hello, Mr. Henson. Hello, Paulie. I am, Doctor Salami."

"Geez, Doc Salami, do ya have to introduce yaself every damn time? Ya the only Salami 'round here!"

"That will be four dollars, please. Do you need any stitches today, Paulie?"

"No. thank you, Doctor Salami. No hockey games today. In fact, the hockey season is over until fall."

Doctor Salami was quite the entrepreneur.

"Oh, too bad. Perhaps, you will whip up an injury or two by just practicing shooting in the off-season. I have my needle and thread ready. See you soon. Next! Hi! I am, Doctor Salami. . .."

Spring came, went, and summer came and went, too. As usual, despite the late summer return of Hoppleburger from his hangnail, the poor New York Bugs finished in last place and the baseball season was happily over. Ole Iron Gut Henson prevailed, and despite the stomach-turning season of his beloved Bugs, the old man, equipped with the faithful assistance of his magic potion, could swallow down anything as fast as he could chew it. When an eruption occurred, he would then just swig down a few tablespoons of the nectar of the gods and all would be well.

As far as the belches go, we became used to rearranging the overturned kitchen furniture from the impact of the resonations.

"Ah geez, what a pain-in-the-ass this hockey bullshit is! Why can't ya play checkers or something like that? I can't stop it from bleeding. C'mon, I will take ya little wounded ass over to Doctor Salami's for a few stitches. I swear this stupid hockey stuff is gonna make me go broke. Anyway, I got to ask him when the next shipment of goo is coming in. I only got a half a bottle left, and I want to have a few, all the way hot dogs next week."

The old man was examining my latest cut, a deep nick above my right eye, from a slap shot that caught me high and hard. He rather quickly conceded defeat by trying to stop the bleeding on his own, with his oft-times primitive, yet sometimes effective methods. Thankfully, this time, he stopped short of stitching it on his own. The only benefit of that rather painful experience was the whiskey the old man would make me swig before grabbing his "special" needle and thread.

"I worked some overtime last week, so I got me a few bucks stashed in my beer money account."

Off we went, across the street, with me holding an ice pack above my eye, and the old man hollering and yelling the entire way, about how much playing hockey was costing him in medical bills. Off we went again, to see the magical Doctor Salami. Yes, it was now October, and it was hockey season once again.

"Hello, Mr. Henson. Hello, Paulie. I see that it is hockey season again. Please sit down, and I will tell Doctor Salami that you are spewing blood all over the waiting room. He is in with Mr. Quigley, who just has trapped gas again. We told him not to eat those franks and beans, but Mr. Quigley is a stubborn one. He will be right out." Doctor Salami's longtime assistant, Nurse Grudley, instructed us.

Privacy laws regulating health care did not exist back then and now, we all know of poor, Mr. Quigley's malady. At least, he was a step above the now revitalized Henry!

A few minutes later, after some rather disturbing noises that emitted through the closed door of the examination room, Mr. Quigley appeared. He seemed to have a bounce in his step and a smile upon his face.

"Go ahead inside, Paulie and Mr. Henson. Doctor Salami is ready for you."

"Say, Dad, maybe, we should wait a minute until it airs out?"

The old man ignored me and pushed me towards the room while commenting, "Get ya little pineapple ass in there. Salami might charge per minute. A little gas eruption ain't gonna matter much."

Off we hustled, and when we walked into the examination room, we both stopped dead in our tracks. Even with an ice pack over my eyes, between whiffs or two of suspicious reminders of Mr. Quigley's troubles, which remained in the air, and the swelling from the cut now closing down on my vision, I could see that the doctor standing in front of us, was not, Doctor Salami!

The old man, in the typical old man fashion, cut right to the chase, "Who the hell are you? Nurse Grudley said Salami was in here."

The doctor, who was standing in front of us, did have a similar appearance to *the* Doctor Salami. His facial features were similar. He was younger, as well as shorter and thinner than Doctor Salami was, but there was a definite resemblance.

The doctor smiled, he held out his hand and said, "Hello. I am, Doctor Salami. Doctor Harem Salami. I am Doctor Salami's younger brother."

"Younger brother? Harem, what kind of name is that? Ain't that a bunch of bare-ass twigeons? You ain't the regular Salami, huh? Where is the other Salami?"

"Oh, my brother is taking some time off. Yes, well, I see that it is hockey season. Please, sit up here, young man. Let's get that numbed up for you. My brother has mentioned you and the Henson family to me many times," the new Doctor Salami said to me, while he patted the examination table in a slightly precarious invitation.

I imagined the real Doctor Salami had briefed his brother as to which patients were whackos and which ones were normal.

I had a feeling that I knew where we placed on that list.

As far as the stitches and procedure, I knew the drill; this would be about one hundred stitches in my head alone.

"Time off? No one 'round here takes time off," the old man commented on a well-known old neighborhood fact and he added, "that's why God invented Sunday."

Vacations did not exist in our lives.

"My brother, well, he unfortunately took ill, and he had to have an operation. He will be out for a few months and until he gets back on his feet, I will cover his medical practice."

"Took ill! Geez, an operation. Youse guys are doctors, Youse is not supposed to get sick."

"We are doctors, Mr. Henson, not gods. We get sick too."

The old man nodded. It seemed as if he had some pangs of sympathy for his old nemesis and our humble family doctor. He stood there watching while Doctor Salami numbed my cut as a prelude to the needle and thread.

"So, are all youse Salamis's docs?"

"Yes, most of us are, Mr. Henson. We come from a long line of medical practitioners."

"Over in Cereal, huh?"

"What? Where?" The new Doctor Salami required a New Jersey translation.

I intervened to streamline the situation. Between cringing as the needle and the thread passed through my skin, I squeaked out, "My father means, Syria, Doctor Salami."

"Oh yes. That is correct. Syria."

"Say, new Doc Salami, ya brother gives me a discount on taking out these stitches. Ya know about that, right?"

"Yes, Mr. Henson."

"Good, good, good. Say, what went flewwie wid ya brother? Please, tell him that I hope he feels better."

"Thank you. I will extend your well wishes, Mr. Henson. He had two troubles. One was a stomach problem, and the other was a gallbladder attack. He had to have his gallbladder removed and they hope his stomach ulcer will heal on its own. Time will tell."

"Stomach otter and glass blotter trouble, huh? Sounds

kinda serious."

Neither Doctor Salami nor I corrected the old man on his anatomical identification. The good doctor already knew that it was futile.

The old man pondered it for a moment, and then his face perked up as a thought crossed his mind. It was the same thought that I had. I almost said something first, but the needle went in for the last pass, and the old man beat me to the statement.

"Say, ya brother, he does not drink his own magic goo or what the hell it is that he calls it . . . does he?"

"Well, he used to take two tablespoons a day, but I have to inform you, as well as everyone else, unfortunately, we no longer will be producing or selling Doctor Salami's Magic Elixir. It might cause some . . . side effects. I think you need to learn to eat slower, Mr. Henson. Chew your food and enjoy it."

The old man's eyes almost popped out of his head! Steam blew out of his ears. The four hairs remaining on the top of his head stood straight up, and his ears turned beet red.

"SIDE EFFECTS! SIDE EFFECTS! WHAT THE HELL DO WE DO NOW? GEEZ NOW, I NEED A NEW GLASS BLOTTER TOO! ALL YOOSE SALAMIS ARE BUMS!"

When we returned home, the old man, much to the sheer amazement of Mum, ran through the back door. He tore open the cupboard, took his bottle of Doctor Salami's Magic Elixir and ran over to the sink with it. He unscrewed the top and proceeded to pour the remaining contents of the former heavenly magical liquid down the drain.

"Honey, honey, honey! What are you doing?"

I leaned in, motioned to Mum, and whispered in her ear, "I will tell you later, Mum. You had better go to the Foodworld and stock up on Big Bob's Super, Whiz-Bang, Tummy, Fizzly Whizzly pills."

The old man finished pouring the remainder of the

former magic goo down the drain; he looked at Mum and asked, "Can ya look up in your little medical book, for the symptoms of when ya glass blotter is going flewwie? Check out stomach otters too! Quick! I might need an operation!"

I stood there, and despite the stitches and slight throbbing in my head, I could not help but laugh a bit at the latest wild Henson family adventure.

Dear Mum hustled off to find her medical book, and I smiled. I guess Ole Iron Gut Henson was running into some trouble, but in retrospect, it could be a whole lot worse.

After all, the old man could be poor Henry. . ..

THE END

Experience Counts

Old Hank pulled his car into the parking lot of the worldwide headquarters for Substantial Industries Worldwide LLC. Substantial Industries ruled the world. The company manufactured everything from cars to coffee mugs and anything in between. Anything that a person could ever imagine or want.

The ultimate company, an empire. Every product they made was of the highest quality, no corners cut, topnotch all the way! One would assume that the streets on the properties owned by Substantial Industries had pavements of gold and curbs made of diamond-plated stainless steel. In fact, their sales pitch was the pointed statement, "When the wimpy stuff just will not do the job, then go Substantial!"

That about summed it all up.

The corporate headquarters buildings were a collection of shining fortresses in the sky. The campus sprawled over thousands of acres, all of it set upon a hill in the suburbs of New Jersey. Towering into the sky, a preeminent testimony to the success of the company, and the dedication and money that was required to build it all and maintain it. Warehouses, office buildings, factories, and research and development laboratories, most every type of building in which you could ever imagine.

A pinnacle of American success!

Old Hank felt as if he had been a cornerstone of at least part of the success. You see, for almost forty-nine years, he pulled his car into the parking lot of Substantial Industries. When there were only two small buildings on the campus and Substantial Industries was still in the infancy, Old Hank was here. Around forty-nine years ago, Old Hank had answered an advertisement for a job opening to be the Plant Electrician and Power Plant Operator for an "up-and-coming company."

Old Hank had been here ever since.

He was an expert in the operation of the complex mechanical and electrical systems of the sprawling city in the sky. He enjoyed the work, he never aspired to be a supervisor or a manager. Hank passed by on those job offers whenever they came along. Instead, he kept the entire place ticking as if it were a fine watch. Over the many years, he responded to countless emergencies, restored plant operations after floods, thunderstorms, blizzards, power outages, blazing summer heat, and through bitter cold winter winds. Old Hank had seen many managers, supervisors and directors of the building maintenance and operations department come and go. Young men, old men, experienced men, not so experienced men, smart men, not so smart men; they all passed through time as if they were painters creating their own tapestries as they went on through one door and out the other.

He was a legend. Old Hank was the "go-to guy" when it all went south, the magic man who knew every creak and blip that the buildings and equipment would make and how to bring it all back to life when it did not want to cooperate.

You see, experience counts.

The previous director of the department, unfortunately, had passed away a few months earlier, and he had been a good one. Old Hank greatly missed him. He, too, knew the buildings like the back of his hand. He relied on Hank for the operation and maintenance of the main power plant and the mechanical systems, but the director surely knew all the other aspects of the building's infrastructure. He had the experience of a lifetime to support him, and the smarts to rely on old hands such as Old Hank when he needed him most.

Now, in his place, a new department director was hired. A young, cocky, recent graduate of a prestigious technical university, and he came along with a collection of degrees to wallpaper his office from floor to ceiling. Old Hank was sure that his family, and the young man, had the bills from endless student loans to pay for the tuition in order to prove his worth. "Mortgages without houses," was what it amounted to in Old Hank's opinion.

Oh, yes, and they made for nice wallpaper too.

What the young director enjoyed hearing the most was his own voice. He would hold endless meetings in order to ramble on and on endlessly in some useless babble, which made little sense, but was an all-out effort to show all the maintenance and operations employees just how brilliant the young man was. New methods, new computer programs, corrections to all the procedures and methods they were currently doing wrong, things he was changing, all the old ways were no longer any good. A university had taught him this, and taught him that, he knew all the theories of operation of every piece of equipment in the entire complex, and he intended to prove it to all the dull-minded and non-educated employees who reported to him!

New, new, and newer!

Old Hank just laughed and observed all the nonsensical chatter. He had seen it all before. In fact, he had seen it countless times throughout his long career. He called these types of guys "Meteorites." They flash in the sky in a brief moment of time and then burn themselves out as quickly as they appeared.

He was a quiet man, he and his wife lived modestly, they raised two children who were now all grown and living on their own. Substantial Industries had been good for him, he made a very good living, and he still enjoyed the work. After all, the equipment and all the buildings had become a part of him, a part of his life, and he intended to work as long as his health was still good and his mind was still sharp.

Old Hank had outlasted all the employees that started in Substantial Industries when he began his career. Newer employees would stop Old Hank in the hallways, or in the main cafeteria, and they would marvel at his employment identification badge with the number one hundred and twelve stamped upon it. Currently, no one has a lower number. They all were gone now.

Hank outlasted them all.

Yet, each day, with a great amount of sadness, he watched the young director dismiss a few more long-term employees of the maintenance and operations department. One of the longtime supervisors of the crew had also recently moved on, a middle-aged man named Tommy McKee. McKee was a good one, but he saw some writing on the wall too, and he took a severance package and moved on.

To replace them, the young manager would bring in younger people such as he was, all with big resumes full of degrees and no experience.

Smart, young, educated and . . . clueless.

They all started at the top, no longer did an employee work their way up from the entry levels, you see, the degrees elevated them to a higher status so all these new recruits would be supervisors, assistant managers and lead persons of the crews right away.

Old Hank wondered when his time would come. The old timer could feel it. In fact, he told his wife just the other night that it should not be too much longer now. Hank climbed out of his car, locked the door behind him, and made the long walk down the employee's path to the side door leading to the main chiller and boiler plant room. He carried his lunch pail, a small tool bag full of tools that he had kept since he graduated vocational school, and his building keys. It was early in the morning, around five or thereabouts, Hank was always one of the first maintenance employees to report for duty. It was late April now, a transition time of the year for the mechanical systems. He had seen it all many years before, heat in the morning, and then roll the big chillers for cooling in the afternoon.

Spring weather can never make up its mind.

Old Hank fiddled with the master key in the door lock, pushed the door open, and walked down the stairs into the huge main chiller and boiler plant. He flipped a light switch on and a quick turn of his head, a sharp listen with his ears, and a scan of the indicator lights on the equipment engineering boards, was all that Hank required to be convinced that all was well. The young director had recently installed a new building automation system, with the latest and greatest in whiz-bang controls to automate all the equipment, but Old Hank did not need all those fancy interfaces to tell him how the equipment was running.

He had his own interface.

Old Hank strode over to the workbench in the room, set his lunch pail on the work surface, and glanced through the overnight logbook. The night security officer was a sharp and a very reliable man. While conducting his building rounds, the security officer checked the systems during the graveyard shift, when the last plant operator went off duty. Hank knew any minor issues would be in the logbook and with Tommy McKee gone; he relied upon the security officer to call him at home for any major or emergency troubles. Hank went down the log entries, and he saw that all was well. The main plant was in good shape; it was time to put his gear away and make the rounds of all the other buildings and systems within the huge complex.

When Hank arrived at his locker in the locker room for the maintenance employees, he saw a small note posted upon the door of his locker. Hank peeled it off, held it and read the note: "Come and see me, first thing in the morning, when I arrive in my office. Around ten o'clock this morning is good." The young director signed the note with his flamboyant and rather silly scrawling signature.

Hank chuckled, crumbled the note in his hand, while simultaneously saying aloud, "He starts his day at ten and is out by four thirty to beat the traffic. I have already worked five hours when he is just coming in."

Hank knew what the meeting was all about. The train was going to pull into the station and make one, last, stop. It had finally come to the end of the tracks.

Ten o'clock found Old Hank sitting in the fancy office of the young director. The same office with all the degrees covering the walls. The young director was dressed in a wonderful, fitted suit, with a fancy watch on his wrist, a fresh, spiffy, fancy haircut, a fresh spray tan and his initials inscribed upon his tie clasp. On his feet, he wore fancy black shoes; they were highly polished and equipped with fancy wingtips. Hank had seen a similar pair in the store window a few weeks ago while browsing in the shopping mall with his wife, and he marveled at the high price tag on them.

The young director had a different fancy suit for each day of the week. Each one was a different color, but they sure looked good. He also had a gorgeous young woman for each day of the week. The young man was a handsome man and Old Hank was quite sure that he had all the young women fooled into thinking that he was quite the catch. Yup, fancy suits, big paychecks, and spray tans lure them in. Old Hank smiled a bit at the thought that the previous director, the old timer, had worn work boots and a uniform, a different color scheme than his crew wore, but a uniform nonetheless.

As the young director began to babble, Hank found his mind started to wander. Hank thought about how he had one good suit to wear. He wore it to church and funerals, and he hoped that it would last long enough for his family to bury him in it. As far as fancy shoes, he would just ask his family to bury him in his work boots. After all, the casket would cover his feet up anyhow.

"Thank you for your many years of service, Hank. It is hard for me to tell you this, but with our new whiz-bang automation system, I am afraid your services will no longer be required here in the maintenance department. I have here a packet that contains all the information you will require. The company will be having a retirement celebration for you. Please clean out your locker, turn in any company issued tools, and see Darlene in the Human Resources Department for your retirement and severance packet." With that, the young director stood up, smiled a fake smile, handed a packet to Old Hank, and shook his hand.

"Wow! Forty-nine years! Congratulations."

Yup, forty-nine years and the train had indeed pulled into the station.

Hank did exactly what the young director told him to do; he cleaned out his locker, handed in a few tools, bid farewell to coworkers, said goodbye to his pumps and machines, and processed out with the nice, young woman named Darlene in the Human Resource Department. Old Hank unconcernedly listened to the sales pitch and glowing words of honor from Darlene at his long career. When she mentioned that she was only twenty-five years of age, all Old Hank could think of was that he had already been working at Substantial Industries for about twenty-five years when she was born.

A week or so later, Substantial Industries threw a big retirement party in Old Hank's honor at some fancy restaurant. Long-winded speeches, a gold watch, a big certificate, a few more shares of company stock, and more important people who enjoyed hearing each other speak.

Old Hank's wife wore her church dress, and Hank wore his only suit with his work boots. He spilled a little bit of a cocktail on the suit's lapel, but his wife told him the stain would come out by dry cleaning. Old Hank hoped that it would. He would hate to have a stained lapel while lying there in his casket.

A few months later, August arrived in New Jersey, and with it, along came a horrendous heat wave. They do occur in New Jersey and sometimes they will light your socks and your hair on fire.

This heat wave was a doozy. . ..

"WHAT DO YOU STUPID-ASS DOPES MEAN YOU CANNOT FIGURE OUT WHY THE MAIN CHILLERS AND THE BACK UP CHILLERS WILL NOT START? ALL THOSE DEGREES ON THE WALL AND YOU IDIOTS COME IN HERE WITH NO ANSWERS!"

The Executive Vice President of Substantial Industries, a certain Mr. Arnold Plank, had the young director and his stalwart team of young assistants lined up in his office, while he popped every blood vessel in his head at the news that the main chiller plant had failed, and the maintenance team could not figure out what the reason was.

To say that the buildings were becoming a little warm was a bit of an understatement. It was also very warm around the collar of a fancy suit worn by a certain young director of the maintenance department.

"Well, Mr. Plank, in our defense, it is an unusual trouble. We are waiting for a top-tier technician to be dispatched from the Super Wizard Control Company, but he is coming from Long Branch and it may take him an hour or two to arrive," the young director told Mr. Plank, while he nervously fingered his golden tie clasp.

That was the fancy clasp with his initials inscribed on it.

The operations manager for the critical data center

buzzed in on Mr. Plank's two-way radio, and the operation's manager reported the latest news from inside the center, "Two more degrees without cooling boss, and we lose the critical production servers in the data center. We will be dark in there, when the equipment shuts down due to the high temperature, and Substantial Industries will be losing approximately twenty-two-thousand dollars per second if we go another hour without cooling. We have never had a dark incident before in the history of our data center operations at Substantial Industries."

Mr. Plank was beside himself at the happy news and he leaned over his desk and yelled, "WELL, ISN'T THIS JUST WONDERFUL! PLAN MEN! WHAT IS THE PLAN?"

One of the young supervisors of the technical end of the maintenance group, whose name was Bradley McDermott, gingerly raised his hand and spoke up when Mr. Plank waved his hands at him to give him permission to speak.

"Well, sir, if we could bypass the automation controls, we could manually run the chillers, just as we did for many years . . . before . . . we installed the Wizard Control System."

"WELL, DO IT THEN, YOU DUMB-ASS IDIOTS!"

Bradley McDermott looked back and forth at his managers and directors, looking for someone to admit the truth. Not one of them was willing to be the sacrificial lamb.

The young man figured that at this point, they were all toast anyway, so he put his neck out there and reported the truth, "We do not know how to do it. Only, Old Hank knew how to do that."

Mr. Plank knew time was of the essence now, and he lowered his voice a little and tried very hard to remain calm.

Mr. Plank breathed in deeply and exhaled.

"Ya mean the supposed too old and too confused guy that you jackasses told me that we no longer needed, huh?"

He picked up the telephone on his desk, dialed his assistant and screamed into the telephone, "I need right now from Human Resources, the home telephone number of Old Hank. NOW, I DO MEAN RIGHT NOW! AS IN, IMMEDIATELY!" Mr. Plank slammed the telephone down and waved his hands in the air.

"You had better hope to you know what in your mess kits, that Old Hank is home!"

Old Hank was snoozing in his easy chair in his living room in front of the television. A daytime talk show had put him to sleep.

"Wake up, honey! It is Mr. Plank from Substantial Industries on the phone. He says it is a dire emergency. He needs to speak with you right away." Old Hank's wife was fervently shaking her husband in an effort to wake him from his nap.

Old Hank woke up, staggered from his easy chair, made his way to the telephone and said, "Hello, Mr. Plank."

"Hello, Hank. Say, we can chit chat another time. Right now, we are about to have the data center and buildings go down. It is horrible here and none of these stupid idiots here knows what the hell to do. The main chillers will not run, the buildings are a million degrees, the backups are down, the critical chillers are down and we are about one hour away from losing the damn data center. Hank, please, please, please, tell me that you can come and help us and save our ass. You are still a retiree. I will make sure we stick a huge bonus check in your pension check. Please, Hank! I do not care how much you will charge!"

"Sure, sure, sure, Mr. Plank. I am on my way and will be glad to help. I will be there as soon as I can."

"Thank you! Thank you, Hank. We will wait for you in the main chiller plant."

Hank hung up the telephone and calmly called out to his wife, "Say honey, do you know where my work boots and my little tool bag are? I gotta go in, dear."

You see, this was not his first emergency call.

Luckily, Old Hank had a short ride.

He parked his car in his old space, grabbed his tool bag, and made his way to the familiar side door. He found it open, walked inside, and climbed down the familiar staircase. A staircase that he could walk down blindfolded, and a team of men led by Mr. Plank anxiously greeted him.

Mr. Plank fervently shook Old Hank's hand as he proclaimed, "Thank goodness you are here, Hank! Please do what you can do as quickly as you can."

The young director came over and started to babble with his technical synopsis of the situation.

Hank held his arms and hands up in the air, and then he waved them violently, to indicate that the young director needed to stop talking.

Hank said, "Please, please, please, I can say this now, because you need me, more than I need you. So, just shut the hell up. I need to concentrate, and your jaws flapping around are not going to help me. In fact, why don't you go in your office, polish the glass on your diplomas on the wall, and touch up your spray tan. Besides, ya might get your fancy suit all dirty standing in here, for what I am sure is the first time that you have ever actually even seen machines like these."

Old Hank then mumbled just loud enough, "Dumb-ass punk."

The young director immediately shut up and a quiet hush came over the entire room. There was no equipment running, not even a pump, so the stillness was deafening.

Everyone watched as Old Hank set his tool bag down, and he removed an electrical meter from the bag. His eyes scanned the entire room, looking for the telltale lights on the control panels. He tilted his ears, listened carefully, looked here and there and checked the pulse of a room, in which he knew so well. Hank walked over to one of the control panels for the main chillers, opened the door, took his meter probes and made a few quick electrical measurements inside the panel.

No one said a word.

Old Hank walked over to the location of the new Whiz-Bang Wizard Automation Controls. While shaking his head, he studied the maze of cables, and then he reached over, pulled out the plug for the main control computer and watched the screen go dark. He then took his meter, opened another electrical panel box for the electronic controls, and took a few more electrical readings. He took a little screwdriver out of his bag, and slowly turned a control, while still eyeing and watching the meter very carefully. Hank moved the control with his screwdriver carefully and slowly. The needle on his meter bounced a little higher, and Old Hank turned the control in another direction. He moved the control back the other way until the needle on the meter steadied out and Old Hank seemed satisfied. Then, the old master electrician reached into another section of the panel and gently flipped three switches in a row.

"BOOOM! BOOOM!"

The sound of electrical relays and contactors closing echoed throughout the chiller plant. Then another noise, then another, and the lights on the main chillers started to glow softly, and then they increased to a brilliant glow.

"BANG! BANG!" Pumps turned on, gauges started to bounce and move and then, then, then, the sound of the main chiller starting to fill the room with noise.

"WHHHHIIIIIIRRRRRR!"

The centrifugal motor roared and came up to speed. The huge chiller machine shifted into high gear as it worked to capture the heat from the hot water that the pumps sent into the machine for cooling. Everyone in the room carefully watched a temperature gauge on the chiller as the water temperature slowly dropped a few degrees at a time, right in front of their eyes.

"You did it, Hank! You did it!" Mr. Plank led a group cheer as the collected group of employees back slapped and congratulated the old master.

Hank smiled, walked over to his tool bag, put his meter and screwdriver back in the bag and said, "Yeah, yeah, yeah. I told youse guys not to put that system in without an override switch. Good thing, before I left that I put one in. But no . . . all you punk-ass, jackleg, ding-dongs, nowadays think you know it all. Cuz that is what the diplomas hanging on ya walls say. Diplomas handed out by clueless professors who teach bullshit. They charge ya a fortune for it, but they never actually worked on one of these machines. They can tell ya the theory of how they work, but they can't work on 'em. We have over-educated everyone, but no one knows shit anymore unless it glows on a computer screen at 'em. Yup, youse guys know everything. When in reality, you don't know your asses from holes in the ground."

An hour later, Old Hank sat in the chair in front of the desk of Mr. Plank's fancy desk in his fancy office.

It was a lot cooler than it had been.

"Hank, old boy, we cannot thank you enough for saving the data center and all of our asses! How much do we need to put in your pension check for next month, my old friend? I am sure that Mr. Kingly Topgun, the CEO of Substantial Industries Worldwide LLC, will be calling you and thanking you with a gift too."

Old Hank sat back in the chair and smiled.

"Let's see now . . . I was watching my favorite show on television when ya called me. Hm, how about five thousand and two dollars, Mr. Plank? That ought to cover it."

Mr. Plank sat back hard in his chair. He appeared to be just a bit startled at the amount of money requested by Old Hank. Hank looked at him and noticed the apprehension.

"Ah, Mr. Plank. You did say on the telephone—

whatever amount that I required."

"Of course, Hank, of course. Believe me when I tell you that we cannot thank you enough and tell you how much we appreciate all that you did for us here today. It is just a very unusual amount. After all, not to minimize what you did, but you only pulled a plug or two, diddled some knob on a control, and flipped some switches, so five thousand dollars and a few bucks more, well, that is an awful lot of dough for that. However, I did say. . .."

"Oh no, Mr. Plank," Hank said, while shaking his head back and forth adamantly.

"You misunderstood me. I am only charging you two dollars to pull the plug, adjust the control, and to flip the switches. I am charging you five thousand dollars for the experience to know, which plugs to pull, control to turn, and switches to flip. You see, Mr. Plank, what those jackleg, smart-ass, young punks just don't get and understand, is that experience counts."

Mr. Plank smiled; he leaned forward, rubbed at his chin a bit and asked, "Say, there, Hank, how would ya like to make it to fifty years of service?"

The next week, the young director and the majority of his staff had all cleaned out their offices; all the fancy degrees and diplomas were gone from the walls. Instead, pictures of chillers and boilers, and logos from favorite baseball, hockey, and football teams, pictures of families, a picture of a girlfriend in a risqué pose and a picture of an old hound dog, now hung on the walls of the locker room and the shop.

Tommy McKee was back running around the hallways of Substantial Industries Worldwide LLC, along with a few old timers who recently returned along with him.

The young supervisor, Mr. Bradley McDermott, who was the only guy who had enough courage to tell the truth, well, he was now working with Tommy McKee, while watching and learning for a few bucks over minimum wage.

In the director's office, Old Hank sat behind the fancy desk. Upon the front of his uniform shirt, he proudly displayed his employee identification badge. The badge with the number one hundred and twelve stamped upon it. Old Hank put his hands behind his head, chuckled a bit, put his work boots up on the desk and smiled.

You see, Old Hank was correct.

Experience counts.

THE END

Under the Pomp and Splendor

1

A Memory from the Past

As I grow older, and live this crazy life, day-by-day, indeed, at times, minute-by-minute, I realize that perhaps, the greatest gift God has given to us all, is the gift of each other. I mean that in the most profound and deepest of thoughts. Each person who we meet, speak with, interact with, share love and share moments with, all are part of God's plan. God sends people into our lives for a reason, to touch us, to influence us and help us make decisions, which shape our entire life.

"Oh, Pastor Paul, I do so enjoy speaking with you. Your quiet calm, it relaxes me, the way in which you explain things, helps me to shed the guilt and the shame, of which the church has put on me. It is quite a burden."

I did not answer Maria, but instead, I fiddled with my pen in my hand, while I floated the pen above the pad on which I was taking notes. So far, I had only written one word "Conflicted" on the pad.

Maria Tooteroni sat opposite me, in a guest chair in front of my desk, in the pastor's office of Reunion Lutheran Church on a rather gloomy, cold, and nasty late February afternoon. It smelled like snow outside, but no flakes were falling yet. Ever since a chance and rather weird encounter in a local supermarket where my best friend, Harry M. Redmond Junior and I ran into Maria and her husband

Salvatore, while they shopped for toilet tissue, (yes that is a story for another time and place) Maria and Salvatore were on and off attendees of church services here. Although they were members of a local Catholic church, they often felt the need to visit and share in our services. As of late, Maria would make appointments and come in to speak with me in some counseling sessions, where we would speak of religious topics, share scripture, but we would speak of general subjects too. Occasionally, Salvatore would attend our sessions, but most of the time, Maria would come by and visit without her husband. I enjoyed meeting with her. She was very intelligent, well-spoken and dynamic in her personality.

The remarkably wide variety of topics in which her mind would roll through made me, at times, quite exasperated. She was difficult to keep up with; high energy and fast-talking, did not even do justice in describing her.

Maria was a beautiful woman, and she had an engaging and captivating personality, with keen intelligence and a good sense of humor. She also was rather forthright, and her counseling sessions were, well, how shall we say, at times, rather, "honest" and open in nature. There were not too many subjects of which Maria did not cover, from her wild thoughts after consuming too much white wine on a recent Saturday night, to her past adventures, to her up and down sex life and relationship with her husband, it was at times, a bit difficult!

I had solid training in dealing with counseling, and between my dealings with my best friend, Harry and his (before he finally settled down in his married life) wandering ways, and my seminary training, I felt well equipped and prepared to handle most situations.

However, Maria could create a bit of steam under my pastor's collar and lift my eyebrows a bit, too. She meant no harm, I was sure of that, or I would have begged out of trying to help her, and pointed her back to the priests at her main parish. In addition, Maria had spoken to me on many occasions about how she looked up to me and admired me as a person, as well as a pastor.

Please understand that it was certainly not that she made any inappropriate advances towards me, nor I to her. It was just that her personality was so blatantly open and honest that the conversation could quickly become rather awkward. It was something of which I was very careful to be aware of and keep in front of me at all times. I had received hours and hours of training, as well as warnings on these types of situations, and I remained always mindful of the perception of how skewed these types of interactions could become in this world nowadays!

When Maria would first request counseling sessions on her own, and would arrive without her husband, I had to admit to being a little uncomfortable with the solo sessions. Therefore, I would purposely leave the door to my office open and request my administrative assistant, Ms. Martha Wiggins, to remain at her desk, which we strategically positioned directly in front of the door. When Martha complained a bit, since the subject matters were at times, confidential, I took a tip from my boss, Bishop Von Houten, and had my facility manager, Dave Sharp cut a viewing glass on the side of the door, so you could see rather well into my office.

"Oh, Pastor Paul, I think it is so cute that you cut that glass in your office door! I do admit that I am pretty cute, and you are an incredible looking man, but you should not fear being alone with me. We are both married and you are a man of the cloth."

"Oh no, Maria, it was not anything like that. I, well, I . . . meant to have Dave cut that glass a long time ago. You see, Martha asked me. . .."

Maria was too smart to buy my explanation, and she proceeded to stomp all over my stumbling reply.

"I would never, well, you know, make any type of

inappropriate advances! I would be lying if I said the thought has not crossed my mind though! You cannot fool me! I know the real reason why you cut the glass in the door. I certainly hope that Mrs. Henson realizes how lucky a woman she is, because you are a gift. I also know that you realize how precious a woman that you have as your wife."

I watched as Maria's eyes danced and moved, as she first studied the new glass in the door, and then she looked at me, carefully studied my eyes, and waved her hands in the air rather emphatically. I did not say a word, nor did I intend to. It seemed as if she had arrived at some type of conclusion.

Maria immediately moved into the latest subject that she had on her mind, "Regardless, let's move on. Here is my trouble with the stuffy and manmade rules obsessed, Catholic Church, as opposed to the beliefs of Pastor Paul John Henson. You have this sign out in front of your church that proclaims your affiliation with the Lutheran Church, but you speak, preach, and you interact with people, as if you see all sides of religion, all denominations, and all views. You do not dwell upon manmade rules. You only trust God and what is in your heart."

Maria leaned in closer to my desk. She grew more intense, and her face glowed with passion at the subject of which she was speaking.

After a slight pause to collect her thoughts, she continued to speak her mind, "I think you convey that God is above the pomp and the splendor. You know, Jesus was Jewish. When it all boils down, are we not all Jewish? He never owned a home, only some clothes on his back, wandered here and there, stayed with friends, never traveled very far from where he was born. Such a simple life. He was, for the most part, homeless. Sort of a beggar, actually. Candles, hymns, choirs, towering steeples to the sky, chants, and liturgies. I do not know why it is all so complicated, Pastor Paul. You made it so simple in that tape of which I listened to a few days ago. That was the most marvelous homily that I have ever listened to in my entire life. For the most part, it summed up all of my thoughts."

This conversation, for some reason, struck a chord. I had heard these types of words before somewhere, perhaps, a long time ago. I tried to remember, but with Maria speaking at a very rapid pace, I could not find the time to recall the memory in my mind.

Maria finished speaking. She looked at me as if I should know what tape she was speaking of, but I had no clue what she was referring to in this conversation.

I must have looked puzzled, because she smiled at me and waited for me to ask, therefore I did, "Tape? What tape is that, Maria?"

She leaned back in the chair, satisfied that her mention of the tape, and then purposely dangling the conversation, had led me to the point where she obviously wanted the conversation to arrive. Maria played me as if I was a fine violin.

"The tape of your first sermon, of course. You know, when you convinced that old crab-ass, Bishop Von Houten to ordain you. Your brother-in-law, Tinky, recommended that I borrow it from the church library. We had a great conversation one day, when I ran into him and I asked him for advice of what, in his opinion, this amazing Pastor Paul and his religious views were really all about. You know, to understand you. Tinky told me that I needed to listen to the tape of this particular sermon. The words you spoke summed up all of Pastor Paul John Henson in one sermon. I must say, your words affected me in ways of which I cannot describe, my dear Pastor Paul. The ending is where I felt the most connected. It sums up where I feel I am right now in my spiritual life."

Maria lifted her eyes to the ceiling of the office, and then she closed them. She was gathering her thoughts. I surmised at this point she had somehow memorized something and now was going to recall it.

Maria spoke softly as she kept her eyes closed, and her head lifted towards the ceiling, "You see, it really is so simple, all of this, all of these hymns, choirs, worship services, fantastic buildings, candles, and all the other things all around us here today. Actually, it all comes down to a very simple thing. It comes down to a sort of blind faith that leads us to follow a light, a guide, a way, and a purpose. A faith that comes from within each of us. It is no different from love, kindness, joy, and hope. Faith in the Holy Trinity is really not very different at all. To understand and have it make sense, all each one of us has to do, is believe it, and it will happen."

She stopped speaking, lowered her head, looked at me, and smiled. I smiled back; I now knew the sermon of which she just recalled from her memory.

I felt compelled to answer with a bit more than a smile, "Very remarkable and an impressive memory, Maria. You are amazingly brilliant, and a deep thinker, Maria. I must say that, I am sure that Salvatore, in his own special way, realizes how remarkable and precious you are. Thank you for the compliment, however, you give me way too much credit."

"Thank you. I hope he does. Oh, no, I don't give you too much credit. You hit it all on the head, right there, at least for me, and many others. Right there, you make it all so simple. That is where I am at right now in my life. I no longer need the pomp and splendor of elaborate church services in order to feel the love of God. Perhaps, on Easter and Christmas, Good Friday, those are the only times that I need them. Now, I stand on my faith alone. I feel the guidance and see the light of God. That is all. Is that wrong, Pastor Paul?"

I shook my head to show that I understood her

thoughts.

"No, Maria, it is not wrong. Church can be anywhere you want it to be. In your mind, in your heart, or even in your own backyard, watching and admiring the sunrise or the sunset."

Now, in my mind, I think I may have found the lost thoughts and events! I felt a memory roll through the index of my mind, a roundabout return to someone who had at one time told me the same words, the same reasoning. It was a memory of a long time ago, and involved a person who came into my life and affected me in ways that I did not realize until many years later.

The ghosts of the past never left me alone.

The rest of the meeting went well, but the conversation had indeed stirred my memory, as well as invoked some deep thoughts within me.

After work, I made a rather pensive journey from my office at the rear of the church office building, across the parking lot to the parsonage tucked on a small hill in the corner of the property. I wandered along with my head down, my hands in my pockets, making mental notes that something deep was stirring inside of me.

I always had this connection of some sort, a connection to God's plan, a plan, of which I now knew to sit back and understand that sometime later, the direction would become clearer to me. Right now, I just continued to keep an open mind, index the memory banks and think.

I walked into the back door of the parsonage, walked up a few steps, and entered into the kitchen. The smell of the dinner that my lovely wife, Binky, was preparing floated about the room, and made me realize how hungry I was. I tried to place the dinner by sampling the smell and guessed it to be a beef stew.

I guessed wrong, of course.

"I hear you, twenty-seven!" I heard Binky shout from the dining room. "I am running late. The Shepherd's Pie is not quite ready yet. You are late, the children and I have eaten already. We had a pizza at the after-school party!"

I could hear Binky's steps upon the hardwood floors and while I stood next to the kitchen table, she appeared from around the corner and she walked into the kitchen. She wore a wide smile, her long blonde hair fell down all about her, and she looked amazing in a tight blue dress and an apron tied around her waist. Binky was an amazing woman. She enjoyed cooking and well, what more could a man ask for? I had a gorgeous, brilliant, and amazing wife, great children, and on top of everything else, my wife was a marvelous cook, too.

Heaven does indeed exist upon Earth.

"Hi, Binky. Yeah, yeah, yeah. Sorry, I am so late. A counseling session with Maria Tooteroni went a bit longer than what I expected."

"Oh, no trouble at all, my dear Paul. I saw her leaving the rear of the church and knew she had most likely lingered longer than expected."

Binky never missed a trick.

I waved for her to come closer, and she did. I held her tightly, kissed her warmly and then held onto her and enjoyed her warmth and smell. My wife always smelled so good. I whispered to her that I loved her and missed her, and she squeezed me tightly. She leaned back, smiled, kissed me on the cheek, and broke away from my grasp.

"Please sit, dear Paul. I will get you a beer and your mail. Relax, please, the dinner will need to cook quite a bit longer. I am sorry, a late start, dear Paul. Was Maria difficult today?"

Binky walked over to the counter, picked up a stack of mail, then made her way to the refrigerator.

"A Big Boulder, twenty-seven, or would you like to try a Dingleberry beer?"

Geez, talk about ghosts. Those stupid Dingleberries are always around too. Someday, I would try one, but not today.

"A Big Boulder, Binky. Thanks." I sat at the table, pulled my collar off, and sighed. "No, quite the opposite today. Maria was not difficult at all. In fact, she has mixed feelings in where and how she wants to worship and how she perceives religion in her life, but her thoughts are so profound. Amazingly, profound in fact. She really stirred my thoughts up today, Binky."

Binky handed me the beer and my favorite beer mug and she watched as I spun the top off the bottle and poured it into the mug.

"How so, Paul?"

I did not know how to answer her. Instead, I thought for a short time as I watched the beer foaming in the mug.

"Not too sure, Binky. Something she said, told me that I was about to visit a subject of which I had been to before. You know how it goes, my love."

"I see. A subject from long ago. More ghosts from the past. Maria does have quite the crush on you, dear Paul. I hope you realize that. It is harmless, and she means no harm. She has attached to you for advice. People always tap your strength and steal what they are able to steal. I do it too. It is only one reason why you are so amazing. You lend parts of your soul and expect no payment in return for doing so. Maria also wants you to lend your emotions to her while she works things out in her life. I must emphasize that she means no ill will. You will help her and figure it all out. You always do."

Binky then stood in front of me. She fluffed her hair and pulled her dress down to reveal a bit of her astounding cleavage. I knew what was coming out of her mouth now; I knew my wife and her poses very well.

"After all, who can blame her? Unlucky, for her that I beat her, and many others to the punch, eh?"

"Ah yes, you did, my dear. Yes, you did!" I tapped her playfully on her backside while she wiggled by me. I watched as she picked the daily mail off the counter and glanced at it.

Binky smiled, and she handed me the mail. She knew me well enough, and we had been through so many of my adventures that she knew the answers would come and that we would venture through them together.

Soulmates are always connected. She knew my soul, and I knew hers.

"Paul, I have to say that I did not know you had an Uncle Heinrich. I never heard you mention him before . . . ever. I know that I never met him. In fact, I never even heard anyone in your family ever mention him before."

My head spun around; my mouth dropped open. I must have shocked Binky, because she handed me the mail and suddenly gripped my shoulder and held onto me.

"You received a card today, or what I surmise to be a card, because of the size . . . yes, from your Uncle Heinrich. At least that is what the return address says. Uncle Heinrich Clovenhofen." Binky paused because she noticed the startled look on my face. She then asked, "Are you okay, my dear number twenty-seven?"

I looked at the card that Binky just handed me and smiled. God's plan just became clearer. Never question it, twenty-seven, just go with it all.

"I do not have an Uncle Heinrich Clovenhofen, dear Binky. That is why, I never mentioned him."

I looked up at my wife. She now was very puzzled.

"But Harry does. . .."

2

The Amazing Uncle Heinrich Clovenhofen

"Oh, I see," Binky smiled and loosened her grip upon my shoulder.

As soon as she heard my explanation, and the fact that it had something to do with the world-famous Harry M. Redmond Junior, then, Binky knew this was going to be a story of which she knew would be long, somewhat strange, and quite involved.

She had traveled these roads many times before. In fact, she was my constant companion on these journeys!

"I will leave you to open the card alone, twenty-seven. I need to help the children with homework and check on them. Please enjoy your beer and memories. There is plenty of more beer in the refrigerator. If this has something to do with Harry, then chances are that you will need it. I will be back in a short time, to check on you and to check on dinner."

She kissed the top of my head; I nodded my head and watched and admired her remarkable figure from my chair as she wiggled out of the kitchen and disappeared into the dining room. Yes, she knew the adventures of Harry and Paul all too well.

Sometimes, there is not enough beer in the world to soften the impact.

I reached down and slipped my finger under the seal of the envelope as my memory bank turned on to full open mode.

"Hey, twenty-seven, did I tell you that my Uncle Heinrich is coming over today?"

I looked first at the face of my gal, Ms. Maureen Zipperelli, who sat upon my lap with her arms draped over my shoulders; she shrugged her shoulders in a vague response to Harry's statement. Puzzled, I looked back at Harry, and then gave the same reaction as my girlfriend just did. Joyce Dilber, the on again, and off again, best gal of my long-time best friend, shrugged her shoulders too.

I commented, "Okay, Harry. I never knew that you had an Uncle Heinrich. I must admit that I never heard you mention him before today."

Joyce, who was sitting next to Harry, set her glass of wine down upon the picnic table in the backyard of Harry's house and said, "I have been dating you for almost four years, Harry. Oh, wait, not true. Four years, except for a lapse here and there, when you chased another skirt or two or three, or four, and I agree with Paul, in that I never heard of him either."

We were all enjoying some drinks and food while gathered in the backyard of the world-famous Redmond family for a late spring cookout and party. This current party was another one of the legendary Redmond shindigs during one of their party-filled weekends. It was the middle of May; the days were growing warmer and summer loomed closer. Today was a perfect day, sunny, warm, and dry, with a gentle breeze that floated around us.

Harry was quiet for a moment or two; he seemed to be pondering our statements. He then shook his head; he appeared to be very surprised that we were previously not aware of Uncle Heinrich.

"I never mentioned him before? Damn, I find that hard to believe. But he is sort of the black sheep of the family, so that might be true."

Harry took a sip of his cocktail and he looked at me over his glass.

He pointed his one finger towards me, while he held the glass and said, "He is like you are there, twenty-seven. He is kinda weird, super smart, a hippie, and a nonconformist type of guy. He is also like you are and is a bit off the wall."

Coming from Harry, those types of statements about me generally caused me a little to no reaction. I guess I was used to them by now. I did have to admit that this mysterious, long, lost uncle was now of some type of interest to me. Just the fact that he appeared so suddenly on this day was enough to pique my curiosity. Now, the description of him and the comparison to me, well, that was a different subject.

Maureen reached over; she grabbed my face and proceeded to lock my lips in a powerful, suction type kiss. Admittedly, it was a kiss that took me quite by surprise.

After she finished extracting my lips from my face, Maureen let go of me, smiled and proclaimed, "Paulie is not weird. He is a little eccentric, and what is the word in Welsh . . . rhyfedd, but he is a goaltender. All goalies are like that. Besides, that is what I love about him. That and a lot of other things that I will not go into here." She winked seductively at me, smoothed her hair out, tugged at her blouse to reveal her ample cleavage, and put her arms back around me.

Oh, geezzzz . . . Maureen was so aggressive.

She also had a bit of the fruit of the vine floating about her bloodstream at this point.

"I love it when Paulie turns all red in the face!" Joyce pointed out.

Harry continued to sip his drink and between sips he explained, "Yeah, well, spin it however ya want, but twenty-seven is a little whacked out from all those blows to the head from hockey pucks bouncing off 'em, but anyway,

Uncle Heinrich is coming over. He is my Mom's half-brother. When my grandfather passed away, my grandmother met some German guy who was a widower. They married, and Uncle Heinrich came along. He is a whacko, kinda cool, but really, really rich. He invented some kind of safety device for cars and got a patent for it. He owned some kind of store in Paterson, and when some old battleaxe put her car in a forward gear when she thought she was in reverse, and went straight through the storefront of his establishment, he invented this interlock whoosie. He sold it to the big car manufacturers, and he made millions."

"Sounds like he actually has it together, Harry. Why do you say he is so whacked out?" I asked.

"Ha! Of course, you will think he is normal. You will see! Let me see, he plays all kinds of musical instruments, he looks like a mad scientist, with long hair sticking out in all directions, he has a long, stringy, beard that is almost down to his chest."

Harry stopped speaking and held his hands up to his neck and body to show the length of his uncle's beard. He then continued in his description of his uncle, "All that he ever wears are open-toed sandals, torn dungarees, and rock-and-roll tee shirts, along with hippie beads around his neck. He and twenty-seven will get along great, with the mutual hippie thing going on there. He owns property all over the place, but he lives most of the time, like some hippie hermit, in a log cabin on an island in the middle of some big lake in New Hampshire."

Harry took a breath, sipped his drink, waved his hands to indicate for us to listen and not comment.

"There is more! He never married, he has tons of girlfriends that he shacks up with, but never got married. He travels all over the place with some old, smelly hound dog named James, and drives a car, which is also a boat. If that is not enough, just to put the icing on the cake, he used to be a Catholic priest."

"Oh my, I see," was at first, all Joyce could manage to say, before she added, "sounds as if he is a boring type of fellow." Maureen almost spit her wine out at Joyce's sarcastic comment.

I looked at Maureen and she smiled, while she said to me, "By the description of Uncle Heinrich, I think he might have you beat on the weirdness thing, Paulie. But no way, can he be as cute as you are."

I felt much better and said, "Thanks, Maureen."

Harry's brother-in-law, the equally world famous Ronzo Boatmann wandered over, smiled at me, dipped his eyes at Maureen and asked, "Ya ready for another beer, Paul? Another wine there, Maureen, Joyce . . . Harry, are you good?"

"Sure thanks, Ronzo. Since ya offered, and are up, please a Big Boulder beer and red wine for Maureen, no Dingleberries, Ronzo."

"I know, I know, I know, too sweet," I heard Ronzo saying as he walked to the cooler. "Ya will thank me later for feeding Maureen all of these wines." Maureen heard his comment and whispered in my ear that Ronzo was correct.

Maureen was always so aggressive.

Ronzo returned with the drinks. I saw him stop. He looked down the driveway and he shook his head.

He handed us our drinks and said, "Well, hold on tight because youse guys are about to meet, Uncle Heinrich. He just pulled up."

I watched Harry's faithful dog, the world-famous Cocoa take off for the front of the house, his ever-present toy pig stuck in his mouth. Mr. Redmond, Ronzo, Patty, and Linda all set aside their merrymaking and made their way towards the top of the driveway.

Suddenly, the air filled with the sound of a trumpet playing some kind of marching music, interlaced with the loud baying of a hound dog, followed by Cocoa barking.

Joyce, Maureen and I all looked at Harry, who put his head in his hands and then looked at us and said, "I told you that he was a weirdo. You can judge for ya self!"

The trumpet playing became louder, and turning the corner from the top of the driveway, there appeared a rather short man, whose appearance was quite like Harry's description of just a few minutes earlier. Besides having a brass trumpet stuck in his mouth, of which he was playing not only very well, but very loudly too, he looked much as described. Long, gray hair, stuck out in all directions from his head, the long beard, all kinds of facial hair. In fact, it was hard to see anything but hair. He dressed exactly as Harry had described him and yes, an old hound dog followed behind him, merrily baying in time with the trumpet music. Cocoa trotted happily behind the strange parade, as if he knew Uncle Heinrich and James, the hound dog forever.

Uncle Heinrich stopped playing; he put the trumpet down at his side, stood at attention, and then he saluted everyone with a right-hand salute.

He then gracefully bowed and loudly proclaimed, "Greetings, salutations, and best wishes! I am so glad to see everyone again! I lost count, but I do declare that it may have been a few years, which have passed, since we laid eyes upon each other. I do apologize for my waywardness and intend to make it all up to you when I pass from this world and leave you all a tidy sum of money. Until that time, you will have to suffer a meeting with me every ten or fifteen years or thereabouts. After all, I love you all dearly, but the lure of African safaris and dog-sledding in Alaska with pretty young ladies, whose hearts are aflame with passion, sometimes, outweigh these visits!"

The entire Redmond family rushed in to greet him and to exchange hugs with him. Patty and Linda appeared thrilled to see him, and the two women gave him kisses and hugs. After listening to the grand entry speech, Cocoa dashed off chasing and playing with his new friend, which I soon learned was indeed the world famous, James, the hound dog. The two dogs were, as if they too were, just old friends.

Harry said while slowly rising out of his chair, "I guess that I better go say hello to him." He walked over to the family circle, awaiting his turn to greet the wayward uncle.

Now that Harry was out of an earshot, I leaned into Joyce and Maureen and said, "This is all so strange. I have known this family for years, in fact, since I was ten years old. I have been over here every day for most of those years, too. Christmas, Thanksgiving, countless holidays and parties. Never once, have I ever heard them mention this oddball chap."

Joyce shook her head. And all she could say was, "Paulie, please remember that it is Harry and his family. And, they call *you* weird? Kinda like the pot calling the kettle black in my opinion."

Joyce had made a propitious point.

After a long greeting, smiles, back slapping and one more trumpet solo, Uncle Heinrich finally greeted his nephew.

"Harry, my boy! You are so big. Strong, muscular and handsome, too. You look a lot different now from how you looked the last time that I saw you. Which was, as far as my memory can recall, quite a few years ago, now."

Harry frowned a bit, reached out his hand to shake Uncle Heinrich's hand and commented, "Yeah, well, that makes a lot of sense. I think the last time ya saw me there, Uncle Heinrich, was when I was about ten years old. Ya could not make my mom's funeral because ya were in the North Pole or some bullshit excuse like that."

Oh, boy, I cringed a bit. That explains a little bit to me. The girls both looked at me and they cringed, too. There was a bit of pain leftover here. At least, this explains just a bit as to why I did not recall seeing him before now, even at the funeral.

"I still deeply regret that fact, Harry. You know how much I loved your mom. She was near and dear to my heart and she always will be. Please understand that flights out of the Yukon Territory are a bit rough to find on short notice."

Harry studied his uncle, and the big guy folded his arms across his chest as he pondered the situation. "I guess, and Mom loved you, too. She always said that she loved you."

"C'mon then, Harry. My dear sister is looking down from her lofty perch and she would want us to show love, only love. I am your only relative on your mother's side, left on this side of Heaven, and Linny, Patty, and you, are my only relatives left too. I love you, Harry. You make your mother very proud. Tall, strong, fearless, and you are not afraid to speak your mind. Your mother wants us to reunite."

Harry smiled and waved his hands in the air, while saying, "Ah, hell yeah, she would!"

The two of them shook hands, then embraced, and all seemed well in the world. The rest of the Redmond clan cheered at the sight of the reunion. They had, until this point, remained silent, and my assumption was that they knew that Harry held onto some acrimonious feelings towards Uncle Heinrich. The family remained content to stand by to allow the two men to settle their differences. I never knew Harry M. Redmond Junior to hold a grudge for very long. Harry actually possessed a heart of gold!

"C'mon over here, Uncle Heinrich. I would like you to meet my best buddy in the entire world, the famous ice hockey goaltender, Paul John Henson and his gorgeous and voluptuous girlfriend, Maureen Zipperelli. Then I want to introduce you to my gal, the fantastic, and very put together, Joyce Dilber! Check out the chest sizes and when they stand up, check out the perfect asses on these two gals!"

Harry and his legendary, bombastic, and usually embarrassing introductions—they never ceased to amaze nor disappoint! Each time, they grew in intensity and lewdness.

Uncle Heinrich looked over towards us. He whistled for James, the faithful hound dog, who responded by stopping his play with Cocoa and immediately running over to his master's side. Once, James, the old hound dog had joined Uncle Heinrich, Uncle Heinrich lifted his trumpet once again to his lips and while everyone watched and listened, he blew a loud charge call into the instrument. James joined in on the accompaniment, with a loud hound baying type call.

Maureen shifted on my lap uneasily and she whispered into my ear, "Well, Harry usually exaggerates, but this time, Paulie, I am afraid he did not. This guy is a friggin' whacko. Please, protect me. He has his eyes locked upon my chest."

I nodded and squeezed her hand to show that I had her protected as well as covered.

Uncle Heinrich finished his charge call, placed his trumpet back down at his side, and quickly walked over to us.

While standing directly in front of us, he reached out his hand and with Maureen tightly gripping my neck, he said, "Ah yes, indeed! The world famous, Paul John Henson. Indeed, it is my pleasure. Uncle Heinrich Clovenhofen at your service, kind Paul. I am a big fan. I have been following your fledging, yet promising career, young man. I am a big ice hockey fan, and my nephew, who is prone to immense and incredible exaggerations of an all-encompassing nature, has in your case made an exception and he has not fudged your skills at all."

I was a little stunned, and I reached out and carefully shook his hand. I was not exactly sure how he knew of my career since he lived in New Hampshire. At this point, I was only in a local semiprofessional league, or a pickup league or two, as a hired ringer, but nonetheless, I took it as a compliment.

Uncle Heinrich had a wild look in his eye, his hair stuck out in all directions. His hair was wild, poorly groomed was a vast understatement. It was, as if he had placed a dusty tumbleweed upon his head. He was strange, slightly ominous, and from a distance, he seemed unapproachable, without some type of weapon in your hand. However, as he came closer to us and I now had the chance to meet him face-to-face and closer up, he actually did not seem quite as weird. He actually seemed to be quite likable.

There was something about him. . ..

His facial hair and beard seemed to cover his entire face. Buried in and amongst the field of white and gray hair, there moved some lips, of which his voice came out of, a voice that was loud in volume and gravelly in delivery. His eyes were set deep in his head, they were dark, and his nose was short and round. It almost seemed as if he was hundreds of years old, he gave the appearance of being very old, but the manner in which he moved, his speed, his upright stance, his physical being and energy, actually was that of a very young man.

"In addition, I feel that we are kindred souls. I love the beard, the long hair, the canvas sneakers and the No Way tee shirt. Love their music. The lyrics are right on, man! I have written many papers on the in-depth meaning of the lyrics and have published many reviews of their music."

Oh, geez, I had been studying the lyrics of my favorite rock-and-roll band for years, and still, I had not been able to decipher them. I made a mental note to read his papers. Uncle Heinrich then continued his rant, while all the time waving his hands in the air and over his head in a wild and uncontrolled manner.

"I must show you my Moonbeam boat-car. I drove it down from Black Cat Island where I live on the big lake in

New Hampshire. It maintains over forty miles per gallon of gas, or petrol, as your grandfather would say. It is a boat, and it is a car, too. Quite unusual."

Uncle Heinrich stopped short in his motions and speech. He let go of my hand and tilted his head. I sensed Uncle Heinrich studying me very carefully.

He smiled, and then spoke a little softer, "More to you than meets the eye, young Henson. You are so large, very tall and powerfully strong. You are quite imposing to most people. You are an athlete, yet, you are a deep thinker. Your eyes are full of emotion and they are most unusual. I see the hand of God upon you, Paulie. That is what most people call you, is it not? That, or your uniform number, which if I recall correctly, is the number twenty-seven. I might add that is a very wonderful number. A wise selection. Am, I correct?"

Maureen tightened her grasp on me, and I felt her pull in tightly to me. Her large breasts moved and heaved as she snuggled in closer; I think she felt as if she needed to hide them from Uncle Heinrich's stare. I suddenly realized that this was an unusual man, but a man of amazing intelligence. To discount him as a wild eccentric might be a grave error. This was not a chance meeting of one of the Redmond's long-lost relatives. We all have met for a greater purpose. This strange, but very insightful man had something to teach and lend to all of us.

All I could manage to say was a weak and feeble, "Yes, Paulie or twenty-seven is correct." I added, "Very few people ever use my actual name."

Uncle Heinrich leaned back and clapped his hands loudly together as James bayed in delight at his owner's correct statement. The dog remained keenly aware of Uncle Heinrich's every move.

"Yes! I knew it! I must tell you that I once was involved quite deeply in the matters of the church. It did not work out exactly as we all had planned, but the teachings and the spirit never left me. You are a spiritual one and your eyes tell your story. It is my immense pleasure to meet you."

I did not know what to say; therefore, I kept it rather generic, "Nice to meet you too, Uncle Heinrich. I would like to see your boat or car . . . whichever one comes first. Thank you for the kind words, but I am sure that I have not earned such accolades."

This was not the first time in my life that I had heard someone tell me the same thing about my eyes, as well as my relationship with God. My mother often mentioned it to me. Harry's mom, right before she passed away had told me the exact same thing, as did the Redmond's family friend and priest, Father Mark. Even my old man had mentioned it many times to me.

Indeed, I did feel something in my heart for religion, but at this moment in time, I could not put my finger upon it or understand what I was supposed to do with my beliefs. Right for now, I kept them to myself.

I shifted in my chair and pointed towards Maureen, anxious to divert the attention from me to Maureen.

"This stunningly gorgeous woman here is Maureen Zipperelli. She is the subject of my love."

"Yes, correct! Maureen! Love! Fantastic introduction and wordsmithing! Maureen is amazing and truly gorgeous!" Uncle Heinrich agreed.

He lifted the trumpet to his lips and played a few notes of a song, of which I did not recognize, and then he stopped playing and lowered the trumpet back to his side. I tried hard to place the few bars of the tune in which he played, but I could not come up with it. I prided myself on my vast knowledge of music, but that tune I could not place.

I continued to try.

"What a gorgeous and captivating woman! It is my pleasure to meet you, Maureen. My, why should I be surprised at all? I would only expect the incredibly handsome and dynamic goalie to have such a beautiful woman as a companion at his side. Young and in love, there is nothing like it in the entire world. No feeling can duplicate it. In fact, old and in love is not too bad either. I am older now, but I still date my share of women. They are all gorgeous, passionate, and they are mostly younger than I am. Time means nothing when you boil it all down. I have already foreseen my own demise."

Maureen looked at me and smiled, as she now seemed to sense that Uncle Heinrich was harmless.

Joyce laughed aloud and Harry shouted out to his uncle, "Got to hear this one!"

Uncle Heinrich placed his fingers to his lips to indicate it was some kind of secret as the entire clan gathered around to hear his prediction.

He spoke in a reduced tone, "As you shall hear, my precious family! My precarious plan is to be shot in the back by a jealous husband, at the ripe old age of ninety-five, while climbing out of a bedroom window and his wife lies happy on the bed, with an immense smile on her face! Love conquers time. Time has no power over love! Rules and the normal, as you might have been able to detect at this point, mean very little to me!"

After his lewd, but incredibly profound speech and unusual death wish, Uncle Heinrich reached out for Maureen's hand, and she slowly reached towards him and allowed him to kiss her hand. This guy could lay it on thick. However, there was much more to it. Underneath all the fluff, something that was, in fact, very genuine. He then bowed once again, whirled, and turned his attention to Joyce.

"Thank you. My pleasure too, Uncle Heinrich," was all that Maureen could muster up to say in response to his introduction.

"And, Ms. Dilber. Oh, my, oh my! Such, a captivating and gorgeous woman, who is rare and precious and beyond description in your beauty and love. You have somehow managed to capture my nephew's wandering heart. It is my pleasure to meet you, too. I am beside myself with seeing such beauty! Uncle Heinrich Clovenhofen is thrilled to meet such amazing and captivating young women."

I had heard Harry's playboy tendencies described in many ways, but this was definitely a first. Uncle Heinrich repeated the hand kissing and bowing behavior, and then he blew a few more notes of the same tune on his trumpet, excused himself, and joined Ronzo in a discussion and a cocktail. I watched as Ronzo handed Uncle Heinrich what appeared to be whisky of some sort, straight up in a glass. Maureen looked at me, and then she looked at Harry, Joyce, and then returned her gaze to me.

She simply said, "Oh my, he is quite the character. Somehow, I knew his boat would be a car, or vice versa. It is only fitting."

We all nodded. Maureen leaned in and put her head upon my chest and she held me tightly.

She whispered to me, "That is the first time you ever introduced me as your love, Paulie. I know now, that I am in love with you, more than ever."

Oh no! Uncle Heinrich's overwhelming entrance might have forced me into a strategic error in my romantic life. Until tonight, I was not quite ready to admit that I was in love with Maureen. Now, after my loose-lipped ramblings, then it seemed as if I had revealed my true feelings. Oh, well, too late now.

Harry's description of Uncle Heinrich was dead on. This time he had not exaggerated one bit about what a character he was. The party went on, the dancing, the music, all the usual Redmond festivities. Uncle Heinrich proved to be the life of the party, and then some!

"Would you like to see my boat that is actually a car, or vice versa?" Uncle Heinrich asked us as he wobbled, teetered and tottered over to us. He swayed back and forth, his trusty trumpet in his left hand and a glass of whiskey in his right hand.

He seemed as if he was well on his way to being half in the bag. I guess that drinking whiskey straight for a few hours could do that to you, but since we knew it was a fact that such a car, or actually, a boat existed, we all nodded our heads and followed him down the driveway. Sure enough, there it sat at the curb in front of the house. It was small; it looked to be about the size of a typical subcompact car, with some exceptions, because it had two little chrome propellers in the rear where the exhaust pipes usually come out of an "ordinary" vehicle. The front sloped up, very similar to how the hull of a boat would slope, and it had rudders, water intake and output pipes, and an engine under a hood. The color of the vehicle was an amazing aquamarine blue color, it was a flawless coating with not a nick or a dent upon the surface. The interior of the "thing" was clean, actually immaculate, with crisp, white bucket seats and a dashboard filled with gauges and chrome trim. The color schemes seemed so appropriate for a boat or a car.

Amazing.

Harry was unfazed. After all, he was a member of the Redmond clan, and weirdness was a usual byproduct of their normal lifestyle. Nothing was too amazing for them, they would greet an alien's spaceship that was landing in the neighborhood, first by sending Cocoa holding Piggy out to meet the alien visitors, and then Mr. Redmond would hand them a beer and invite them in the backyard for hamburgers and hot dogs on the grille.

Harry leaned over and peered inside the boat. Or car, depending upon your point of view on the "thing."

"Nice rig, Uncle Heinrich. We need to take a spin in this puppy, or a float or two. Ya just drive on up to the lake and go into the water, huh?"

"That's right, Harry. She is seaworthy too."

Harry continued to examine the "thing" while the rest of us could not even comment at the thought of driving a car into the water and going for a boat ride in it!

"Seaworthy, huh? Ya go in the ocean with it?"

"Once or twice, sure . . . I mean, I would not venture to England in it, but it is good for a spin or two around the bay."

Harry smiled and nodded his head. A million horrible thoughts went through my head. Oh, geez! I knew that look all too well. Harry now wants one of these contraptions of his own! Joyce had a shocked look on her gorgeous face. Her mouth hung open because Joyce knew all that her world-famous boyfriend was capable of when he had those types of stars in his eyes. Joyce quickly alternated her gaze from Harry and Uncle Heinrich over to Maureen and me. Yes, there remained little doubt that Joyce knew that look, too. In my mind, as Harry and Uncle Heinrich spoke about and mutually admired the thing, I could see us sinking in the bay, in our aquamarine car, or boat or whatever it is, all the while as we are sinking; Harry calls me an old lady for worrying and we slowly sink into the murky depths.

Maureen gripped my arm tightly, and she whispered in my ear, "I think I have had too much wine, Paulie. Did he just say he goes into the ocean with his car?"

"Ah yes, indeed, Maureen, he did. But not to England, just around the bay."

Maureen shook her head, pulled me by my hand and led me towards the backyard as she mumbled, "Oh well, if it is just around a bay then! Shit, this is unreal. Oh, please, come along, Paulie. I have seen and heard enough. Even for Harry and his family, this is a bit much to understand. The weirdness factor is too high to take. I need more wine. We can neck, and probe each other, in all the right spots for the rest of the night. Later on, when we are alone, I plan to make love to you, until I turn you inside out. After tonight, you will walk like a cowboy for a week. That love comment has me on fire."

Maureen was so aggressive.

As the afternoon waned and nighttime arrived, it suddenly came to me. I quickly sat up in my chair and loudly announced, to everyone's surprise, "Beautiful! The tune that Uncle Heinrich keeps playing is a song called, Beautiful!"

Uncle Heinrich nodded and faintly smiled to confirm my correctly identifying the tune.

Alcohol was in full effect now; Harry smiled and shouted out, "I love it! This is what I am talking 'bout! These gals *are* beautiful!"

He then reached over and lip locked Joyce.

I figured I might as well do the same with the all too willing, and very gorgeous, Maureen Zipperelli.

As we kissed, I could hear in the background Uncle Heinrich blowing that same soft tune on his trumpet.

3

A Trip to New Hampshire

"Hello, Harry. What's going on?"

"Uncle Heinrich called, and he invited all of us up to his cabin in New Hampshire. I told him we would be up this weekend. He sure likes you, Paul. I think he was amazed that you knew the tune that he was playing on his trumpet. The size of the girl's chests, and how they look, might also have something to do with the invitation. Ya better call Maureen and make the date! I am going to pick Joyce up around six in the morning on Friday. Ya need to get the day off and if you can't get the day off, then do not let your typical Old Lady Syndrome consume you and just call in sick. It is a long ride. Be ready with Maureen over my house by seven. I will pick ya up! Make sure that Cocoa knows we are going on a long trip to see Uncle Heinrich and James, the hound dog. You and Maureen need to explain it to him. Make sure that he has his water and food dish and Piggy ready to go. I am not going to tell him ahead of time. He will be too excited and have to pee every few minutes. I will drive the Sonicmobile, cuz, if you drove, by the time we got there then it would be time to come on back."

"CLICK!"

The telephone line went dead.

Another typical conversation with Harry M. Redmond Junior. In all the years that we have known one another, if we had a conversation which lasted more than five minutes and I said more than just a few mere words, I would be shocked.

There was very little sense in arguing. I had to admit that Harry planned all of our adventures. I simply went along for the ride! I always looked reflectively upon my role as a life coach and recorder of these adventures. It seems as if all of these years later that it has served me rather well.

It was easy to ask for a day off at my employment in the electronics and electrical service shop where I worked. I had been there for a few years now. I had apprenticed there and stayed after my vocational training ended, and I seldom, if ever, took a day off. My boss appreciated my diligent and dedicated attendance.

Maureen, however, might be a different story. She had a lucrative position as a hairstylist, and she rented a chair at a local salon. The end of the week was usually busy for her, and Saturday was the most lucrative day for Maureen. I was not too sure she would be able to pass up those types of earnings; she was just now beginning to establish a loyal client base.

I made the telephone call, and we were in luck! The salon planned to close on Friday and Saturday for some construction remodeling. Therefore, Maureen had moved most, if not all, of her appointments to earlier in the week. She planned on working very late on Wednesday and Thursday, in order to fit in her clients. She also told me that even if this construction were not occurring, she still would have given up her appointments to spend the weekend with me. She lowered her voice and whispered in the phone with a husky and amorous voice. While telling me that she loved all of me, but various parts of me were simply amazing. Oh boy.

Maureen was so aggressive.

I picked Maureen up; she was waiting for me in front of her house. I double-parked and I grabbed her bags and suitcases. I also grabbed, and very carefully loaded up, the ever-present gifts of jugs of homemade wine that her uncle and father made in the basement of their home. Whenever we had a special event or a holiday, Maureen always insisted on presenting the wine as gifts to our hosts. It was a tradition for the Zipperelli family. We shared a quick hug, a kiss, and jumped back into the van. From Maureen's house, it was a short drive over to Harry's house and once we arrived, we waited for him and Joyce to arrive.

Maureen was quite the talker, she could wear your ears out, and despite the early hour, she was very excited and in topnotch babbling form today. I parked in front of Harry's house and Maureen climbed out of the passenger side while I jumped out to find Cocoa and explain to him where we were going. Cocoa was our constant companion throughout our youth and even now that we were young men, he was still by our sides. Harry and I would never dream of going on a long adventure without him.

"I will be right back, Maureen. I need to find Cocoa and tell him we are leaving."

I stopped and thought about it as Maureen stood on the sidewalk and she stared at me.

I thought about it again, waved and said, "Please, you come along too. C'mon, Maureen." She smiled and quickly ran up to me, anxious to be included on the adventure.

Maureen slipped her arm inside of mine as I opened the gate to the Redmond's driveway and she leaned in and whispered, "I love you dearly, Paulie. I really do. You are an incredible man."

I did not know how to answer her, but leaned in and kissed her gently on the cheek.

Everyone throughout our neighborhood and beyond knew Harry's dog, Cocoa. They knew that in addition to being Harry's dog, he also was the world's smartest dog. He understood everything you told him, and people always spoke to him as if he was just a human with four legs and some paws.

It was still early in the morning and the sun slowly appeared over the roofs of the factories and mills, which lined our old neighborhood. It seemed as if it would be a perfect day.

The Redmonds were already off to work, Mr. Redmond left around three in the morning, and Ronzo was right behind him. They all worked from dusk to dawn, literally. I knew I would find Cocoa in the yard, and I was correct. He must have heard my voice and the van pull up because he came happily trotting around the corner and then he sped up as he saw me. He was as much my dog as he was Harry's dog.

I bent down, hugged him, and held him. After greeting each other, I said, "Hey, Cocoa. How are you doing, boy?"

I looked over at Maureen; she followed my actions and bent down and petted him too.

"Hi, Cocoa! It is so nice to see you today." Cocoa sat, and he looked at us. He knew that it was unusual to see the two of us this early in the day. As I said, he was the world's smartest dog.

"Go and get Piggy, your water and your food dish. Bring them all to the front of the house. We are all going to visit James, the hound dog, and Uncle Heinrich. Hurry!"

Cocoa barked twice and wagged his tail three times to show that he understood, and he ran off to fetch the items. At first, it amazed you when you saw the world's smartest dog in action, but now, I took it all in stride. Cocoa was smarter than most people were. We walked back to the front of the house, leaving the gate open for Cocoa to come out and join us. Maureen came over to me and wrapped her arms around me as we leaned upon the fence in front of the house. As usual, she looked gorgeous. Maureen was dressed in a loose fitting, summer-type, dark red blouse, with tight black dungarees on that enhanced her amazing curves.

She hugged me as she said, "Oh, Paulie, I am so looking forward to visiting New Hampshire. I have never been there. I visited Vermont one time when I was very young, but we never made it to New Hampshire. I hear it is so beautiful there."

We watched as Cocoa came running out, dropped his water dish at our feet, then turned and ran back into the yard. He returned in a flash with his food dish and he dropped that, too. All that remained for him to fetch was Piggy, his favorite plastic squeaky toy. Cocoa never allowed Piggy to be very far away and he would never dream of leaving him home.

Maureen laughed at watching the world's smartest dog actually pack his belongings for a road trip, but she, too, was used to it and took it all in stride.

After Cocoa ran off to find Piggy, Maureen looked at me, somewhat starry-eyed, and said, "Ever since you introduced me as the subject of your love, and we made such glorious love that same night, I have been so giddy. Just the thought that we are actually committed to one another now, is a thought of which I relish."

Oh, geez. That was not exactly what I meant when I said that to Uncle Heinrich, and I do admit that we did share an amazing evening of passion, but wow, this was a bit much. Still, I did have to admit that I loved Maureen. I started to explain a bit more while we stood in front of 20 John Street waiting for Harry, Joyce, and Cocoa.

"Yes, about that Maureen. I wanted to explain that to you. What I was actually saying was. . .."

"Oh, look! Here they are, Paulie! HI, JOYCE! HI, HARRY!" Maureen bounced off the fence and ran out towards the street while she was waving her arms frantically to attract their attention.

The roar of Harry's giant engine in his Sonicmobile shattered the calm of the morning, while his gear shifting told the entire neighborhood that he arrived and was flying up the road towards the house. I didn't even have to see the car to know that it was Harry making a grand appearance.

Speed limits were merely suggestions to Harry M. Redmond Junior.

Oh, well, timing is everything in life. I did not have time to voice my side of the statement that I had made about Maureen being my love and my gal. I guess it was going to have to stand now. What is the harm in allowing Maureen's happiness to perpetuate a bit longer and allow her to bask in the glow of our love? I shrugged my shoulders and rubbed my whiskers as I watched Maureen and Joyce hug each other and Harry jump out of the driver's door. I thought how as of late; it seems as if no one actually lets me speak. They all tell me what impressive words I say and how smart I am, but I seldom, if ever, get a word in edge wise. Someday, I will actually finish a sentence from start to finish and a person will pay attention to me.

Someday.

Cocoa appeared with Piggy. I walked over, picked up his dishes, and opened the trunk of Harry's car. I grabbed Maureen's suitcases, the jugs of wine, and my bags and tossed them in the trunk too.

Harry was smiling broadly, waving for everyone to jump in, and loudly shouting, "This is going to be one of our greatest adventures ever, gang! Let's go! Jump in! I bought a map; I think I know how to get there."

I stopped and thought about that for a second or two, and I had a suggestion, so I started to speak, "Harry, about the way there. . .."

Harry, of course, ignored me and instead yelled at his faithful dog, "Cocoa! Make sure you pee really well. We ain't stopping every few minutes." Cocoa barked twice and wagged his tail three times and took off for a minute or two. He quickly returned and jumped into the backseat. Harry was satisfied; the big guy clapped his hands and waved us onward and upward.

"We are rolling! LET'S GO!"

Maureen grabbed my hand and pulled me into the backseat while I still had the words on the tip of my tongue. She reached over, kissed me deeply, and squeezed my hands while she buried her lips into mine again.

Maureen was so aggressive.

She stole the words off the tip of my tongue. Ah, forget it, anyhow. I was going to offer to read the road map and would receive the label of an old lady, so I might as well neck a little with Maureen.

Harry would not listen to me, anyway.

"Ya ain't reading the road map on this trip, twenty-seven. Joyce is taking ovah for ya. Ya such an old lady and would take us on the scenic route instead of highways to avoid speeding tickets and irate state troopers."

I knew that already, so I ignored him and enjoyed Maureen's various delights, which always were intoxicating mix of allure and red wine, topped off with a touch of garlic.

Cocoa barked twice and wagged his tail three times in agreement with Harry, and I ignored him too.

Off we rolled, into the sunrise of another Harry and Paul adventure.

Harry blasted music from his tape deck. He sang loudly to every tune that came along and soon enough, New Jersey, rolled into Connecticut, and Massachusetts loomed ahead.

Cups of coffee equaled some rest stops, but for the most part, we did not stop except to refuel, let Cocoa out, and stop for a restroom here and there. A few missed turns, a supposed shortcut right over the Massachusetts border did not exactly work out well, but for the most part, we rolled on and on, without any mishaps. I avoided the Old Lady Syndrome affliction that, according to Harry, had infested my soul. I did not mention the fact that I was usually the road map navigator on these types of trips. Harry claimed that his new navigator looked a helluva lot better than I did, and I had to admit that he had me on that point.

The conversations ranged from every topic you could ever imagine. With the ever vivacious and talkative Maureen Zipperelli around, words and conversations never lacked, she held her end of the conversation up and then some.

Harry, Joyce, and I managed to say, "Uh huh, Maureen" a few thousand times or thereabouts. I could have passed on the weirdness comparison between Uncle Heinrich and myself, but I did feel exonerated when he edged me out because of his hairstyle, being, as Joyce described, "Untamed."

We stopped for lunch; I offered to take over the driving, of which caused an immediate denial of my offer, not only by Harry but also by all four of my companions. My penchant for driving slowly caused all four of my companions to shake their heads (and tail) simultaneously to show that I should not take the wheel.

I heard Joyce mumble something about, "Wanting to get there today, not in a week or so."

I tried not to take these types of criticisms to heart, and instead, I rather prided myself on my perfect driving record.

The scenery was beautiful, the blossoms of spring were giving way to the leaves of summer, and along the roadsides was a view so very different from what we saw in our home state. Massachusetts turned into New Hampshire, and as we rolled north on Interstate 91, I realized that Maureen, Cocoa, and Joyce were all fast asleep.

"Here, twenty-seven. Here is the map. My gorgeous navigator with the amazing chest has conked out on me, so you take over. No old lady shit, straight up the highway," Harry whispered as he handed me the map over the seat.

I nodded that I understood, and smiled. Harry was indeed rolling now. The big engine on his sports car revved up, and it was now sailing along. The big guy managed to avoid speeding tickets. He flirted with the threshold speeds of what would be the breaking point, but Harry was an expert driver and he stayed under control.

Maureen laid her head upon my shoulder; she had tucked her arm into mine and I could hear her soft breathing near my ear. I surmised that she was not only tired from working so hard to complete her appointments in time to leave for our holiday, but I dare say now that she was sleeping, perhaps from talking so much. I did not mind that part of Maureen's personality. In fact, I felt as if it was part of her charm, and there was little doubt that she made up for my lack of conversation. At this point in my life, I studied situations more, before speaking much. Unless it was a topic of which I knew a great deal about, I tended to be more on the quiet side.

It was all of twelve hours for us to make it to the shores of the big lake in New Hampshire, where Uncle Heinrich lived on an island, which apparently was out in the lake. Yes, indeed, he lived on an island called Black Cat Island out in the lake. Not in the exact middle of the lake, but "his" island was over towards one of the inlets. Yet the fact remained that he lived on an island.

In fact, Harry told us that he called it "his" island because he actually owned the entire island.

If it had to do with the Redmond family, it had to be strange. It just had to be.

It was still light outside when we finally arrived. The girls and Cocoa were now waking up, they remained a bit sleepy-eyed, but they were trying to shake off the sleep. Harry parked the car on a street that faced rows upon rows of boat slips, at a place called Weirs Beach. We all climbed out of the car and stood on the sidewalk, looking out at one of the most gorgeous lake scenes that you could ever imagine. Maureen had brought along her camera and she snapped picture after picture.

It was breathtaking.

Deep blue water, waves gently rolling in, framed on a backdrop of pine trees and hardwoods, with the deciduous trees just now, dropping blossoms of spring and growing into their summer covers. We all were now a long way from 20 John Street!

"Geez, twenty-seven, this place is unbelievable. Never imagined a lake could be so perfect, so gorgeous. It makes the Oldham Pond look like a puddle in my driveway," Harry said while standing on the sidewalk. He was holding Joyce's hand, and Joyce looked over to make sure the three of us were walking over to them. We joined up and Joyce signaled for us to gather as a group. We did, and we all hung our arms across each other's shoulders. Cocoa tucked in at our legs. He was a bit too short for the group hug, but we included him anyway.

"It never ceases to amaze me, of how Harry and Paul's adventures seem to spread far and wide. Here we are on the shores of this gorgeous lake, all the way from northern New Jersey! I love all of youse guys," Joyce emphatically told us as we held onto each other.

Harry bellowed, "It is pretty cool, and we are just getting started, there gorgeous, Joyce-a-roo-ski!"

Oh, no! Whenever I heard Harry say the phrase of words, "We are just getting started," I always received a little shudder up and down my spine, a shudder that occurred many times over the many years.

The start of a Harry and Paul adventure was never really the trouble, nor what worried me, but it was always the trouble that began about halfway through, all the way to the ending, which generally gave me some sort of problem.

As I stood there, holding on to Joyce and Maureen, while pondering rather pensively what could, or may, lie on the horizon for us, Harry broke away, he happily scampered off towards a pay telephone hanging on a nearby post next to the sidewalk. Cocoa sensed some type of excitement because he picked himself off our feet and ran off after Harry. Cocoa was barking happily during the entire run.

"I have to call Uncle Heinrich and tell him that we made it!" Harry shouted. He then stopped, turned around and yelled back with a wide smile on his face, "He is going to pick us up in his boat-car! He arranged for me to leave my car right here. Of course, he knows everyone and everyone knows him too!"

Maureen and Joyce both looked at Harry, then at me, and I shrugged my shoulders.

While gently shaking her head, Maureen said, "Oh, shit! We should have known that we would have to ride, drive, sail or whatever, the hell you call it, in that damn boat thingy! Paulie, would you please go get a jug of red wine out of the trunk?"

"Okay, Maureen, but we do not have any wine glasses."

Maureen looked at Joyce. Joyce nodded her head, and she made a motion with her hands as though she was holding an imaginary jug in her hands, tipping it over and drinking out of it.

"We don't need any glasses, Paulie."

I nodded that I understood, turned, and made my way to the car to grab the jug of wine.

Yes, indeed, we were just getting started.

4

God Does Not Only Come Out on Sundays

Once you became used to the tip and roll and the sway of the boat-car, then the ride across the lake was not too bad. You did have to deal with the occasional trumpet playing by the driver, and James's baying and Cocoa barking in tune to Uncle Heinrich's songs. You also were painfully aware of the fact that you were actually sitting in a subcompact automobile, powered by two silver propellers. I kept telling myself that this was fun, and tried very hard to ignore the fact that we were gliding merrily across the surface of a huge lake, which most likely was hundreds of feet deep, in a boat, which was also a car. After all of this pondering and apprehension, it was somewhat enjoyable. Except for the trumpet playing, and dog singing.

I guess perception is a reality, or vice versa, but this was actually some type of boat. It was just that your perception made you think it was a car.

On the other hand, perhaps it was a boat.

In the world of Harry and his rather unique family, this was just another cog in the weirdness wheel. I had been through many weird and wacky adventures with Harry and the Redmonds, and I was sure that this ride across a majestic lake in a car that just changed into a boat was certainly strange, but I swear, there was an adventure in the past which was stranger than this one was. At the moment, I could not think of one, but I knew that I just needed a bit more time to inventory the many adventures in my mind and find one to outdo this one. Give me a few minutes; there are, after all, quite a few of them.

Harry sat happily in the passenger seat, with Cocoa on his lap and James, the hound dog, squeezed between them all. Harry's face had a smile a mile wide on it and I thought that his face would crack because he was smiling so widely. Cocoa was up in front of him, his backside on Harry's lap and his two front paws on the dashboard, enjoying the ride, too.

Uncle Heinrich sat in the driver's seat, His wild, mad scientist-like hair blowing in the open window of the boat-car, his dark eyes set deep in his head. He was alternating between taking sips of whiskey out of a clear whiskey glass, blowing his tune on his trumpet and puffing away on a pipe like a smokestack, with James's baying in delight.

I would imagine that it was illegal for the "captain" of a watercraft, or whatever the authorities would classify this mechanical device as, to be drinking alcohol while piloting the craft. I thought how, since Uncle Heinrich owned an entire island on the lake that would most likely influence and cause the Coast Guard Auxiliary to look the other way. In actuality, the fact that we were all riding in a car-boat made the whiskey nipping seem slightly irrelevant. At least, in the big picture, that is!

Uncle Heinrich put the trumpet down for a moment and instead he broke out singing a loud tune. His voice grew in intensity as we made our way across the lake. James bayed loudly to the obscure tune of which Uncle Heinrich was merrily singing.

It seemed as if it was some type of seafaring song, something that an old sailor would sing on the deck of a ship that was about to sink. The lyrics mentioned something about, "Sinking to the bottom of the deep blue ocean to find some long, lost love."

Despite the fact that even singing a cappella, Uncle

Heinrich had a wonderful singing voice, (he sang in a deep bass that shook the interior of the boat-car), I tried very hard to ignore his rather ominous choice of songs to serenade us on our precarious journey.

Joyce and Maureen sat next to me in the backseat. I sat in the middle, and each of the gals had a death grip on my arms. I could feel my pulse beating in my head as my heart desperately tried to overcome the death grips on my arms and keep blood circulating around my body. The two gals squeezed my arms as if they were tourniquets. Despite the fact that both Joyce and Maureen had downed a few hearty sips of homemade Zipperelli wine to dull their senses as a prelude to the ride, they still were white as ghosts and gripped with fear. I came to the vague conclusion that our lovely women were not finding the boat-car ride very enjoyable.

I reassured them as best I could, with some mindless drivel that I quickly conjured up, "I am sure that Uncle Heinrich has made this trip, thousands and thousands of times. We are fine. Look! We are already halfway across the lake. Look at the shoreline, the trees are so beautiful and I am very sure that. . .." I pointed out towards an island that seemed as if it were a few hundred miles or so away on the horizon and Maureen cut me off.

She removed her death grip on my arm for a second to wave to Joyce, while asking her, "Please hand me that jug, would you, Joyce?"

Joyce handed the wine jug to Maureen, who tipped it over as if she was a seasoned lush and she chugged a few gulps. She then handed it back to Joyce, who did the same.

Just to add to the delight of this precarious joyride, Harry was now familiar with the verses of the song, and he joined in with his uncle and James, the hound dog, in the chorus of the lovely tune:

"Grab me 'nother drink. Down my throat it goes.

I swaller it down with a smile on my face,
and my old pipe stuck in ma mouth!
Her breasts were like gentle mountains!
Her lips were as sweet as red wine!
Her hair was the color of a golden sunset!
My long-lost love, I hear you calling me!
Calling me, from the bottom of da deep blue oceannnnn!"

Now, Cocoa started barking in time to the tune too!

Oh, geezzzz, how the hell long is this friggin' lake?

The boat-car tipped into a steep turn, it rolled and lurched, and I swear, the waterline was almost up to the windows!

Unfazed, Uncle Heinrich and Harry laughed and the two of them, along with James and Cocoa, continued to sing merrily away. The gals both screamed and I had to admit that I held on a bit, too. This was a bit too much for my lifelong affliction with the cursed Old Lady Syndrome, for me to handle, or more importantly, for me to dismiss.

I leaned in and asked between breaths of their singing, "Do you have any life jackets or preservers on board, Uncle Heinrich?"

Without missing a beat or verse, he answered, "Ah yes, my nephew told me ya are sufferin' from the dreaded, Old Lady Syndrome, twenty-seven! Big tough goalie, with hockey pucks knocking into ya head bone all game long, ya would think you would shake that. Nah, we don't need 'em, cuz, this is considered a car!"

A car? On a lake? I mean, what the hell? The proverbial straw that breaks the. . ..

"That's it! If we are going to sink, I will go with you kissing me, Paulie. I will go happy with your lips locked upon mine!" Maureen grabbed my face with both of her hands and lip locked me. I was grateful that for just a brief moment, she let go of my arm. At least the blood could now rush around my body because it was free at last.

Now, the trouble was breathing.

Maureen let go of me, and Joyce grabbed me, while she proclaimed, "Forgive me, Harry, but you are out of reach in the front seat. Maureen, please forgive me, but that is a good idea. I need to borrow Paulie's lips."

"Go ahead. They are amazing and the rest of him is not too shabby either. You are gonna have to take my word for verification of those parts because you can't have them. The lips you can borrow, just give them back when you are done."

Yes, indeed, Maureen and Joyce were now deeply under the influence of a wine-induced haze.

Maureen smiled and nodded while relinquishing my face for a few minutes for their perceived last rites. Joyce now lip locked me as the boat-car tipped back upright and we were now cruising happily towards an island that loomed a bit closer. Joyce let me come up for air, as Harry laughed, and Uncle Heinrich resumed his trumpet blowing and the dogs resumed their accompaniment.

Joyce held my face in her hands and looked into my eyes as she said, "Damn, Paulie, you are a friggin' amazing kisser. I am gonna die happy. Sorry, Maureen, I need a bunch more!"

I had to admit, there did seem to be an intriguing side benefit to this ride.

There we cruised, the seven of us enjoying (a wild supposition on my part, but certain aspects proved somewhat enjoyable) the rest of the journey across the lake, peacefully gliding along in our boat-car. The boat-car slowed as it glided next to a boat dock. A dock, which currently held a massive forty-foot boat with an impressive flying bridge.

As we glided by the massive boat at the dock, Maureen paused for a moment from her last rites and slurred out, "Sssso, wwwwhy the hhhhell could we have not gone on that damn thing instead of this floating-ass tuna fish can?"

I shrugged my shoulders, and no one answered her before we bumped, jumped, and the boat-car rolled along and it continued to roll right up on the shore, we rolled to a soft and gentle stop in the center of a long driveway!

There was something very strange, yet sublime, about this entire situation. As we slowed to a stop, Harry jumped out of the passenger's door, followed by Cocoa. Uncle Heinrich and James then opened their doors and jumped out, too. The backseat dwellers were still greatly under the influence of Zipperelli wine, as well as shell-shocked from the entire experience. My lips and arms ached, and now, I had to fend off the two wine-influenced women who were arguing over my lips, as well as to try to stop Maureen and Joyce from placing their hands in and on certain spots upon my body. After all, parts of me started to react to the extra attention. When the two women realized that we had safely made it to shore, they giggled, whispered some coy comments about my anatomy to each other, and then allowed me to convince them to exit the boat-car. Being the least enthusiastic of our group, we slowly clambered out of the backseats.

Harry stood next to the boat-car beaming as if he was a Halloween pumpkin, while shouting out, "I have just got to get me one of these rigs!"

"No trouble! I'll fix ya up wid one nephew!"

When a wobbly and slightly intoxicated Joyce heard Harry's comments, as well as his uncle's reply, she leaned over me and into Maureen and whispered, "You do that ya big blowhard, and after one ride in the backseat of it, Maureen and I will both be happily pregnant with Paul's children."

Maureen, who was only slightly soberer than Joyce was, grabbed me forcibly by the backside and laughed uproariously, while answering Joyce, "You know it. Maybe *we should* buy it for Harry. I can guarantee that it will be worth it!"

Oh brother, too much wine made these women a bit on the wild side. To say the least.

Out of earshot of the drunken drivel and undaunted in his quest for a boat-car, Harry spouted, "That would be great! Say, this is some nice little shack in the woods that ya got here, Uncle Hein-a-roo-ski! And, ya own the island too! Damn sure is impressive! Don't know what ya invented, but it sure musta worked! Joyce and me gotta come and hang with ya all the time!"

Joyce took a break from probing my body; she stood wearily up on her legs, wobbling a bit from the futile attempt to dull some reality of the boat-car ride.

When she heard her beau declare his intentions, and Uncle Heinrich's reply, she shook her head and said, "Oh, shit, that is just what I knew he would say! I swear that there is not enough wine in the world to be Harry M. Redmond Junior's girlfriend."

We stood there in the driveway; a driveway leading up to a majestic log cabin towering to the sky, nestled within a bed of stately pine trees. It was not really a log cabin; more of a log mansion was a better description. Massive, glowing, a full front porch that stretched from one end to the other. The house had to be at least three thousand or more square feet. It had a peaked roof; with a chimney, puffing some entrancing aroma of smoke, while looming miles and miles above the structure.

It was difficult to tell how large the island actually was, but forests of pines and hardwoods stretched everywhere, and the views of the lake were amazing. In front of the home, there was a huge front yard of deep, lush green turf, trimmed in a perfect and immaculate manner. The yard, which gently sloped away from the front porch, passed rows upon rows of trimmed and blooming rose shrubs, gardens with brick paths dotted with annual flowers and blooming perennials of all kinds. The front yard ended at the edge of the lake, where it gave way to a small patch of a sandy beach.

Uncle Heinrich stopped in his driveway, waved his arms over the land, raised his trumpet to his lips, and played a loud tune of some type of charge call or a military tune of some sort. At this point, it was difficult to tell what the hell he was playing.

Once he finished the tune, he shouted out, "Welcome to Black Cat Island, where the joy of nature is prevalent and the gentle waves of the big lake lull you into peace and complacency. James and I maintain all of this. We plant the gardens, we mow the turf, and we plant the flowers, the trees and tend to all of God's grand creation! It is a testimony to his greatness. God created it all and we just tend to it!"

I was unsure how an old hound dog assisted in ground maintenance, but at this point, nothing seemed impossible for Uncle Heinrich. Besides, I had to admit that the grounds were spectacular.

It was awe-inspiring.

Uncle Heinrich owned his own island! An island within a slice of Heaven on Earth. It was a concept for this city guy that was indeed a bit hard to accept.

I watched as Harry, still mesmerized by the boat-car, put his arm around Uncle Heinrich and they made their way to the front porch while still singing the chorus to that stupid song. The dogs jumped, played, and followed behind their masters.

Harry was too enthralled in the euphoria of unique transportation to think about the mere fact that we had tons of luggage packed for this adventure!

"I guess that Harry is not going to help with the luggage," I said, while making my way to the trunk of the boat-car, fiddling a bit with the lock and finally, opening it up to reveal the mountains of luggage inside.

It is a miracle that we did not sink.

Slightly more sober versions of Joyce and Maureen

helped me, while the three of us collectively pulled, tugged, and bumped the luggage up and into the cabin. Maureen clung to the jugs of the homemade Zipperelli wine as if it were more precious than gold. She knew that in a day or so, we had to return to the mainland and that meant a reverse trip in the boat-car. I prayed that my lips and male anatomy held up.

The inside of the log mansion was even more impressive than the outside was. The first floor was an open floor plan, with floor to ceiling windows looking out in all directions on the forests, the lake, and the front and backyards. Gleaming hardwood floors, polished as if they were mirrors, glowed at us; I could see our reflections in them while we stood there in awe. Even Cocoa stopped in his tracks, dropped Piggy on the floor and looked around because the world's smartest dog never imagined such a sight!

On one end of the floor was an open gourmet kitchen, equipped with gleaming appliances, and rows-upon-rows of spice canisters and other cooking supplies, which lined the counters. A large, stone countertop spread from one end to the other, wrapping around and ending in a full, wet bar, even equipped with a sprawling, wooden rack stocked with wine, liquor and other alcoholic delights.

Some type of food was cooking. The aroma floated around the inside of the room as enticing as a fine perfume on a beautiful woman. In the center of the floor was a large granite fireplace (we were in New Hampshire) with a glowing fire inside. The hearth was so large that you could play a football game on it. The chimney rose through the mansion, with additional fireplace openings on the second-floor loft as the stone reached to the sky.

"Here, let me show ya around the place," Uncle Heinrich proclaimed while waving us onward. "We've got plenty of room here! Let's see, eight bedrooms, six bathrooms, and it is only James and Uncle Heinrich. Well, I do entertain a few women here and there too, but that might be a subject that we do not dwell on right at the moment. Please come and look at the other side of the fireplace. Check out my band room where James and I serenade the women who visit us."

We all followed behind Uncle Heinrich, still mesmerized by the interior of his mansion. I held Maureen's hand as we gasped at the sight on the other side of the fireplace. The rest of the first floor consisted of what appeared to be a stage, equipped with all types of musical instruments, from a grand piano to stringed instruments, such as a large string bass guitar, violins, and even a harp! There were electric guitars on stands, amplifiers, acoustic guitars, you name it, and it was here.

"My, goodness. Do you actually play all of these instruments, Uncle Heinrich?" Joyce asked.

"Why, of course, my dear pretty lady. James and I do play all of them together." The old hound dog sat and bayed loudly, displaying his prolific vocal skills. I was not surprised. After all, if he could maintain the grounds, flowers, and turf, why would James not have musical abilities too.

Harry stood there nodding his head in acknowledgement to all of his uncle's claims as Cocoa sat next to him looking up at his master for guidance. Cocoa seemed to acknowledge that his dog cousin had some unique talents.

"This is actually James the tenth. He is the current James Clovenhofen. However, of all of his descendants, this James actually is the best singer. By far, in fact, his vocal tones as well as his range are amazing."

By now, our temperance and defense shields for weirdness had reached their maximum output; therefore, all four of us were not fazed one bit by his statement and his dog's reaction. We were now quite battle hardened and sufficiently fortified, and the gals were full of enough wine that it did not much matter what Uncle Heinrich managed to whip up in the bizarre department. Maureen only giggled and held onto my arm as she listened to the testimony.

She did lean in and whisper to me, "I am not sure that this is not all bullshit, Paulie. But with the Redmonds you just never know."

I only nodded, as I was not yet willing to admit that it was indeed bullshit.

Uncle Heinrich stood in the middle of the room, and he held his hands and arms straight out from his body and outstretched towards the heavens. It seemed as if he was trying to capture all of his surroundings. It was then that I reminded myself that Uncle Heinrich had been sipping his whiskey.

We watched as he slowly spun in circles, his long hair wildly projecting in all directions, while he shouted, "First we shall eat and drink. I have cooked a gourmet meal for us to enjoy. Yes, indeed, roast beef, potatoes, asparagus and sweet corn smothered in my own, secret recipe butter sauce, green salads, all veggies grown right here in our gardens here on Black Cat Island! Homemade biscuits, fresh-baked bread, and a dessert of apple pie from apple trees grown here on the island."

He stopped spinning, pointed at the stage, and continued to explain, "Then, after dinner, we will jam together. Harry plays a mean banjo and guitar, and the gorgeous women, Cocoa, and James can sing. Paulie cannot carry a tune in a bucket, but Harry tells me that ya can strum three chords on a twelve-string guitar. Bands always need guys like you, Paulie. Ya, just eye candy for the women. You can stand in the corner, let your long hair down, wave your instrument around and make as if you know what you are doing!"

"Well, in my defense, I do not. . .."

As usual, I did not complete my statement. I stood there

like a dope with my mouth open and one of my pointer fingers extended in the air as I tried to make a point. Harry cut me off as he jumped in and joined in a round of backslapping laughter at my expense.

Everyone headed off towards the kitchen, however, Maureen stayed behind, she leaned in for a kiss, and then she slapped me on the backside and gently whispered, "I can assure you the dessert that I have for you, is a whole bunch better there, twenty-seven. I couldn't care less if you can sing or not. You sing to my heart like no other man. Ever."

Maureen was so aggressive.

Dinner was beyond words to describe. Maureen's Italian family happened to be experts in the cooking department, and when Maureen was in awe of the culinary delights, of which Uncle Heinrich whipped up for us, then you can imagine how wonderful his cooking was.

Dinnertime was memorable for many reasons. However, one moment stuck out above the rest. When the table was set, and the food laid out for consumption, right before we began to eat, Uncle Heinrich paused.

He bowed his head in a slow reverence, he asked us to join hands and he recited a heartfelt and powerful prayer, "Lord in Heaven and our Lord on Earth, bless this food which came from not only our toil, but from your creation. Bless it to our bodies, but most of all, bless our souls to your service. We have friends and family gathered here, at your table, in your kingdom. A kingdom, which exists not only in churches and in the tallest steeples where proud bells peal in your honor, but it exists on the very soil of which produced this food. In Jesus' name, we pray, to God be all the glory! Amen!"

I placed that particular memory in my mind for future reference.

For some reason, it sent shivers down my spine, and for the second time since we had met, it made me look at

Uncle Heinrich as more than just some eccentric character. There was a great deal of depth to this man's soul and beliefs. It resonated with me and I felt a strange, yet powerful connection to his words and to him, too.

I also recalled Harry telling us that in addition to all of his other adventures and his endless vocations, he, at one time, was a priest. After dinner, we wandered the home, gazing in admiration, while Uncle Heinrich showed us his collection of oil paintings. They were all magnificent oil paintings that he painted! He showed us books of poetry and prose, of which he wrote and published, and a collection of incredible photographs that he snapped and framed. All of this was mesmerizing; the talent that the man possessed was remarkable. He was, without any doubt, a genius. He was a painter, inventor, a millionaire, an expert gardener, a gourmet chef, a writer, a poet, a photographer, a musician, my goodness, it was exhausting, just listening to him and trying in vain, to keep up with his seemingly, boundless energy.

I would guess Uncle Heinrich to be about sixty years of age or thereabouts, but his energy level was that of a twenty-year-old man. He was a very difficult man to keep up with, between his wanderings and meanderings between subjects, the high level of his vocabulary and his intelligence level. He was indeed an eccentric chap, but there was no doubt that God had set a special hand upon Uncle Heinrich Clovenhofen.

After our tour, while fueled by a great deal of Zipperelli wine, beer, and whiskey, we did jam with a memorable hodgepodge of music. I strummed, as best that I could, my feeble chords. What I had tried previously to convey in vain was that I actually knew four chords, on a twelve-string guitar, as opposed to the three that Harry claimed were all that I knew. My numerous broken fingers from playing hockey made working a fret-board a bit difficult, therefore, I conceded relegation to the role of a four-chord strummer. Harry played the six-string acoustic guitar and the banjo. The women and dogs sang, and Uncle Heinrich played every other instrument there were and a few more.

His solo on the harp of a piece that he wrote himself, in which he titled, "On God's Good Earth" moved you to tears. After we finished our music, we all realized, even in our alcohol-induced haze, that this incredibly long day was finally ending.

Uncle Heinrich tossed a few more logs into the fireplace as the night loomed and the air grew chilly. When the fire roared back to life, he then stood in the center of his grand palace.

Uncle Heinrich smiled and loudly told us, "It is now time to retire for the day and night, my dear family and friends, and far be it from me to be called a prude. I surely have my share of closet dwelling skeletons, that God provides me daily forgiveness for the weakness of my mind and flesh. You are all adults! I say to you that tonight, I would gladly close my eyes to your individual sleeping arrangements. I am sure that even twenty-seven and his chronic affliction with the Old Lady Syndrome, could overcome its grips for the prospect of making love to such a lovely lady such as Maureen is, however, that pondering might be for debate upon another horizon. Despite the fact that I have more than enough bedrooms here, I will throw a bit of a twist in this for all of us!"

Harry, after hearing and calculating, in his rather devious mind, his uncle's proclamation and staring at Joyce, cleared his throat and spoke, "Oh geez! That is okay there, Uncle Heinrich. I am fine with no twists. I kinda like your first suggestion."

Joyce punched Harry playfully in the arm, as Maureen circled in close to me while batting her eyes and rubbing up against me.

Since I did have my affliction and my reputation to honor, I spoke up, "I think the women would rather enjoy their own rooms. Harry snores terribly, and Harry, Cocoa, and I can. . ..''

Of course, I never finished my statement.

"Surprise! Outside we go, gang! Bring your sweaters and hoodies. I will show you where we will rest our heads tonight. Back to nature, sleeping on God's grand creation. The night air produces the most wonderful rest!"

None of us had any hoodies packed with us, but it did not matter. Uncle Heinrich handed out a selection to each of us as we followed him out the back door, around the house to a side yard. There, in front of an immense stone fire pit, where within the stone confines of the pit a warm and dazzling fire erupted, were seven sleeping bags.

Harry groaned while his visions of lust fizzled as he realized his fate.

Uncle Heinrich tended to the roaring fire and there we sat, sipping the last remnants of Zipperelli wine, toasting marshmallows, talking and watching the flames dance in our eyes.

As the conversation lagged solely from a lack of energy, and the alcoholic influences took their toll on us, I finally commented, "That was a wonderful prayer you said at dinner, Uncle Heinrich. Thank you for sharing it."

Uncle Heinrich stared at me for a long time; he seemed to be studying my eyes rather intensely in the dim light of the flames. Maureen noticed it too, and she squeezed my hand tightly.

He spoke gently, quietly, "God is great, my dear Paul. You know this too, in your heart, you know it, and remember this, someday, when the lure of ice hockey no longer flows in your bloodstream, you will answer a call. The call will be your ultimate mission. Hockey is merely a vehicle for you to ride in for now. The call will be powerful and it will consume your heart and soul. You will touch many lives, and then, for a reason, out of your control, God's plan will twist and turn you. Eventually, you will trust and obey your heart. It is in your soul. It will never expire, Paul. There is nothing that you can do to control it, because it is God's plan for you. Much as it was for me. I answered the call once, and despite my love of God, it did not work out. My own heart shattered."

"Why, Uncle Heinrich? Why did you quit the priesthood?" Harry asked.

Uncle Heinrich stood up; he spun around slowly, much as he did inside the house earlier this same evening.

He held his arms outstretched with his hands and palms facing up in the air.

He suddenly stopped and said, "Because of all of this! Look around at this wonderful creation. A world, and our God, is far too wonderful for humankind to understand. Therefore, we rebel and we create religion. Along with religion, come man's opinions and confusion. Too many rules, too many threats, all-man made, all in some futile and hapless attempt to shoehorn God into some kind of tidy box. Religion is so different from God! Can you really tell me that God keeps track of all of those rules, all of those rituals? When they interview a professional athlete on the television after the big game and he looks in the camera and proudly tells the reporter that God helped him win the game. Those types of statements make me sick to my stomach. My goodness, I do not think the glory of God is involved in the outcome of sporting events."

Uncle Heinrich grew even more animated, and he pointed, first towards the heavens, and then to all of us individually.

He then continued with his sermon, "It is all some type of feeble effort on man's part to categorize and quantify God. To understand how great, God is, how wonderful the real things in which he created are! Realize that Jesus is Lord, Abraham is too, as is Moses, and all the prophets and spirits combined! God is everywhere and in everyone!"

Uncle Heinrich leaned in, and he pointed first at

Maureen and then to Joyce, and he continued his amazing sermon. I could not help but to think that some bishop somewhere made a grave error when he stripped this man of his collar and qualifications.

"Look! Behold! A woman's beauty. Profound and unparalleled. Her heart hanging on her sleeve, all given for a man that she loves, for him to take. God smiles on her love. God does not frown upon her sharing her body in the name of love. God created it. This is all part of the plan, not something she needs to hide or to be ashamed about in any way. Oh, my, when I wrote that thesis for my Master of Divinity degree, and expounded upon the virtues of a woman's love in the most detailed, and in my opinion, a Biblical manner, the bishops frowned a bit. They gave me a one-hundred percent grade on the paper, but went away horrified after reading my opinions. When I stated in my homilies that Jesus was love, that we all are still as Jewish as our Savior is, and our religion remains severely flawed, well that did not go over so well. It was good enough to have me excommunicated . . . and they did. Let me tell you! They collectively tore my collar off when they read my papers and listened to my words. Set their hair on fire! Sent me packing! Yet, all these years later, when I observe the beauty and the love of a woman, I stand by what I wrote. How, if not for a woman's beauty and a man's appeal, do you think the world will perpetuate? You see, it is all part of God's great and flawless plan! These leaders per se, are merely men, who are too ignorant to admit that they are making these rules up as they go along."

He waved to simulate that "they" threw his belongings away, tore his collar off and tossed them both into some imaginary place.

He now, if it were even possible, became even more animated as he continued to speak, "Church is here, in the glory and splendor of this lake, in the wind whispering in the pines, in the love in a young woman's eyes. In the moonlight, in the sunlight, and in the glory of sunsets and sunrises. Church is wherever you want it to be! Not only in some grand structure, with towering spires that are lifting towards the clouds, in some foolish testimony of wasted money. I assure you, to save one soul or one life, is more important to God, than a manmade structure created in his honor is! Church is in the cry of a baby longing for their mother's breast, it is in the desire, and the joy of lovers joined as one during and after a night of passion. Look above our heads. Look to the glory of Heaven, and beyond, and try to tell me that God is not real or is not great. I know that love is the greatest power of all and that God loves us and wants us to love each other in return. I know this is true. His glory is all around us. Even, right now."

Uncle Heinrich paused, and we all sat there stunned. His words were too mesmerizing for any of us to move.

He then took a deep breath and continued, "Jesus owned nothing more than his shoes and the clothes on his back. He never traveled far, never owned his own home. He stayed with friends, walked the earth humbly, wept when his best friend died, and slept, as we will tonight, upon the very dirt that God created. Silly churches built with millions of dollars, while babies starve and die from lack of medicine, shelter and food. It is a farce! I tell you that it is! It is all around us and this is a church, and glory should be only to God."

Uncle Heinrich relaxed now, while his voice lowered to a whisper, "That will be the true measure of my soul's worth—how I recognized God's love. What all of organized religion has to understand is that God does not only come out on Sundays. God is here with us every day and not buried under the pomp and splendor."

He fell silent, but not before his speech mesmerized all of us so deeply that none of us had a reply. What else could you actually say? Uncle Heinrich summed it all up for all of us and then some. It was, and is, even to this day, the greatest sermon that I have ever heard.

We all climbed into our sleeping bags on the ground, bid and kissed one another goodnight, and we slowly drifted off to sleep. Before sleep overcame us, we all stared at the clearest and most beautiful sky that we had ever seen. The belt of Orion glowed as if the stars were only a mile or two away.

They were so bright.

Magnificent did not even describe it.

I reached over and grasped Maureen's hand. In the rippling glow of the flames, I could see her face and her smile.

She stared at me, until she finally said, "Goodnight, Paulie. I do love you with all of my heart and all of my soul. We do not have to honor it tonight or prove it in any other manner. It is in our hearts. My, the sky is so magnificent. I have never seen anything so clear, so brilliant. It truly is God's work. Uncle Heinrich is so correct when he says that God does not only come out on Sundays. God is here right now, with all of us. This is all so unforgettable."

I nodded and said, "He is indeed. Goodnight, Maureen. I love you too."

While we drifted off to sleep, I could hear Uncle Heinrich singing gently, low, almost to himself,

"Grab me 'nother drink. Down my throat it goes.
I swaller it down with a smile on my face,
and my old pipe stuck in ma mouth!
Her breasts were like gentle mountains!
Her lips were as sweet as red wine!
Her hair was the color of a golden sunset!
My long-lost love, I hear you calling me!
Calling me, from the bottom of da deep blue oceannnnn!"

"I do think that dinner is finally ready, my dear Paul."

Binky's voice shook me back to reality.

Startled, I nearly jumped out of my chair.

"I am so sorry, Paul. I did not mean to startle you so badly! You must have been very deep in your thoughts. Are you okay?"

I looked up at my lovely wife and smiled. "Yes, so sorry, dear Binky. I was thinking that I just came up with an amazing title for my sermon for this Sunday. At least, I think that I did."

I tore open the rest of the envelope and pulled the card out. Printed on the cover there was a simple, yet stunning print of a sunset over a lake.

I already knew who the photographer was. I did not have to read the credits or examine the copyright.

I opened it, and read the contents aloud, as Binky walked over to see, and to listen to me read, what the card said:

"Hello, dear number, twenty-seven. I have to apologize for the time between our communications, but by now, Harry and you know that Uncle Heinrich only makes occasional appearances. No matter, our bond is strong and my love for all of you remains great. Sorry about the hockey career, but I guess by now, you know that it is all part of the plan. I told you that, someday, you would answer the call. I could tell by the emotion that God planted within your eyes. My sincere hope is that all is well. A week or so ago, I sent in a donation to your church of a few thousand dollars, and your tape committee sent me a recorded tape or two of your sermons. I am sure that the bookkeeper fainted, when she opened that envelope and that eventually, she will report the donation to you. I must say that your sermon work is very impressive. Well, worth a few grand or two. Please, keep up the good work. Never tire or falter until God tells you that all of it is over.

Remember, church is everywhere within this grand creation. God does not only come out on Sundays. Say hey to my nephew for me and be sure to tell him that I love him, as well as everyone, with all of my heart and soul. By the grace of God, I will write to you again in twenty years or thereabouts!

Signed with all of my love, respect, and my best wishes, Uncle Heinrich Clovenhofen."

I closed the card and smiled.

Even after all of these years, I knew that those lessons he taught to me were still very valid and profound. In addition, it seemed as if Maria Tooteroni and a certain long-haired Lutheran pastor shared some of the same exact thoughts and words as did Uncle Heinrich.

Hidden under the pomp and the splendor is where you might need to look to find the God that you are looking for. Always remember that God does not only come out on Sundays.

Thank you, Uncle Heinrich. I too, within all of God's glory, love you and respect you. Indeed, you might be unconventional, but you are full of God's glory.

Yes, indeed, I just came up with a sermon title.

I have to think that I have a good one too.

THE END

The Great Beach Adventure

"Traffic is backed up on the Garden State Parkway for miles. All the way from exit 138, Galloping Hill Road all the way into the Bergen Toll area. It is mostly heavy volume with Friday afternoon shore traffic and due to an overheating and disabled car in the center lane near exit 143. Use the turnpike or alternate routes."

I leaned in, listened to the radio traffic report, and even fiddled with the volume knob to turn it up a bit. The afternoon rush hour report on my favorite local radio station was of interest to me, primarily because my faithful assistant of more years than I could recall, Martha Wiggins and her husband, were heading out on their annual summer holiday to the Jersey shore. They had left shortly after lunch and I hoped that by now, they had made it past exit 100 and were cruising easily on the long trek to Cape May, New Jersey. There is nothing worse than being stuck in Friday afternoon Jersey shore traffic on the Garden State Parkway.

I turned the volume down on the radio, leaned back in my chair, and glanced at my watch. It had been a long week and now the end was near. I sat at my desk in my office and pondered my next move. Martha was already away. I am the big boss, the bishop. . ..

It was close to three in the afternoon, a Friday, and it was a hot, "Dog Day of August" type of day in downtown Newark, New Jersey. In my heart, I knew that I should quit for the day, pack my briefcase with the rest of these papers and call it a weekend. A trip around the corner to "The Elusive Lion," pub and a long afternoon chat with the engaging and friendly bartender, Jennifer, while sharing a few cold ones would be nice. I could enjoy a warm visit with the locals while hanging out there and Pastor Paul John Henson, or specifically, Bishop Paul John Henson, could enjoy the weekend a bit early.

Even after all of these years in this position, I stayed far away from using the "bishop" title. It is too stuffy. Pastor Paul works just fine for me. No, I cannot quit yet. Sorry, cold, frosty beers and engaging conversation with Jennifer. I had to plow through a few more emails, and then I could call it a day. The emails never stopped coming in. Often, it seemed as if they were part of one of those electronic video games, where the aliens continued to envelope the Earth and for every single one you shot down, ten more would appear on the screen.

I fiddled with the mouse of my computer to wake up the screen and placed my hands on the mouse buttons to click on my emails. Suddenly, I found my mind drifting back to Martha, and the traffic along the Garden State Parkway, and overheating car engines. Then, as these types of afternoons often do to me, I drifted even farther back in time, drifting back to an adventure with my family and a summer's day excursion to the Jersey shore.

If I typed the word "disaster" on the big internet search engine, then perhaps I would read a description of that day and see a picture of the centerpiece of our adventure, which was our glorious family car.

A 1964 Putter Classic model 200 was the Henson family car from around when I was an infant until, well, until I moved out, married, and might even have had my own children.

Mum swore that my first words were, "The stupid Putter won't start!"

Despite the car's slightly dubious and less than sterling reputation, to say that the old man loved the car would be an understatement.

He adored it.

Looking back on the relationship, I guess that I would classify it as a love-hate type of relationship. I think the old man loved to hate the car, and he hated the fact that he loved it so much. He had the car forever and then some. In those days, if you looked up the definition of "Unreliable" in the dictionary, there was a picture of the 1964 Putter Classic model 200 automobile listed there to reinforce the definition. Everyone understood the reputation of the Putter except the Chief Executive Officer and the Chairman of the Board of Putter Motors, Inc. and my old man. They were all certified Putter lovers and were all under the common delusion that the cars just had a "few quirks." Putter Motors, Inc. is the only American automobile manufacturer ever asked to leave Detroit, Michigan. The automobile magnates banished Putter Motors, Inc. forever from the Motor City and forced the company to produce cars in a makeshift manufacturing plant located near High Point, New Jersey. A local dairy farmer in Sussex County, New Jersey, allowed them to make the cars in a barn that he added an assembly line in, right next to his cows.

Most of my childhood from when I could walk and talk and fetch tools, involved working with my old man while repairing, painting, resurrecting, doing body work, or some type of other activity on the Putter in the driveway of our home at 182 Belmont Avenue in Haledon, New Jersey. One of those city slicker guys who painted any car for fifty bucks in a dark shop in some hidden enclave of Paterson, New Jersey painted the car. For some unknown reason, the old man chose to paint the car a weird shade of powder blue or something similar to powder blue. The car was an unusual blue color that no one could never, ever duplicate or match. Therefore, touch up of the paint job was an adventure and as a result, the car was seventy-nine different shades of blue.

The 1964 Putter Classic model 200 did have some cool and unique features.

Well, let me rephrase that sentence because it had one cool feature.

Forget the plural.

The car had a push button transmission with these very cool and neat buttons mounted on the dashboard. If you wanted to go in reverse, you simply pushed the "REVERSE" button. If you wanted to go into drive, then you pushed the "DRIVE" button. Neutral and Park were buttons on the dashboard, too. The buttons were very cool, until eventually, the label paint wore off and the old man, in a moment of haze, forgot the proper functions of each button. After he repaired the damage from that little errant excursion in the wrong direction from pushing the incorrect button, the old man stuck labels with adhesive tape on the buttons, and in black ink, he wrote, "THIS IS THE DAMN DRIVE BUTTON" and "THIS IS THE DAMN REVERSE BUTTON" on the tapes. Mum always wanted him to eliminate the overly descriptive words from the labels, but the old man refused to do so.

Luckily for the Putter, and our meager bank account, as well as our family, the old man served in the United States Army as a sergeant in the motor pool. As a result of his military training, he was an expert car mechanic and his skills as a driveway mechanic spread from Burhans Avenue all the way to Henry Street. Primarily on weekends, in the middle of the night or on holidays, the old man rebuilt or replaced most every part on the Putter. He even made some new parts and modified parts in his machine shop during his lunch breaks. Specialized parts for 1964 Putter Classic model 200 cars were difficult to find.

According to legend, there remained a total of only sixteen of the model 200s registered in the entire State of New Jersey.

The old man was a legend amongst car repair aficionados, and in one very famous old neighborhood incident, after downing too many beers with my grandfather (Gramps) at the Widow's Pub and placing a bet with an old drunk named Mr. Oliver J. Buddley, the old man changed the water pump on the Putter while wearing a blindfold. Mr. Buddley bought Gramps and the old man a beer each for a year after that demonstration.

The old man swore that the Putter could determine temperature and what day of the week that it was. The car never broke down on a nice, gentle, warm spring day. It only broke down when it was ten degrees below zero with a raging, howling blizzard bearing down on us, or it broke down on the hottest summer day with stifling humidity and 100-degree heat. The car also never broke down on Saturdays when you had the weekend to repair it. It always broke down on Mondays. Or on Christmas Day or New Year's Day, or when you wanted to go on a family trip.

I heard the back door to our house open; the old man's lunch pail made a distinctive noise as the metal bottom settled in on the kitchen shelf, and the loud voice of the old man bellowed, "Home! What the hell is for supper? I am starving."

"Oh hi, dear. We are having stewed chop meat and tomatoes over mashed potatoes. How was your day? Do you want a nice cold Big Boulder beer or would you like to try a Dingleberry for a change?"

"Change? I never change. Dingleberries are too sweet. Give me a Big Boulder. Why the hell do you even buy Dingleberry beer? How was my day? The same as all the days are in the shop in August in the summer. It was hotter than fourteen Hells. Stewed chop meat. Sounds hot. Did you use the tomatoes from the garden?"

"Yes, of course. They are a nice crop this year. Paulie picked a few more this afternoon. I will get your Big Boulder beer for you. Sit, relax, and cool off a little now. It is already Thursday. Only one more work day and you have the whole weekend to cool off, work in your garden, watch baseball and have a few beers."

I was sitting on the edge of my bed in my bedroom right next to the kitchen, where I could hear the arrival of the old man and the conversations very clearly. Every night, the conversations were about the same. Hot day, Big Boulder, no stupid Dingleberries, supper, the shop, no change in the words. The old man sounded a little grouchy tonight.

I tossed my hockey magazine aside, looked over at Skippy, my faithful fox terrier, and asked him, "So Skip, the old man is home. Do we wait until he settles in or brave it now?"

Skippy jumped to his feet, looked at me, jumped off the bed, and headed for the kitchen. I guess that was my answer. If Skippy was up for it then so was I. The two of us walked into the kitchen, and by the time we arrived, the old man was already in his chair at the table with his nose buried in the *Paterson Evening News*.

Without even looking out from behind the newspaper, the old man asked me, "Did you weed the garden and cut off the suckers on the tomatoes?"

"Yup."

"Edge the lawn?"

"Yup."

"Paint the side of the shed where I put the new boards in last week?"

"Yup."

"Hit your plastic baseball on the roof?"

"No, not today."

"Really? Son-of-a-bitch. First day in a week that I don't gotta climb my ass up on the roof after work and get your plastic baseball."

"My football is up there."

"WHAT THE HELL IS THIS BULLSHIT? IT AIN'T FOOTBALL SEASON YET! Every day, I gotta come home from a hot day at working in that stifling shop, and get the ladder out, and climb up on the roof to retrieve sumthin'!"

"While you are up there, dear, can you spin the television antenna a little bit? That little ghost came back on channel two, and I want to see Ted's funeral tomorrow on *Nights of Our Lives*. Ted was such a nice guy."

Mum always had ghosts that haunted her afternoon soap operas.

I was around ten years of age now and my summer vacations filled up very quickly with assorted tasks and chores that the old man assigned to me. He was very proud of his urban garden. He cut it in along the edges of our small backyard and it was a remarkable garden, which provided us with fresh vegetables and some glorious flowers. The old man was a highly skilled gardener, and he learned, as a young boy from my grandfather, how to grow and to plant and tend to the small city gardens. During the war, the gardens were very popular, and even in small city lots and backyards found in old cities such as Paterson, New Jersey, the gardens were an important aspect of summer life. My father passed many of his skills onto me and I tended to the garden during the day while the old man was at work. We grew corn, tomatoes, green and red peppers, and cucumbers. In the spring and fall, during the cooler weather, the old man grew radishes, lettuce and various sprouts. The amount of food we raised out of such a small amount of dirt was amazing, and when money was tight and hard to come by, the garden provided us with nutritious food.

In the flower section of the garden, the old man planted his zinnias, asters, marigolds, four o'clocks and his prized cockscombs. Most of the flowers, the old man would cut for fresh bouquets for flowers to place on our relative's graves when we visited the graveyard after church on Sundays.

"See any more of those damn tomato hornworms? That one hungry, little, son-of-a-bitch, carved up my Bloppee Big Boy pretty good before I nailed his ass."

"No more hornworms. All clear."

My sister, Dorothy, or as we called her by her nickname of Dottie, appeared on the scene. When my sister was not hanging out with her best friend, an Italian-American gal named Maureen Zipperelli, my sister usually held up inside of her bedroom during the summer, with window fans stuck in both of her windows in a vain and futile effort to keep her room below ninety-seven degrees. There she stayed, curling her hair and listening to rock-and-roll records and the top 40 radio stations. With the seventy-two electric fans whirring about our house, it was sometimes difficult to hear, so my sister usually got away with blasting her music loudly. During the non-electric fan season, her music was a constant source of agitation to the old man. He was a Harvey Crooner fan, and loud rock-and-roll did not make the cut with him.

Air conditioning was an unfulfilled dream in our house, but the gentle whir of the fans as they propelled hot air around the rooms had some sort of comforting quality to them. Most of the time, they simply blew the hot air into corners of the room and actually made the rooms more uncomfortable. I came to realize that the fans were just a psychological comfort and while they did little to offset the heat, the blowing of the hot, humid and stagnant air directly in your face provided the illusion of cooling you. In addition, when you are a dopey kid, you had a blast speaking into the blades and listening to your voice echo within the rotations of them.

My sister was around three years older or thereabouts than I was, and she was on the borderline rebellious stage of life, where she spoke very little to our parents and when she did, it was usually very general discussion of a neutral nature. Tonight, while sensing the old man's mood, Dorothy did not say a word, but she smiled at me and settled into her chair for supper.

Mum dished out the stewed chop meat with the tomatoes and mashed potatoes on our plates and we all chewed. It was a strange phenomenon, but once food was set in front of us then a deep, dark silence overcame the entire Henson family. All we did after the food plopped onto our plates was to shovel the food in and chew.

Skippy begged, and we chewed.

Only an occasional mutter of, "Please pass the butter, or the bread, or whatever," interrupted the sound of chewing.

Usually, our grandfather, or as we called him, "Gramps" would be eating supper with us, but at the moment, Gramps was off to visit his sister, the amazing Aunt Alma in his semiannual adventure to Bloody Hot, Florida. Gramps was Mum's father, and he was English born and bred. Gramps grew up in and around Sherwood Forest in Nottingham, England. If there was one season that Gramps despised above all the others, it was summer. His English blood much preferred creepy fog and cold, clammy, murky weather. The colder and clammier the temperature, and the thicker the fogs were in the old neighborhood, the happier Gramps was. He thrived in fog. It was home to Gramps. Aunt Alma was his younger sister, and his sister married some chap across the pond that came over to America and opened a very successful chain of shoe stores. When her husband suddenly and tragically passed away, Aunt Alma sold the stores off, banked all the money and traveled (travelled) around the world. She did her best to drag her brother along, but Gramps seldom went on the trips. He much preferred staying in his apartment, that was on the second floor of our family home. They would take turns visiting each other a few times a year, at each other's homes and when Gramp's turn came to visit his sister; he did his best to plan the trip in the cooler months. It never worked. Gramps despised Florida. It was not until I was much older in age did I even realize that Aunt Alma actually lived in Vero Beach, Florida, not Bloody Hot, Florida.

We neared the end of the chewing session when it happened. It was unexpected, unannounced, and by the look upon Mum's face, it was unplanned.

Spontaneous.

The old man, put down his fork and spoon, belched a little backfire of stewed tomatoes, quenched the backfire with a swig of beer and announced, "Oh yeah, I put in for a vacation day next Monday. We are gonna go to Brady Beach for the day."

Mum was replenishing my plate with the last remnants of the mashed potatoes, and she stopped in mid-shovel as the shock of what the old man just said rippled through all of our bodies and minds. I dropped my fork, and it impaled straight up through the center of the lump of mashed potatoes, Dorothy's left eye spun clockwise and her right eye spun counter clockwise, and even Skippy stopped begging next to me to sit and listen to the old man. I swore the old dog shook his head and poked at his ears to make sure he heard our father correctly. Out of all of us, Mum managed to sputter out a few words to double-check that we all were not dreaming and the old man actually said that he was taking a VACATION DAY!

"Ah . . . did you say . . . that you were . . . ah . . . taking Monday off?" Mum squeaked as the wooden potato spoon slipped out of her hand and dropped on the floor. Errant blobs of mashed potato splattered on my sneakers and on the legs of the kitchen table.

Ordinarily, Skippy would have pounced on the spoon and potatoes like moths circle a flame, but even old Skip was too shocked to move.

In a cavalier and matter-of-fact manner, the old man

pushed his plate aside, licked a blob of mashed potato off his lips, took another swig of the frosty brew, and quietly said, "Yup. We are packin' up the Putter and headin' for Brady Beach for the day. It is time to take a day off."

"Oh, okay, I guess that I will miss Ted's funeral on Monday afternoon."

"You won't. Those bullshit soap operas put everythin' off and show ya ass tease clips of the next day, so ya tune in. They gotta show ya commercial after commercial selling laundry and dish detergent and push up and shape up bras for gals with outta shape breasts. The funeral won't be until Friday. His ten secret mistresses and six illegitimate kids will show up to interrupt the service 'till then."

My old man never watched the show, but he knew the inside scoop of plots, as well as the secret modus operandi of soap opera teasers.

"Oh, okay, dear. I think that Ted actually had eleven mistresses."

I thought about how Ted must have been exhausted all the time.

Now, my old man always had off from Christmas Eve until the day after New Year's Day, every year for an extended vacation. This was an era in which we actually made things other than fast food and prefabricated pizzas in this country, and New Jersey was a hotbed of manufacturing. The old man worked as a machinist in a shop that made parts for military aircraft, and his shop as well as most others closed during that time. It was primarily to allow maintenance and repairs of the machines, but it also was a tradition of sorts. Other than those times, no one, and I do mean no one, took a vacation day. The old man had not missed a single day of scheduled work in forty-two years. No sick days, no leave days, no funeral days, no bereavement leaves.

Nothing. Nada. Zilch.

Only scheduled and approved vacation days.

All the men in our neighborhood were the same. My best friend's father, Mr. Harry M. Redmond Senior, had not missed a day of scheduled work since his mother first put a diaper on his ass. Maureen's dad, Mr. Salvatore Zipperelli, came out of the womb with a mason's trowel in his hand.

Needless to say, that made for a bit of a troublesome delivery.

Work was a way of life.

A religion.

Beer, arguing over everything, church services, fixing your junky car on weekends, baseball, football, hockey, dodging bullets and crime, hanging out on the front porch and work. All of them were a way of life in the neighborhood. Even passionate sex received a pre-approved schedule around work. Spontaneous sex was against the neighborhood's laws.

If you did not go to work at five o'clock in the morning and you returned before six at night, you received the label of a slacker in the old neighborhood.

If someone keeled over and croaked in the old neighborhood, they had better do it late on Friday, the services completed, and over by the following Monday morning, or it would be the least attended funeral service in history.

We only allowed scheduled and pre-approved dying in our neighborhood.

My sister stood up and did a happy dance when she heard of the old man's proclamation. She sensed the salt water, fresh ocean breezes and actual air in her lungs, rather than fan-powered recycled city air.

My sister loved the beach and later in her life, she would escape New Jersey and flee to the beach in southern California. That is indeed another story!

I was a bit more subdued at the news, surprised, but subdued. Mum coaxed Skippy out of his shock and into potato cleanup duty while she asked the logical and forthright question that was the one question on all of our minds.

"But, dear, will the Putter make it all the way to Brady Beach? The Garden State Parkway could be bumper-to-bumper traffic, it will be hot and the car *could potentially overheat.*"

The old man scoffed at the mere suggestion of the malfunction of the beloved 1964 Putter Classic model 200.

He shook his head and picked up the newspaper, waved to Mum for a replacement beer and proudly and sincerely proclaimed, "Nah, no way. Shit, that car is bulletproof. It just has *a few minor quirks*. Paulie and I will check it out on Saturday. Ya know, make sure the hoses and belts are good, the water in the radiator is up to snuff, and we will be good to go. Say, shake ya pretty, little ass there and get me a'nudder Big Boulder. Make sure ya got lots of quarters for those money-grubbing tolls. C'mon, Joan, get me a beer! Please."

Saturday morning found us combing over the 1964 Putter Classic model 200 Putter with a fine-tooth toolbox. Away from the influence of my mother, my sister and beer, the old man spewed confessions more than a Catholic gal did after the night of her high school prom. The hood was up; the heat was on and the old man carefully studied the belts and cooling system of our family vehicle. His eyes darted back and forth, while he squeezed hoses to test for any squishiness, he peeled belts back to examine them for nicks and checked the seams of the radiator for spurious spurts of coolant.

I could hear him mumble under his breath, "Damn, son-of-a-bitchin' Putter will overheat in the middle of a blizzard in Alaska and breakdown in the bay at the service garage. Piece of. . .."

Suddenly, I had my doubts in *the few minor quirks* of the Putter.

"Gotta get ovah to the Golf station and get me a tank of

high-test in this puppy. High test will stop all those rattles in the valves."

After four hours in the blazing sun, and Paul John Henson fetching every single tool from the old man's basement workshop and tool stash, and the old man hurling a million obscenities, while telling me not to tell Mum that I heard *that particular* word, the old man pronounced the Putter was roadworthy for the long haul. After all, Brady Beach was exit 100 on the Garden State Parkway, so it might as well be as if we were flying nonstop to Jupiter. With the Putter, able to do a top speed of forty miles per hour with a tail wind and high-test gasoline in the tank, we might just make it to Brady Beach by next August.

On Sunday evening, we packed the Putter with ten beach towels, four hundred and twenty-two bottles of suntan lotion, one umbrella, fifteen plastic shovels, an old bedspread to place on the sand, forty-two pairs of sunglasses, one pair of flip-flops, a baseball and two baseball gloves, a football, water pails, foam coolers packed with ice, sandwiches, soda, candy bars, and ten six-packs of Big Boulder beer (no Dingleberries) and jugs and jugs and jugs of coolant and water in empty glass jugs that Mr. Zipperelli lent to the old man. The glass jugs usually held homemade Zipperelli wine, but right now, they held pure water. We needed the water, just in case, under the unlikely instance that *the Putter overheated*. Oh, yes, we also put all the old man's toolboxes in the trunk, along with ten rolls of Big Bob's Death Grip Tape, and four spare coolant hoses. Just in case the putter *broke down or overheated.*

We were ready to go. The 1964 Putter Classic model 200 was ready to go. The day of reckoning lay bare and naked on the horizon of life.

We stumbled bleary-eyed out of bed at 4 A.M. on Monday morning to the sound of the old man banging pots and pans together while bellowing, "C'mon get your lily-white asses outta of the rack! Time to eat. Time to hit the road. We gotta beat the southbound traffic into Newark!"

We were going to drop Skippy off at my best friend, Harry M. Redmond Junior's house, for the day. Harry and Skippy got along quite well, and Skippy would enjoy the visit and play around with Harry's dogs, Cocoa and Marshmallow.

Vacation days were rare, and they were such fun. We ate a hearty breakfast, grabbed Skippy and his leash and collar, and headed joyfully out to the driveway to begin the journey to the far side of the moon.

Sort of.

"WHAT THE HELL IS THIS BULLSHIT?" The old man hollered and pointed at a flat rear tire on the 1964 Putter Classic Model 200.

A very flat tire.

"Ah, it is a flat tire dear." Mum observed. "But it is only flat on the bottom." Mum tried to joke a bit. Jokes were not going to work right now.

"I CAN SEE THAT IT IS A DAMN FLAT TIRE! BUT IT WAS NOT FLAT YESTERDAY!"

No one amongst us had the courage to tell the old man that, well, it was bloody well flat now. The old man kept ten spare tires in a dark corner of the basement, or as the old man called it, the cellar of our family home. None of them had much of any in the way of treads left, but nonetheless, they were his spares. He also had two "snow tires." Spare tires were not the issue, but the rims of the wheels were. Since the 1964, Putter Classic model 200 was a rare car, not rare because of demand, but because of the less than sterling reputation of the car, parts were often difficult to find. Even the roving gangs of parts strippers that prowled the neighborhood, anxiously waiting for a car to be pushed off to the side of the road, where they could strip it bare in ten minutes, ignored the Putter. There simply remained a little to no demand for the parts.

Luckily, for the old man, spare tires were in stock! Somehow, of which the methods of procurement will forever remain shadowy, the old man cornered the market on Putter steel rims.

One year, when we had extra money, the old man bought snow tires with steel whoosies that made a bizarre noise when they spun on the road. They called them, "ice and snow studs" or something similar. But, in reality, it sounded like the nicknames for the male strippers at the Hitchin' Post Club on lower Belmont Avenue on a Friday night.

The old man stood with his hands on his hips, shaking his head, while the temples on the side of his head pounded as if they were tom-tom drums.

"Paulie, go into the cellar, in the back room and pick out the best of the spares. Bring 'em up, while I spin this one off. Musta picked up a nail. C'mon, shake ya ass! Joan, do ya have lots of quarters for those money grubbing-son-of-a'bitchin' tolls?"

"Yes, dear. Lots of quarters, but right now we need air."

"Daddy, since as usual the Putter is dead, can we just stay home and I can listen to my records in my room and curl my hair? I think Maureen is around and we. . .."

"No! We are going to Brady Beach! The car is fine. It just has a few quirks."

The old man gave me the order and while our parents debated quarters versus air and my sister made her request for an alternate adventure, off I dashed to the hidden stash of spare tires. I spent most of my childhood years and part of my adulthood fetching tools and spare parts from the old man's stash. They build luxury ocean liners with fewer tools than was required to perform repairs on the Putter. Picking out the "best" tires out of the old man's stash of spares was an arbitrary decision to make. It was similar to asking a convicted killer how he wanted to meet his demise. Let's see, Old Sparky, lethal injection, guillotine. . ..

Picking the best from the worse, seemed illogical. I scanned the dubious collection of the tires, spinning them while studying for a tire that did not feel as if it was a polished bowling ball, knowing full well that the old man had already removed the flat tire and soon he would be bellowing to me, "Where the hell are ya?"

I gave up, picked the two "best" tires, two which seemed to have at least one or two lines of tread, mumbled "Oh, what the hell, they all suck" and rolled them out of the basement (cellar) and over to the foot of the stairs. It was a good thing that I was very big and strong for my age.

In two minutes, flat, I had the tires out to the old man and, predictably, he frowned at me, took a tire from me and mumbled, "Shit. Where the hell were ya? Traffic is building up out there. Took ya forever. Oh, good, this tire here looks good. Lots of treads left on this one. Put the other one in the trunk for the spare while I put this on the car."

Finally, we were off. A push of the "DAMN REVERSE" button, a spin of the steering wheel with the old man hunched over the wheel, a few puffs of a smoky oil from the exhaust pipe and we were on the way to the moon. Oh, wait, no, I mean the Jersey shore.

We dropped Skippy off to play with his pals and because Cocoa was the world's smartest dog, there Cocoa sat at the front gate of the Redmond's house. Cocoa was waiting for us. When Harry told Cocoa that Skippy was coming over to visit, Cocoa set his doggie alarm. The Redmond's family dog was a neighborhood legend for his intelligence and everyone knew he was indeed the world's smartest dog. The stories of the legendary Cocoa will someday fill many pages. No need to wake Harry up. Cocoa was waiting inside the front gate for Skippy to arrive and I dropped our family dog off, along with his supplies and knew that all would be well. Off the two of them dashed into the wild world of the Redmonds.

A trail of blue and black smoke followed along us as we made our way out of the outskirts of Paterson, up Union Avenue to Route 46, then we wandered onto Route 3. So far so good, and as we rolled onto the entrance ramp for the Garden State Parkway at the amazing top speed of about thirty-eight miles per hour, the old man wiggled his backside deeply into the seat and hunched over the steering wheel even more.

He stood on the gas pedal and mumbled, "Here we go. Do ya have the quarters for those damn tolls? This trip is costin' me a fortune."

"Yes, dear, I have the quarters."

The Putter slid into the Granny Lane, into a speed just above a slow crawl and immediately, horns blared and a roar of obscenities sounded above the Garden State Parkway. Forty-seven million and sixteen cars backed up behind the Putter. All the way from the Route 3 entrance ramp merge to the tollbooths at the Bergen County line, it was now a solid line of jammed up cars. Once the old man settled into the right lane and caught a bit of a tailwind, the old man reached over, turned the radio knob to the "on" position, and turned the volume up. He always kept the radio tuned onto station, WPAT broadcasting out of Paterson. WPAT was an "Easy Listening" station and when Dottie heard the first crackles of sounds emit from the speaker, she leaned into her seat, rolled her eyes at me and settled in for the long haul of listening to soft mellow sounds, sleepy strings of orchestra music and the entire collection of Harvey Crooner's greatest hits.

However, right now, it was the top of the hour and time for news and a traffic break, "There is a back-up on the Garden State Parkway, from the Route 3 merge to the Bergen toll. It appears to be due to a very slow car in the right lane just past the merge."

"Great! Damn, I knew it. Paulie took too long gettin' the tires outta the cellar. Shit. Traffic buildin' up already. Some piece of shit car, holding stuff up," the old man mumbled, seemingly unaware of his sudden celebrity status of being the main feature on the radio. Mum glanced at the old man and she almost smirked. Dottie rolled her eyes and I sat perfectly still and kept my mouth shut. I was the old man's primary assistant in battle. I had to work side-by-side with him and in a testimony to the basic instinct of self-preservation; I knew when to shut the hell up.

Silence can truly be golden.

The radio announcer at WPAT was unrelenting in his torturous news. He continued in a happy and melodious voice to add layers and layers of joy upon the old man's, "I finally took a damn day off celebration cake."

Once he overcame the shock and awe of the traffic jam news, the old man fiddled with the volume control of the radio as the speaker broadcasted the glorious news of, "Today will be the hottest day of the summer so far. Temperatures all around the Garden State will soar near one hundred degrees with stifling humidity and incredibly oppressive conditions. Even in the cooler mountain elevations of Sussex County the temperature will be near one hundred degrees and it will be difficult to breathe. . .."

Yes! The happy frosting of heat and humidity on the celebration cake!

"WHAT THE HELL IS THIS BULLSHIT?" The old man dug in even more on the gas pedal as the traffic sped up to around forty miles per hour. "The hottest day of the year! Why the hell did you suggest me taking this day off?"

At the muttering of that amazing proclamation, Mum's head spun around and an immediate, intense glare of a death ray beam emitted from her eyes. Mum was a dear, sweet woman, but it was best not to test her.

Oh, no!

"Me? I do not think so! I had nothing to do with this day! all of a sudden, without warning, you come home from work, drop your lunch pail and proclaim like some, big blowhard hero, oh, by the way gang, we are going to Brady Beach on Monday! Big jerk! I had nothing to do with this trip. If I did, knowing that we have this crummy, hunk of junk car, with, as you say, a few quirks, some of which are overheating in the middle of a blizzard and breaking down while in the bay of the service garage, then I would have checked the weather forecast first. But noooo, when you are a big blowhard hero, you just do stupid things!"

The old man retreated a bit. Sometimes, the best offense is a defense, and he stayed hunched over the steering wheel, his eyes glued on the crawling traffic ahead of him. WPAT shifted gears and let up on the torture pedal, while the radio announcer gently uttered, "Now, back to the mellow sounds of Harvey Crooner and his number one hit from the hottest week of July in 1942, 'When Our Lips Finally Meet.'"

The old man fiddled with the radio knob as his favorite singer crooned in glorious, monaural sound from the whopping two-inch speaker, his favorite, weepy-eyed ballad, "When your blue eyes reflect the glorious sunset and our lips finally meet. . .."

Without admitting total defeat, the old man invoked self-preservation and revised his previous stance with a bit of a soft-shoe shuffle of words, "Well, you might not have picked this *exact* day, but the other night when we were listenin' to the news, ya said it has been a long time since we went to the beach."

Mum folded her arms across her chest, stared deeply at the old man, while turning the knob up on her death ray beam. The old man shut right up. The debate was over. Mum had notched a shutout. Unsurprisingly, the score was in dear Mum's favor. Mum: ten thousand, seven hundred and fifty-six, and the old man: zero.

"When your blue eyes reflect the glorious sunset and our lips finally meet. . .."

A diversionary tactic now was in order as the old man

whistled to the Harvey Crooner tune, fiddled with the knob and pointed at the radio. "What a great song, huh, honey? Da ya 'member the first time we heard it? On that date when we went to the. . .."

"NO! I CAN'T STAND THIS STUPID SONG!

The heat bore down in many ways.

As we crawled along with 80 percent of the total population of northern New Jersey, mixed in with the rest of mankind, toward the blessed Essex Tollbooths, the sun beat down on the 1964 Putter Classic Model 200. With no breeze passing through the car, the inside of the car quickly reached blast furnace temperatures. In theory, the Putter had "4-55 air conditioning," you just rolled down the four windows, the vehicle went fifty-five miles per hour, you stuck your head out the window, and took deep gasps of car exhausts mixed in with generally polluted air. The trouble was that the Putter seldom, if ever, could roll along at fifty-five miles per hour and even at the Putter's top speed, without the car actually moving more than five miles per hour; there was very little "wind."

GULP, GULP, GULP. We took turns sticking our head out the windows and gasping.

These little family getaways were such fun.

"When your blue eyes reflect the glorious sunset and our lips finally meet. . .."

"Paulie and Dorothy, now, please be very careful when sticking your head out the car windows in order to breathe because a car could come by and take your head off. There was an article in the newspaper just last week about a man losing his hand out his car window on this road here," Mum strategically warned of the ominous and precarious nature of bumper-to-bumper traffic on the Garden State Parkway. Hm, let's see now, stay in the car and swelter and die of heat and no air, or risk losing your head on a sideswipe. Such difficult decisions we had to make at such a young age.

These little family getaways were such fun.

GULP, GULP, GULP.

I made my life choice and with a shrug of her shoulders so did my sister.

GULP, GULP, GULP.

Tollbooths are a devious, yet creative invention of politicians. In secret and covert meetings, in the dark basements of dreary, New Jersey government buildings, beady-eyed politicians, with bad breath and horrible toupees, who are not up for reelection, cast their "YES" votes to construct the evil, coin extracting obstacles and plant them along the most heavily traveled sections of the magnanimous road systems of the Garden State and beyond. They construct tollbooths on the entrance and the exit ramps too. That way, they successfully get ya when ya are coming and going too. In the darkness of this shrouded secrecy, the tollbooths receive approval amidst fiendish cackles of money-grubbing politicians. Then they summon expert wordsmiths who create carefully woven cover stories in order to release to the newspapers some pieces of the evil plan. Amongst the ranks of the conniving, beady-eyed bunch, they choose a short, overly educated accountant type politician, who constantly blinks and has a phony smile with a gap in his front teeth. The poor sap stands in front of the television, radio, and newspaper reporters, while wearing black horn-rimmed black glasses that keep slipping onto the end of his nose, while reading from a prepared statement.

"The tollbooths are only temporary and once the roadway extension, asphalt paving projects and other improvements are funded and completed, we will remove the tollbooths."

And so, it goes, and since in New Jersey, they have five seasons, which are winter, spring, summer, autumn, and construction season, the roadway extension, asphalt paving projects and other improvements are NEVER completed!

Within seventeen days after the press conference ends, the new tollbooth is constructed and commissioned and it is sucking all the spare coins from the pockets, piggybanks, and vehicle storage cups of road-weary New Jersey travelers. No bid packages, no material delays, no union negotiations, no pre-approvals or construction permits required. Sal Zucchini's Tollbooth Construction and Pasta Making Company, mysteriously wins the nonexistent bid under suspicious conditions and has it up in a blink of an eye. This *is* New Jersey and we all know who wins all the construction bids. No newspapers in the entire state ever question these types of construction bids or dare to do investigations on them.

Cement shoes fit everyone.

GULP, GULP, GULP.

Within every family there are always a few bad genes passed on from one generation to the next one. There is always a kid, who despite constant bathing and cologne masking, smells like urine, a kid whose nose always runs, and there is always a kid who is overly observant and incredibly annoying. Thankfully, my sister and I missed the urine smelling gene (that dubious honor went to our Cousin Bibby over in England) and the nose issues, (Cousin Pat) however, I received the overly observant and incredibly annoying genes.

"Hey, Dad, the sign says, Essex Toll booth two miles ahead. The toll is twenty-five cents. Quarters only."

Since losing the battle and narrowly surviving Mum's death ray beam, the old man was feeling a little spunkier, "What the hell do you think I am? Blind? Do ya think that I can't see and read the sign?"

"Now, now, dear. Paulie, is only trying to help you a little. He is very smart and observes everything."

"Oh, bullshit. It is so annoying. Da kid got the annoying gene from your side of the family. I am an expert driver and seasoned traveler. I never miss a sign or a turn. Ya kidding me, or what? He is just a kid. Say, Joan, do ya have a quarter?"

"Yes, dear. Here is your quarter. What do you mean by my side of the family?"

The old man pretended to fiddle with the radio knob to avoid the death ray beam and Mum wanted to sooth her son's supposed hurtsy-wurtsy feelings, so our father successfully avoided answering the question.

Mum handed off the precious coin and turned to face me while instructing me on the rules of the happy family getaway, "Paulie, it is okay. Your father appreciates and loves you very much. Thank you very much for helping and observing everything, but your father can see the road signs. You do not have to read them out to your father."

My feelings were not hurt. When you were the old man's offspring, it was impossible to have sensitive feelings. Deep down, I also inherited the old neighborhood, son-of-a-bitch gene; it just takes until a little past puberty for that gene to manifest itself. Instead, I simply knew the truth. The old man could get lost in the frozen food aisle of the local supermarket. Knowing our fate, I nodded my head, faked a smile and sunk deeply into the rear seat of the Putter, while my sister rolled her eyes.

Now for the tricky part while forty-seven million and sixteen cars converged upon four tollbooths that are each about nine feet wide. The other seventeen tollbooths spanning the entire width of the Garden State Parkway were out of order. Within a half mile or thereabouts of the tollbooths, the four lanes of the Garden State Parkway widened to what appeared to be the width of ten football fields stacked end-to-end. In theory, this would be quick and easy, except we all had to squeeze back down to pass through the four operating tollbooths. A road sign (which I did not read aloud) apologized by stating something about maintenance on the other tollbooths.

Therefore, it was here that the battle ensued. We drove

straight into a hair-raising test of the nerves and a roundabout game of "Russian Roulette" or better yet, "Chicken."

In New Jersey, New York, and Connecticut, we call it, *The Merge*.

The Merge was not for the faint of heart and the old man buckled in for the battle.

The dashboard speaker crackled with the voice of the WPAT radio announcer as he announced, "*The Merge* into the Essex Tollbooth on the Garden State Parkway is a rough one this morning!"

The old man's eyes scanned the horizon for wimps, cowards, and old women with silver and blue hair highlights heading out for hair appointments and bridge games, and other easily out maneuvered victims. He wiped his mouth, adjusted the brim of his New York Bugs baseball cap, quickly stuck his head out the window, took a deep gulp of air, and then dove back into the cockpit. His hood ornament pointed in the direction of toll booth number three and come hell, high water, a visit of aliens from the Planet Zutron, or the impromptu return of one of the Biblical prophets of old, the old man and his 1964 Putter Classic Model 200 was going to make it before the other forty-seven million and fourteen cars. He was well equipped for the battle since the Putter could easily be touched up with a can of whatever blue shade of spray paint the corner hardware store had in stock. A few more dings, scrapes, and variations of powder blue did not bother the old man. The driver of the fancy sports car rolling right next to us with the million-dollar finish and New Mexico license plates, quickly spotted and scanned the Putter and its seventy-nine different shades of blue, epoxy welded and duct taped fenders, and he easily yielded the right of the way to the old man.

"Hold on everyone because we are going in!" The old man cackled in glee at the easy defeat of the fancy sports car piloted by the smart, but cowardly driver, and our father gunned the Putter to maneuver it in line with the approach lane for tollbooth number three. The only trouble was as the old man whirled into the lane at a breakneck speed of three miles per hour, was the 1963 Zippymobile Model 50 ZA that rolled in next to us. A Zippymobile, layered in about seventy-nine different shades of red, with duct-taped fenders and a hip-swinging hula girl on the dashboard, piloted by a sweaty guy who was chomping on a cigar and was from a bad section of Port Bayonne. To add to the confusion of *The Merge*, old sweaty also had his eyes set on the approach to tollbooth number three.

As we slammed to a stop and narrowly avoided tapping duct-taped fenders with the Zippymobile, the old man bellowed out the window and shook his fist in the air at the sweaty guy from Port Bayonne.

Our father dug deeply into his bag of New Jersey insults and he leaned out the window with his magnanimous protest, "YA GOTTA BE KIDDIN' ME! WHAT THE HELL ARE YA DOIN? YA BLIND IN ONE EYE AND CAN'T SEE OUTTA DA UDDER?"

"GET THE HELL OUTTA MY WAY WITH THAT PIECE OF SHIT, PUTTER! IS THAT REALLY A PUTTER? THOUGHT THOSE STUPID-ASS CARS HAD TO BE PUSHED NOT DRIVEN!" The sweaty guy from Port Bayonne fired back while the official New Jersey sport of arguing and insulting began. Off they went, exchanging barbs and insults over temporary ownership of two feet of the Garden State Parkway. Car horns blared, fists shook, and the traffic backed up all the way to the entrance ramp near Midland Avenue in Paramus.

The dashboard speaker crackled with the voice of the persistent WPAT radio announcer as he announced, "*The Merge* into the Essex Tollbooth on the Garden State Parkway, has two cars stuck in the center approach to one of the tollbooths. Traffic just stopped dead all the way back to the ramp on Midland Avenue in Paramus."

The battle raged on until the sweaty guy from Port Bayonne noticed that the old man wore a New York Bugs baseball cap. Suddenly, he stopped in mid-insult, leaned closer to the passenger window of his car, pointed at the cap and asked the old man, "Say, rya a Bugs fan?"

"Yeah, why?"

"Did they win last night?"

"Nah, the Minnysoder (Minnesota is an impossible word for a person from New Jersey to pronounce correctly) Retro-Rockets, beat the hell outta 'em."

"Shit! Who pitched for da Bugs?" The sweaty guy from Port Bayonne asked while not missing a beat and lifting his middle finger to the driver next to him, who was leaning on his horn.

"Lard-ass McDermott started. Lasted three innings and gave up seven earned runs. Drunk, I could out pitch his lard-ass," the old man answered.

I have heard it said that love has invoked truces to wars. Maybe so, but in this case, it was not love of a fair-haired, lovely woman, but the mutual love of the pitiful, and hapless, New York Bugs baseball team.

A truce in *The Merge*.

A blessing from Heaven.

Somewhere in Heaven, angels stroked their harps of gold.

"Ya right. Da guy is a bum. Say, ya slide in there first and I will follow right on ya tail and cut off this jack-off with da horn up his ass," the sweaty guy from Port Bayonne proposed to the old man. The old man waved, slipped the Putter into the lane and *The Merge* was over.

The dashboard radio speaker spouted, "*The Merge* into the Essex Tollbooth is slowly moving now."

Our father, the radio star.

The old man waved and out of the corner of my eye, I saw a spent cigar fly out of the Zippymobile's window in the direction of the fancy car with New Mexico license plates.

The old man happily whirled the 1964 Putter Classic Model 200 into the lane. He rolled close to the white basket mounted on the side of the tollbooth with its mouth wide open to accept the magical coin toss, and with a confident flip of the wrist, the old man launched the quarter high in the air in the direction of the coin-eating basket. In horror, we watched the coin hit the edge of the basket and bounce off!

"Shit! How da hell did I miss?" Mum tried a vain attempt to convince the old man that it was not worth it by handing him another quarter. He flung the door open, waved his hand and spouted, "No way! Ain't gonna waste a quarter."

The old man stepped out to retrieve his errant coin, the sweaty guy from Port Bayonne suddenly shifted allegiance, and he hit his horn and yelled out the window, "Geezzzz! C'mon! Ya worse than, lard-ass McDermott!"

The old man deftly picked up the missed toss, slam-dunked the coin and was back in the cockpit in a flash. The green light signaled a goal and for us to go. The old man hit the gas pedal and we finally escaped the confines of the Essex Tollbooth. The old man gunned the Putter and stood on the gas pedal and the little engine whirred in protest at the flood of gas in its carburetor. The road leaving the toll briefly widened to what appeared to be the width of Montana. Then a slight taste of *The Merge*, as we rolled into four lanes and we were off!

The 1963 Zippymobile Model 50 ZA passed us and old sweaty waved out the window and honked his horn. The old man did the same, and it seemed as if all was well.

Brady Beach loomed ahead of us.

Sun, sand, surf and fun!

The inside of the Putter was growing hotter and hotter. At least now, there was some air flowing through our windows and some type of air movement within the car.

Wait just a second. These family getaways are not so easy to find. Hold on now to that sun, sand and surf.

The Putter gained speed until the engine coughed, choked, and our speed declined from thirty miles per hour to about five miles per hour within ten seconds.

Horns blared, fists shook and the radio announcer's voice, once more spoke from deep within the dashboard speaker, "There is a slow car in the right-hand lane, just past the Essex Tollbooths." My goodness, they are very efficient on the traffic reports there at WPAT.

The distinct whiff of coolant filled the cockpit of the Putter, and puffs of steam escaped from under the front of the hood. In reality, *The Merge* won the battle. The dreaded overheating quirk arrived on the scene. Without all the air of the entire Tri-state area passing across the radiator of the Putter at a speed of at least five miles per hour, it would overheat.

"WHAT THE HELL IS THIS BULLSHIT? Damn, Putter would overheat in a blizzard and breakdown in the bay of the service garage. Piece of. . .." The old man leaned in on the glass of the windshield to observe the puffs of steam emitting from under the hood.

My sister could not resist, "Is this one of those little quirks, Daddy?"

"Oh, bullshit! This is New Jersey's fault, cuz them union guys shut down da extra tollbooths to milk da repairs for overtime on our tax money! Collectin' millions of quarters from us workin' guys ain't enough milking."

There was considerable truth to the old man's statement.

"I gotta open the heat up to take the pressure off. It will cool the engine down."

The heat! It was already two thousand degrees inside of the Putter's cockpit. I was beginning to think that it was easier to journey to the planet Jupiter than it was to make it to Brady Beach in a 1964 Putter Classic Model 200.

"And now back to the music on WPAT. Your relaxing music station at ninety-three on your A.M. radio dial."

We rolled to a stop on the shoulder of the roadway, and the old man jumped into action. The faux anger was actually a facade. I knew better because I fought these battles with the old man. In reality, he lived for these moments. A side of the road breakdown and ensuing repair was part of his mojo. If he did not have at least one weekly malfunction of the Putter, he became depressed and sulky.

"C'mon, Paulie. We just gotta add sum wadder. The jam up into the toll steamed it off."

I jumped out of the Putter and ran to the trunk. Once the old man popped the trunk lid, I grabbed some of the glass jars that used to hold homemade Zipperelli wine, but now, in lieu of the fruits of the vine, they held the precious cooling juice of Paterson tap wadder.

I mean, water.

The old man had the hood open, and he emerged from under the hood, while enveloped in layers of billowing steam and splashes of coolant. Popping the radiator cap to add water (wadder) on a Putter when it was under pressure and overheating was the equivalent task to disarming a ten-ton nuclear weapon. A hasty miss-step with an errant twist resulted in blowing the nose off your face. Since the Putter had "a few quirks," the old man was an expert at the practice. He had performed the action about eighty-nine thousand times. A deep twist with two hands standing on the radiator cap, a powerful puff of steam filled the air, a slight pop, and the old man twisted off the cap without any removal of body parts.

"Pour da wadder in the neck there, Paulie. Fill it all da way."

A drink of wadder (water) a spin of coolant around the engine block, and through the heater core, and the 1964 Putter Classic Model 200 was refreshed and happy. As a side benefit, the old man had his emergency breakdown urge satisfied.

Everything was now well in the world.

Now that the bedlam of rush hour passed, we rolled the rest of the way to the exit to Brady Beach without additional trouble. I even heard the old man whistling to a Harvey Crooner tune or two. Everything was going well, the Putter's engine happily whirred under the hood with the one-hundred-degree air flowing over its radiator. The old man and Mum talked and laughed, and my sister rolled her eyes. I sat in my seat watching the road signs and not saying a word. I learned my lesson and knew that the fateful moment would eventually arrive.

When I spotted the road sign proudly proclaiming, "Exit 100 A, B, C, Brady Beach, Ocean Gardens and some other beach that no one ever goes to," I almost shouted with joy and pointed out the directions. However, knowing that the old man was *an expert driver and seasoned traveler, who never missed a sign or a turn,* and I was an annoying kid with the annoying gene; I kept my mouth shut.

As the Putter approached within about five hundred feet of the exit ramp for Brady Beach, I looked over to Dottie, who shrugged her shoulders and rolled her eyes.

I whispered, "Should I say something?"

My sister shook her head and softly answered, "I wouldn't. Not worth it. You will get yelled at no matter what, so you might as well wait until he drives past exit 100C and he has to turn around."

"That sounds like a plan. Or, do you want to tell him?"

"No way, Paulie. You got the annoying gene. I got the straight hair gene."

At the whirlwind speed of forty-seven miles per hour (there was a tailwind) the Putter sailed happily by the exit for Brady Beach and the little engine whirred with glee.

Time to face the music. Drum roll, please. A slow death march to the gallows.

"Ah, Dad. I know that you are an expert and all of that stuff, and that I am supposed to keep my mouth shut and not be pointing out signs, but that was the exit for Brady Beach that ya just passed by."

The old man's head spun around and his eyes caught the last glimpse of the road sign as it sailed by our windows.

"WHAT? WELL, WHY THE HELL WOULD YA NOT SAY SUMTHIN'?"

"Because, you told me not to say anything or point them out to you. You are an expert driver and stuff like that."

"Yeah, but geez! That is not what I meant. I meant that ya got to point them out sometimes. Ya know . . . the signs that these evil road guys hide and make 'em hard to see. Now, we gotta go all the way to the next exit and spin around. And pay a toll on and off too! They hide 'em on purpose to make ya pay more toll dough!"

I am quite sure that Mum and Dottie were just as confused as I was.

Very confused.

We had no idea of what it was that the old man just said, but none of us felt as if it was worth clarifying. Signs that evil road guys tamper with and make them hard to see? The sign for the Brady Beach exit was the size of Texas. Instead, we just kept our mouths shut and chalked it up to his unusual logic.

Or something like that. Our father moaned and groaned the entire roll down the road to the next exit, moaned and complained some more when he paid his toll (thankfully, only a dime on the exits and entrances) and just to stay consistent, he moaned and groaned all the way back up the parkway. This time, dear Mum took one for the team and she pointed out exit 100B to the old man.

"I see it! I see it! What the hell, da ya think I am blind and gonna miss it again?"

"You never know, dear."

The Putter rolled along Route 33 and almost like the lost city of El Dorado; the ocean appeared on the horizon. The sweet ocean breeze blew some of the gruesome humidity and heat away, and the salt air warmed our senses. Even the scowl on the old man's face left, and Dottie stopped rolling her eyes. We had finally reached the Holy Land! My sister did her little beach happy dance in the rear seat! Now, we were all excited, and when the old man parked in a public parking lot and we all happily jumped out of the Putter, it was magical. Our good, old, 1964 Putter Classic Model 200 groaned to a stop. The engine shuddered and coughed up belches of blue smoke when it shut off, but we had made it. Not without incident, but that was normal. If it had been a smooth ride, then that would have been abnormal.

It seemed to be unusual because it was now close to noontime and there was not another car parked in the lot. In fact, the entire area was desolated. Not another soul was in sight. Now, willing to risk the backlash for pointing out logical things, I felt as if I should mention it.

"Doesn't it seem to be weird that there are no other cars, or people around, and the guy who sits in the booth there and collects the dough for parking is not in there?"

We were in the middle of unloading, ten beach towels, four hundred and twenty-two bottles of suntan lotion, one umbrella, fifteen plastic shovels, an old bedspread to place on the sand, forty-two pairs of sunglasses, one pair of flip-flops, a baseball and two baseball gloves, a football, water pails, foam coolers packed with ice, sandwiches, soda, candy bars, and ten six-packs of Big Boulder beer (no Dingleberries) and everyone looked around at my statement.

The old man dismissed my observation and expertly diagnosed the situation, "We came at the right time. Everyone is at lunch."

Huh? Lunch? Apparently, everyone in the entire beach

community of Brady Beach, New Jersey, goes to lunch at the same time.

"C'mon! Everyone take sumthin'. Bend ya lazy asses ovah and help me. I can't carry everythin'," the old man pointed to us and kicked at the "stuff" we unloaded to make a little path away from the car. I thought about how we needed a moving van to help us carry all of this "stuff" to the beach. We picked up and hauled our mountains of supplies, sporting goods, liquid and tum-tum refreshment, and other "stuff" and we made our way across the boardwalk.

Under heavy load, (a vast understatement) we walked over to the little security guard guy, who was happily sitting on a stool under a beach umbrella, at the stairs leading from the boardwalk to the beach. The security guy was the only person around.

I guess that he did not go to lunch with the others.

The old man reached into his wallet to pay, what the old man will call an exorbitant fee of two dollars per person to go on the beach, when I elbowed my sister and pointed to the large sign sitting on a wooden frame next to the security guard.

There, in large and ominous block letters, the sign announced:

WARNING: BEACH CLOSED DUE TO A SEVERE JELLYFISH INVASION. ENTER WATER AT YOUR OWN RISK!

Mum and the old man spotted it at the same time as the security guy pointed to the sign and the old man flipped his cork.

"YOU HAVE GOTTA BE KIDDIN' ME! JELLYFISH! REALLY? JELLYFISH! WHAT THE HELL IS THIS BULLSHIT? JELLYFISH!" YA WOULD THINK THE

RADIO WOULD HAVE TOLD ME 'BOUT AN INVASION!"

In exhaustion, and because our arms were about to fall off our bodies, we dropped the mountains of supplies and stuff onto the boardwalk. Immediately, we stood waist deep in and amongst the heaps of various items around our feet. We all moaned a loud groan. In addition to groaning, Dottie also rolled her eyes.

The old security guy first pointed at all of our "stuff" and asked, "What the hell? Were ya plannin' on stayin' fer a week?"

We did not answer his question.

The old security guy then shook his head, apologized and explained, "Sorry. Yeah, really bad out there. Jellyfish all ovah. Damn heat has been so bad this year and the ocean currents stirred the bastards up from da Golf'O'Mexerco. Ya can go on the beach and put ya toes in the water if ya want. I will only charge ya fifty cents for all of ya."

The old man nodded, looked at the mountains of gear sitting on the boardwalk and said to us, "I guess it is better than nuthin'. Youse guys go. I will stay with the stuff."

Mum, Dottie, and I stripped our shoes and socks off, the old man paid the security guy the fifty cents, and as we sadly walked down the stairs to the glorious sandy beach, I heard the old man ask the security guy, "Say, do ya wanna Big Boulder beer?"

An hour or so later, mostly in silence, we carried the gear back to the Putter and loaded the trunk up. We all climbed in and off we were back to good old Paterson, New Jersey. The old man mumbled as he pushed the "THIS IS THE DAMN DRIVE" button, "Gotta find us a Golf station and get me a tank of high-test in this puppy. High test will stop all those rattles in the valves. Do ya have enuff quarters?"

"Yes, dear."

GULP, GULP, GULP.

The asphalt on the Garden State Parkway was now turning to molten oil in the Granny Lane. The afternoon sun had turned on the afterburners.

When the persistent radio announcer reported on WPAT that most beaches along the Jersey shore were closed due to a severe jellyfish invasion, the old man angrily tuned the dial away from the "relaxing sound of WPAT and landed the radio dial on WLOS, which was the radio station broadcasting the first game of the Bugs doubleheader against Minnysoder. It was the second inning and already the Bugs were losing the game by the score of five to nothing.

The old man was happy when the Bug's famous play-by-play announcer, Blabber Viscardi, reported that the Bug's manager, "Short-leg, Sandy Howell, had banished lard-ass McDermott to the bullpen."

"Geez, Good. Thank goodness. 'Bought damn time that Short-leg Howell got him a set of gonownes and woke the hell up," the old man commented, "worse pitcher we evah had. Worse than even, String-bean Linguini was."

The roll back up the Garden State Parkway was not too bad as far as our trips go. We pulled over at the Sal Zucchini rest stop and munched on our food, drank some sodas, and enjoyed the snacks. The Putter only overheated twice and the old man missed the sign, and then the exit for Route 46 in Clifton, but overall, it was not too bad. Mum put a happy spin on the entire day by pointing out that at least we were not all sunburned and had sand particles stuck in our genitals and our ears.

Whoops!

My mind spun back to reality, and I realized that I had wasted away quite a bit of time here at work, thinking about our great beach adventure.

Or had I?

Those were magical times and despite the oddball adventures, how I wish that I could return there just one more time.

Just one more time.

With all my heart and soul, I wish that I could go back there. One more ride in the beloved, 1964 Putter Classic Model 200, with Mum, the old man, and my sister. This afternoon, I needed to thank the ghosts. This time, the ghosts brought me to a very special place. A place deep within my heart and mind. A place where I was very happy to visit.

Sure, do miss my parents. . ..

With a smile on my face, golden memories in my heart, and a prayer of good luck for dear Martha battling it out there somewhere on the roadways of New Jersey, I pushed the off button for my computer.

Time to call it quits.

I packed up my briefcase, shut the light off in my office, and headed for the hallway. A quick spin of the key in the lock and I turned and headed for my favorite bar stool at "The Elusive Lion."

There, with an ice-cold beer in my hand, I will say a toast to the 1964 Putter Classic Model 200, to foam coolers, to my old man, overheated engines, exit 100B on the G.S.P, wadder in glass jars, sweaty guys from Port Bayonne, lard-ass McDermott, and most of all, to jellyfish.

THE END

One White Duck Left on the Wall

Mr. Henning led me from the front foyer of his home, into a wide, expansive first floor. He then pointed through an open doorway and waved to show that he wanted to meet in this room. I peered into the room and observed a large living room, lavishly decorated with a large amount of furniture and with what appeared to be some expensive paintings and framed photographs hanging upon the walls.

He waved and said to me, "Please sit here in the living room, Pastor Paul. I will be right back. I will prepare a cup of tea. Would you care to join me in afternoon tea? I do have some coffee too, if you would prefer coffee, rather than, tea."

"Oh yes, thank you. I do prefer tea. I grew up drinking it. My bloodstream has an awful lot of tea leaf byproducts floating about in it. Tea would be perfect. Thank you, very much."

"Oh, yes. I forgot. Must admit that your New Jersey accent masks most of your heritage. Your mum is from England, is she not?"

"Yes, she is. You are correct. Nottingham."

"Yes, I do recall, Mrs. Crankshammer mentioning that when she enticed me to attend your services. She told me that fact and a lot more too. I guess that you have noticed how she tends to talk quite a bit."

I waved in the air at the mention of one of our longtime parishioners of Reunion Lutheran Church, Mrs. Edith

Crankshammer, who indeed could talk the ears off an elephant.

"Oh yes, she can get lost in the weeds sometimes, but we love her despite her chattering ways. And I might add that your English accent gives you away as much as my New Jersey accent gives me away too. Northern England, maybe?"

"Very impressive, Pastor Paul. Please do not speak any Welsh to me. I never could follow a lick of it. Yes, I am from Durham."

I nodded and explained, "The nucleus of Mum's side of my family was from the Midlands of England, but I had relatives who either worked or were scattered about, so I can usually come closer with the accents than most people can."

"Interesting, that we have a common heritage of sorts. I will make the tea and be right back. Please, sit and relax."

I nodded and chose an armchair close to the fireplace and settled in. I set my communion kit down next to the chair, placed my Bible and notepad next to the kit, and settled into the chair.

I was here on a Saturday afternoon, on my last call for the day, on my typical pastoral rounds. I mostly visited the elderly or ill of the congregation in their homes on Saturday. In addition to sick calls, I also performed special visits to parishioners who requested my visits, in lieu of one of the elders of the church or other persons who were in a church leadership position. The church membership was growing rapidly, which was a great thing. However, my schedule was becoming increasingly difficult to maintain. There had been recent complaints from members, who were disgruntled that Pastor Paul was so difficult to see or obtain an appointment with as of late. They were correct, and I had discussed the possibilities of calling an assistant pastor to the ranks with my boss, Bishop Von Houten, who initially agreed, but then changed his direction and he rather vaguely told me, "To hold off, until he worked out other plans for me."

Oh, well, I tried, and the bishop was not the type of man whom you pressed for answers. Admittedly, the work schedule was becoming wearisome and a bit stressful for my family, too. My lovely wife and children were missing their husband and their father much too often.

This particular visit was not a sick call or shut-in call; this was a little different because it was a visit to a potential new church member. I was here for my first pastoral visit to spend some time with Mr. Henning at his home. He was a friend and a neighbor of Mrs. Edith Crankshammer. I was sure that, with what was most likely a great deal of talking, as well as what at times could be profound and intense insistence, Edith had managed to persuade Mr. Henning to attend Reunion Lutheran Church.

Mr. Henning had been a rather frequent visitor to our church, and as the head pastor, (in fact, the only pastor) I routinely asked among frequent guests as to whether or not they were interested in a new church, just passing through the area, or in fact, they might be interested in making Reunion Lutheran Church, their home church.

As it turned out, Mr. Henning beat me to the question, as he recently filled out one of our pew cards and requested a visit from the pastor before I could catch up with him.

I was not obsessive about growing the church membership, as some of my leadership and laypersons of the church tended to be these days. The membership was growing quite rapidly; we were running out of space and resources, and with the amount of money that was pouring into the budget, some changes loomed on the horizon. Since I first arrived at Reunion a few years earlier, for my first permanent church assignment, we had managed to take the membership from a failing church with about only thirty members on the roles, to a church bursting at the seams. It had been quite the journey, and I was now at a crossroads of expansion, with an addition planned for the church facilities. Perhaps, we were on the brink of hiring an assistant pastor.

I felt confident, extremely overworked, but confident. I had not done too poor of a job, for a retired professional hockey player, entering the ministry later in my life, keeping my long hair and beard, and all the other obstacles facing me, I thought I had done rather well. I was surely not stereotypical, but instead, I did what I thought was correct and I remained a "hippie pastor."

Now, my aforementioned boss, the famous curmudgeon of all curmudgeons, Bishop Werner Beck Clodhopper Von Houten, well, he would have a much different opinion of my performance.

Looking around the room, I admired the photographs and paintings. Some paintings were in oil paint and they looked as if they were very expensive in nature. The photographs were mostly of landscapes, sunsets, sunrises, and a few photos of objects, such as flower vases or glass bottles, illuminated by spectacular lighting to enhance the colors and effects. All the art on display was quite tasteful and reflected quite a bit of skill on the part of the photographer and painter. I surmised that the artwork was the work of Mr. Henning, but that was indeed supposition on my part. Perhaps a family member?

I shifted in the chair and continued to gaze around the room, which was painted in a rather dark and somewhat drab, dark green, an almost black color. There was a white base trim along the floor, meeting brightly polished hardwoods, a white chair rail and a white molding along the ceiling line, which did help to offset the dark colors.

As my eyes and my gaze traveled around the room, I caught the glimpse of an object, a piece of decor, hanging upon the wall of the living room, and this object sent a little chill down my spine. I knew that it was once again time to invoke a few of those ghosts that haunt me from my past.

The ghosts, which never seem to be very far from the recesses of my mind.

My eye had caught that mounted on the wall, very close to the mantle of the fireplace, was a white porcelain duck. It was polished and shiny, a bright porcelain china replica of a common Mallard Duck. The duck hung there alone because below it, in a vertical row, were three empty picture hooks with picture wire, but there were no other porcelain ducks mounted upon these hangers.

They were empty.

Apparently, there used to be more ducks on the wall, and I could faintly, even in the rather dim light of the room, see outlines in the paint where other porcelain ducks at one time, hung there in a vertical row beneath the first duck.

Now, there was just one white duck left on the wall.

Off my mind went, searching for the memory.

"Have you ever been to a funeral before today, Paulie boy?" Gramps asked me, as he bent down close to me to gauge my reaction.

I shook my head to suggest no and Gramps immediately looked over at my sister, Dorothy, who also shook her head to show to our grandfather the same answer as was mine.

Gramps waved to gather us in close to him. Gramps was dressed in his finest suit, with his traditional English derby sitting upon his head and his black walking stick by his side. Our mother and father stood close by, watching the scene carefully unfold. We were all standing a few feet outside a funeral home in downtown Paterson, New Jersey, on a cold, late February day. I was in, or around ten years of age, and my older sister was around thirteen years old or thereabouts.

"It will be solemn, but do not be afraid. It will look as if Uncle Percival is asleep in the casket. He was very old. He lived a good life and I shall miss him greatly."

Despite Gramp's well-meaning attempts at the comforting of his grandchildren, my sister and I were both frightened out of our minds. I was a tough little kid, and it took an awful lot to rattle me. However, this was a new experience for me, as well as for my sister. Dottie reached over and grabbed my hand, and I took it and held her hand tightly. I love my sister dearly; she and I were often and still are each other's ultimate comfort.

We were attending the funeral of our grandfather's brother-in-law, a chap we called Uncle Percy. He was actually our mum's uncle, and in family roundabouts, he was a distant uncle to my sister and me. While I stood there holding my sister's hand, waiting to go into the funeral home entrance, trembling in my shoes, my mind wandered.

Uncle Percival had dual citizenship, with British and American citizenship papers, and he often went back and forth across the big pond. He, as did most of my family, worked in the lace and silk trades, and when the big wars ravaged England and the mills there required rebuilding, then Paterson, New Jersey, provided a place where my family found work.

Paterson was home to silk, lace, specialty cloth and garment manufacturing during an era where we still manufactured products in America. My relatives were experts in machine repairs of the machines utilized in this type of manufacturing. Uncle Percival was an expert in a type of specific loom machine repair and maintenance, a name of a particular machine, of which I could no longer recall.

He would work in England and Wales, and then he would return and work in the United States for a time. He lived a few blocks away from us when he worked here in

America. He had a small apartment, and very few relatives left. Our grandfather was his only relative left in America. There were some distant cousins and uncles and such still in England, but he always visited alone. His wife and children had all passed away, as had his only sister, who was, of course, our grandmother.

I had fond memories of him visiting Gramps and watching them sit and play cards at a small card table in Gramp's apartment on the second floor of my boyhood home. They would drink beer all night, speak in some heavy English accents and I would learn some Welsh and some other words, which Gramps would make me swear not to repeat in front of Mum.

Then there was the night after, as Gramps would often say, "One, two, three, too many beers," that Uncle Percival challenged Gramps to an amazing test of strength.

The memory of this particular night etched forever in my mind. It was a hot summer's night, or as Gramps would often say, "Bloody awful heat!"

Uncle Percy was now very old, and he had grown a bit feeble as of late. He was still moving around, just noticeably slower. He and Gramps were playing cards in Uncle Percy's apartment, and I tagged along to hang around with them in order to learn some life lessons and some words that I would need to forget before Mum caught me using them.

I enjoyed it all. I was a young sponge at the time.

The beer had flowed since late in the same afternoon, and my grandfather, who had a disabled left arm due to a terrible injury in his youth, took Uncle Percy up on the test. Due to the injury, and primitive, horrible surgery in the countryside of England, Gramp's left arm never grew much longer in length than it was when the injury occurred, when he was around ten years of age. Gramps did not allow his short arm, or his disability, to stop him because he was too powerful, headstrong, and courageous to allow that to happen. His right arm compensated for the weakness on the other side, and it grew strong, powerful, and muscular. Just how strong, well, I was about to find out.

"You cannot do it, John, not at ye age now. It is not like when we were young lads," Uncle Percival said with a chuckle. I do think time has chased away from you, John. Ye are a bit soft now, eh? If ye think that ye can, then go 'head and pick it up, then do it."

Gramps laughed and pushed his chair away from the table, which was a small, steel-legged card table, with a white plastic top.

"Like bloody hell, ye say I can't, Percy. Soft, eh? Well, watch. Paulie boy, please gather those cards and take our beer bottles off the table, eh? I am not steady enough to pick it up without it all tipping a bit and creating a mess."

I quickly jumped up from my chair and removed the items from the tabletop. I then watched in awe, as my grandfather reached down, he groaned and grunted, and with his right hand wrapped around the bottom of one table leg, he picked the entire table up in the air, and held it straight out in the air by the one leg, with his left arm outstretched!

The muscles rippled in his right arm, and Uncle Percival shouted, "Bloody amazing! Strongest man whom I have ever seen!"

All I could say was, a dopey and awestruck, "Wow!"

I played professional sports, met many tough guys both on and off the ice, and I know in my heart, none of them could ever hold a candle to the strength, both physically and emotionally, of my grandfather.

He was amazing.

"Uncle Percival, why do you have a white duck on your wall here, and empty hooks on the wall underneath the one duck?" I wandered into the living room of Uncle Percival's apartment and pointed at a porcelain white duck on the wall. I was a typically annoying little kid, asking too many questions.

"Oh, well, okay, Paulie boy," Uncle Percy said while he looked at Gramps for confirmation, to see if he should tell me the story behind the white ducks. He needed to confirm if I was old enough. Gramps did not say a word, but he nodded while he took another sip of beer.

Uncle Percival continued, "Ah yes, well, Paulie boy. In England, we have a tradition, you see, for each family member, you have a white duck, for each person, ye know what I mean?"

I shrugged my shoulders to suggest that I required more information and did not quite understand.

"Well, Paulie boy, the ducks represent your family. They are merely symbolic. I had two small ducks for my children and one medium size duck for my wife. The large duck is mine."

Uncle Percy swallowed hard; the conversation was going to turn from educational to emotional.

I caught a glimpse of tears in his eyes, and then he said to me, "They have all passed away. Now, Paulie boy, I am the only white duck that is left on the wall. . .."

I heard our father's voice, and it returned me to reality. Our father's voice brought my sister and me some comfort. Our father had been watching us carefully, and he now gauged the reaction on our faces, he put his arms around each of us, and gathered us in while telling us, "Come on now, Paulie, come on along, Dorothy, it will be okay."

Our father knew that it was time for both of us to learn a painful lesson in life: that people are born, and people will die.

The seasons of our lives catch up with all of us.

We were now old enough to learn.

The next day, after the funeral, I stood in the living room of Uncle Percy's apartment and watched as my parents and Gramps packed up his belongings.

"Now, there are no ducks left on the wall," Gramps said as he reached up to remove the last duck from the hook on the wall. I grabbed my sister's hand and held it tightly, and with my other hand, I wiped the tears away from my eyes.

I knew that I was going to miss those card games. Together, we watched as Gramps gently and carefully removed the one white duck from the wall. He wrapped it in some paper, and he lovingly placed it in a moving box.

"Okay, here we go with some tea, Pastor Paul. I apologize, but it took me a bit longer than I thought. I had to take a quick telephone call there. I hope I did not keep you waiting, too long."

I looked up, and Mr. Henning's voice brought me back to reality. I tried hard not to focus my eyes upon the white ducks on the wall.

"No, it is fine. Honestly, I did not notice how much time had passed."

"A bit of Earl Grey. I hope you like it."

"Indeed, it is my favorite. Thank you."

Mr. Henning handed me the tea and while we sipped it, he took a seat in the chair opposite to where I was sitting. We proceeded to engage in some small talk and general chit chat. We chatted about the neighborhood, Mrs. Crankshammer, the weather, and then a little about church, and then slowly, we moved a little deeper into the reason for the request of a pastoral visit. I knew how these types of situations usually played out, and I sensed his uneasiness about the subject.

There was a great deal of pain here somewhere; it would be just a matter of time before it surfaced.

Mr. Chadwick Henning was a handsome man. Lean and mean, his tall frame had not an ounce of extra pounds upon it, his arms were strong and muscular, and his handshake was very strong too. I guessed his age to be in or around fifty years of age, but he could easily pass for his early forties. Only a touch of grey hair above his ears and a few licks of grey in his facial hair, made me think otherwise. He was in good physical shape, and he appeared to be a man who took a great deal of pride in his appearance and kept himself neatly groomed and handsome. His beard was neatly trimmed and close to his face, and not a whisker was out of place.

In carefully studying him, I focused upon his eyes. It was a habit of mine. It was a leftover habit of my days as a hockey goaltender where the eyes of the shooter provided you with all the clues that you required. Mr. Henning's sparkling green eyes had more than just a touch of sadness rimming them, a sadness, of which I suspected had something to do with the missing white ducks on the wall.

Yet, my years of playing the position of a hockey goaltender, and the habit of watching a shooter's eyes for clues on where they were planning on placing the shot upon the net that I was guarding, never betrayed me. It has actually worked quite well in my new career as well as in my daily life in general.

While Mr. Henning spoke, even during our general conversation, I followed his wandering eyes. I watched the manner in which he focused his pleading eyes back to mine, in order to gauge my reactions to his words. His actions gave his inner feelings away. He was searching for something, waiting for me to ask the question, which he wanted me to ask. It was only a matter of time until he felt comfortable enough in my presence to reveal the true reason for his request for my visit on this, now late, Saturday afternoon.

Being aware of my calm style in counseling and not wanting to be the overpowering, high-pressure pastor, yet wanting Mr. Henning to feel comfortable, I decided to move the conversation along quicker. I allowed my eyes to land upon a particular framed photograph on the wall, which I admired. At a slight pause in the conversation, I placed my teacup upon a coaster on the end table next to me and stood up.

"Mr. Henning, I have been looking at these pictures and photographs all around your room, and they are stunning. This particular photograph of a sunset is remarkable. If you do not mind, I want to take a closer look here."

I walked over to the photograph on the wall and studied it. It was a photograph of a sunset, with waves of red and yellow rays of sunlight illuminating clouds in a mysterious and colorful manner. I was not an expert, but I could tell that a professional photographer captured this image. At first, Mr. Henning did not say a word. He watched me standing there studying it, and then he also stood up and walked over to me.

"I always forget how large a man you are, Pastor Paul. All that hair and beard seems to help to make you larger than life. I am six feet two and you are taller than I am. How tall are you?"

"Oh, six four or five. . .."

"You must have covered a lot of that net when you played hockey. Thank you for the compliment on the photograph. It is my own creation. I took that one right here in this neighborhood. In fact, right down the street here at the dead end. The view is wide open to the horizon."

"I did not know that you were a professional photographer. It is fabulous."

Mr. Henning now stood next to me and shook his head a little, "Well, I have published a book containing my best shots, and sold some of my paintings and prints, but the artwork is not my primary source of income."

"A painter too. Yes, indeed, the identity of the painter was going to be the subject of my next question. The paintings are also wonderful. You are a very talented man,

Mr. Henning."

I now sensed and was quite comfortable in determining that the sadness rimming his eyes somehow equated to the empty hooks on the wall. I felt that the study of his artwork would provide an opportunity to allow Mr. Henning a sense of comfort and an avenue to open up his emotions.

I walked around the room, and when I reached the one white duck on the wall and the empty hooks underneath it, I stopped and stared at them for some time.

That was all it took to invoke a response, "We have a common heritage, Pastor Paul. Yet, this is more of a tradition in the north of England, not so much in the Midlands."

I fingered one of the empty hooks, while fighting with some of my own ghosts, and said, "No, I had a relative . . . my mum's uncle, and he too, had some empty hooks on the wall at one point in his life. Yes, I know what it symbolizes."

I turned and looked at Mr. Henning, and he waved back towards the chairs.

"Please, can we sit again?"

We once again returned to our chairs. Mr. Henning let out a deep sigh and started to tell me the actual reason that he requested my visit. His heavy northern English accent was quite a bit different from the accents of my family, however, I could easily follow him.

I spoke many dialects, including fluent northern New Jersey.

"The photos and artwork are merely a diversion, Pastor Paul. Just a way to pass some lonely times. I actually own an investment firm with a longtime partner of mine. It is quite successful and for the most part now, after all of thirty years or thereabouts, the business runs on its own. I am bored with it all. At this point, there is no challenge to running the business, but I am quite fortunate, since I do make a very good living in the business. It provides a healthy income. I live all alone here. My wife left me about ten years ago, we have been estranged for many years now. Yet, I am faithful to her, never a thought of another woman. I love her dearly. We have been married for thirty-five years now. She went to live on her own while she finds herself. She lives close to our oldest child, our son."

I first looked at his hands and made a note of the fact that he wore no wedding ring, and I then looked over at the empty hooks on the wall and counted them. Wife, son, and one more. He followed my eyes and read my mind.

"Yes, indeed, we have a daughter, too. The wife has convinced them that I am worthless and they no longer speak to me either. It has caused me a bit of trouble within my soul. My wife explained to me when she left that she needs to find herself and think about our future. Well, forgive me, but living apart for these many years, 'tis a bloody long time."

"It is. I agree. Do you speak to each other?"

"Yes, and she knows where I stand. I want her to return. I want the hooks to be full of ducks once again. She does not have any actual employment. Therefore, a divorce would tear me, I say, rather tear us up financially, not to mention the emotional confusion. I am a wealthy man. The estate is complicated."

I only responded with a nod; I sensed his need to continue to tell his sad tale of woe.

"At first, I hung in there. Hoping. I kept my spirit intact, but now, the power of the loneliness and the memories of the past have penetrated my inner being. I worked on my photos and art endlessly. After work, on the weekends, it provided me a diversion to keep my mind occupied, but now, it has all run over the top of me. I only removed the other ducks from the wall last week. It was when I came to terms with my situation. I do not understand it. I always provided everything for them. A fine house, education, worked long hours, the best in clothes and food. Perhaps, my mistake was I did not feed their souls or emotions."

Mr. Henning stopped speaking, and I carefully watched as his eyes wandered back over towards the empty hooks on the wall. There was no doubt that the sadness in his eyes was deep and genuine.

He spoke once again, "Do you know the power of loneliness, Pastor Paul? It is horrid. Loneliness is the most powerful of all the human emotions. By far. More powerful than love, more intense than joy, crueler than hate and more gut wrenching than grief is. It is a feeling of being dead while remaining alive. It is intensely cruel, because it tears away at your soul slowly, and then, while it grinds on endlessly, loneliness erodes and warps your mind. Remarkably, over time, loneliness then becomes normal, it becomes commonplace, and it is somewhat like a drug. An escape. Loneliness becomes a haven and a place for your soul to hide inside of a now empty, human shell, in order to escape all the bullshit and absurdness of life. You might disagree with me, but I believe it is the most powerful human emotion. More agonizing than grief or more consuming than love, or hate or any other emotions. Do you know of its power?"

I edged up a bit in the chair; his testimony of loneliness hit a nerve.

"I do know of it, Mr. Henning. I too, went through a stretch in my life where it was not exactly a fresh bed of fantastically scented flowers, waving gently in the breeze, on a warm spring day. I know your pain. How can I help? What do you need from the church? From me?"

He stared at me for a few seconds and did not answer. Then, without hesitation, his voice grew louder and his body posture changed to a more aggressive projection.

"I can tell you what I do not bloody well need. I do not need you to tell me that God loves me, and I can tell that you are a tough guy, Pastor Paul. I connected with you when I first attended services at Reunion. I grew up, as you might expect, in the Church of England, and your book of worship is common to ours, so the liturgies and services are similar. Nevertheless, forgive me but you tell it as it 'tis, so I guess that I will too. You are not some pandering, patsy ass, white washer in the pulpit. Instead, you are a pastor who knows our flaws and tells of the blood dripping off the cross, not about how wonderful life is, and how following Jesus, will solve all your problems in one easy step by tossing money in the collection plate. I rather like that."

"Thank you," I said, as I now sensed another aspect of his emotions. Not only anger at God, anger at his life, but largely, anger at himself too. Masked within supposition, I jumped to a conclusion.

"Do you drink alcohol more than you should?" I asked.

He answered without a moment's hesitation, "Of course, wouldn't you?"

And so, did I, "I would, yes, I would, Mr. Henning. Indeed."

"I appreciate your honesty with that fact. It dulls the pain. I suppose that between her incessant chattering, Mrs. Crankshammer has greatly assisted me. She recommended that I attend a service or two at Reunion and while it has not changed my situation, your preaching has provided some type of comfort. You see, I have gone down the prayer route. Prayed until my bloomin' eyeballs rolled out of my head. I lit candles, waved incense, and prayed to Jesus, the Holy Spirit, God, saints, and sadly, the bottom of many an empty Scotch bottle. Prayed to all of them, and nothing changes. Now, to answer your question, what I need from you and the church, is simply admittance that organized religion does not get it. It does not understand human emotions, or a man who has tried as hard as he could and still, has only one white duck left on the wall. God abandoned me, Pastor Paul. Not a single prayer answered. Vacant, empty, my soul and life are meaningless. The pain, the shattering of a life. . ..”

I cut him off because he hit a powerful nerve with me, and he just praised me as to how I was a different type of pastor. Now, I could shock him back to God and prove his point, too.

I could sense how intensely the mood of the conversation was changing, and I needed to reinforce the fact that I agreed with him, “I agree. It might surprise you that I do agree, but I in many ways, share your despair towards organized religion. That might be shocking coming from a pastor ordained within the Lutheran Church, but I have to be honest. Human beings can make a mess out of many things, Mr. Henning. However, you must remember, God did not create religion . . . man did. God, Jesus, Moses, all of the prophets and saints from every belief or denomination, do not need any specific religion. I am embroiled in it because it is the only vehicle that we have right now to perpetuate God’s plan.”

Initially, Mr. Henning did not react. He simply stared at me.

I was not sure if he was now in shock at my response or was waiting for more of an explanation, so I continued, “I do believe that God has a plan. That fact is what led me to the ministry in the first place. It often does not agree with our own plan, or make us happy, or shiny, or new, but I can assure you that it is all there. I saw it envelop my life, my best friend’s life, and I came out of turmoil, much stronger, and with a better understanding of how all of this is interconnected. All of it. I will not tell you any great words, nor will I quote flowery Bible verses, or unless you request it, provide counseling to you and your wife. She has been gone for a long time. No doubt, that is a fact. People move on in their lives for whatever reason. Right or wrong or indifferent. People make choices. People chart their own courses in life and often they need to stand by those choices. What I will offer you is this.”

I reached down next to the chair, opened my Bible, thumbed, until I found what I wanted, and handed it to Mr. Henning.

My old standby! The game-winning save and the shot that wins it all. I have now used this verse more times than I wanted to recall. I used it, because it actually is all that we need to remember, all summed up in two words.

"I have used this too many times in my career, but in my opinion, it sums it all up. The entire New Testament of the Bible in one verse. Please read it. John, eleven, verse, thirty-five."

Mr. Henning reached over. He took the Bible from my hands, read it, sat for quite a few moments and then he smiled. "I have heard some whispers in my attendance at Reunion from people who think you are a long-haired hippie. You might bloody well be, but you are a smart one. Compassion is what you have offered me, Pastor Paul. Jesus felt the same pain that I feel right now. He knew the salty taste of tears running down his cheeks, and had compassion for his friends. I now feel as if compassion is a more powerful emotion than loneliness will ever be. I know that I cannot change how my wife or children feel. As you say, we are all free to make our own choices. In the big picture, we can only change people very little."

I smiled and nodded, pondered for a bit of time, prayed in my mind for some words, some guidance, and then I looked around the room again. First, I looked at the empty hooks, and then at all the incredible artwork.

Now, I knew what to say.

"I do think that a byproduct of your pain and emotional distress can be seen in all of this incredible awakening of your creativity. Your artwork, your photography, it all reflects your intense admiration of God's creation. The beauties of the sunrises, the sunsets, and the landscape scenes, which you have captured, are remarkable. It is easy to see that your most powerful admiration and dreams are unlocked in your creativity. It is a magnificent outpouring of your love."

Staring within his eyes, I continued, "Your admiration proves that you are not a nonbeliever in God, just a person who has found, maybe later in life, but regardless, you found that despite the perception of unanswered prayers, God has compassion. You have a gift, an emergence of creativity that in my opinion, you should share with the world. Perhaps, this is your religion, Mr. Henning, and while God cannot undo the pain, or change what is in your family's hearts, the plan is for you to share what you obviously appreciate so much. That is a form of worship, a form of showing God that you appreciate the majesty of such a wonderful creation. Religion comes in many forms."

I climbed out of my chair, walked over to where Mr. Henning was sitting, and extended my hand. His eyes were teary, but he was under control. He reached up, took my hand and I clasped it and I placed my other hand tightly over the top of his.

"You might actually someday realize that your prayers have been answered. God just chose to not reveal that fact to you until much later."

For the most part, I ended the counseling there, and decided that now was not the time to offer a communion service. Mr. Henning needed to feel the presence of the Holy Trinity in his heart first, before he experienced the awakening of the presence of it within the blood and wine. Instead, I packed up my Bible and my gear and, for the most part, left him with those words to ponder.

We exchanged a few more pleasantries; the afternoon was waning, so we left one another with some warm greetings and mutual well wishes.

I did notice that Mr. Henning never attended any further worship services at Reunion Lutheran Church. He no longer returned my phone calls, nor did he answer a handwritten note and a card that I sent to him. As a pastor, as it was in my life as a goalie, you learn that you win some, and you lose some too.

Around a year or thereabouts later, after my visit with Mr. Henning, on a late afternoon in the summer, I was in my office working on a sermon when my assistant, Martha Wiggins, buzzed in on my telephone. I answered promptly; this sermon was kicking my backside around, anyway. I often pondered that if I worked at the ministry for another forty years that I would run out of subjects for sermons. It was a very good thing the Bible was very long in length.

"Pastor Paul, there is a man here asking to see you. He does not have an appointment, and that might not be an obstacle, because I know that this current sermon is kicking your ass. I know that because I hear you cussing in there and tossing your pencil. Do not fret, my dear Pastor Paul. This is why I am the greatest assistant of all time because I tell no secrets."

For obvious reasons, I loved Martha Wiggins with all my heart.

She continued to explain, "The man without an appointment has announced himself to be a certain, Mr. Chadwick Henning. The man is, of course, persistent in asking if you are available. He is here in person, standing right over me at my desk."

I had to admire Martha's amazing forthrightness and her protection of me. She made mention, a number of times now, that he did not have an appointment. Martha always lectured me about how I worked too hard and accommodated people too much. She was a guardian of me for sure, and I could not ask for a more capable assistant. If she was not married, and I was not, well. . ..

"His accent is a giveaway that, he could perhaps, be a relative of yours on Mum's side of the family."

I paused for a few seconds. Mr. Henning, my, I had not heard from him in a long, long time.

"Thank you, dear Martha, for your amazing efficiency. I

love you to the moon and Jesus does too."

"I love you too, Pastor Paul, but love and Jesus will not pay my bills. Remember my amazing efficiency at raise and review time."

Between laughs, I managed to say, "I will and of course, please send him in, please, I will meet him at the door."

I jumped up from my chair, hustled over to the door to my office and opened it to hear Mr. Henning explaining the unique differences in his northern accent as opposed to the gentle burr of Mum's accent.

"My goodness, Mr. Henning! It is indeed, quite the surprise to see you this afternoon. I am very glad to see you again. You are looking well."

We shook hands, and he gently chuckled at the firmness of my grip, "You seem as if you are even bigger and stronger than the last time that I saw you, Pastor Paul! Still need a bit of a haircut and a shave, but looking well!"

We exchanged some more pleasantries, and it was then that I noticed that he carried with him two items in wrapping paper. One item was rather small, but the other item was larger, flatter, and rectangular.

The gift-wrapping was a generic wrapping paper, but there was very little doubt that they were gifts of some sort. I also casually noticed that, unlike our last meeting, he was wearing a wedding band on his ring finger.

"Please sit here, in the guest chairs away from my desk."

I watched as he set his packages down and we settled into two chairs in a corner of my office, chairs that I typically used for meetings, which required me to soften up the harshness of meeting over my desk.

We settled in and Mr. Henning spoke right away, "I need to fill you in on the past year or so. I apologize for never returning to another worship service at Reunion, for not calling ahead of time for an appointment, and for many other past mistakes. The Pastor Paul that I know is not judgmental and I suspect that he too, has made a few mistakes in his past."

Mr. Henning looked at me for confirmation, and I nodded my head.

I softly answered him, "For sure. I hung my old goalie mask on the fact that our God is a forgiving God. Otherwise, I am doomed."

He smiled at me and continued, "Pastor Paul, I have to thank you for our meeting on that fateful afternoon. I am sure that once I never returned your calls or contacted you that you felt as if I was a lost cause. I did not return your calls, or cards, or letters, mostly because I am a coward, but I did find the courage in my soul to turn my life around. I quit drinking the hard stuff. Oh, I still dabble a bit here and there with some beer, but I no longer drink to become numb or to ease the pain. I faced the fact that the one duck left on the wall would always remain in my life. I drew a line in the sand right then and there. There was no real hope for any reconciliation. I sold my business to my partner, and strongly admitted to my mind and my soul that my wife and children were, for whatever reason, never planning to return to my life."

His eyes filled with tears. Despite his strong pronunciation, the pain was still quite strong and still remained. It was a powerful and profound pain. I did not say a word. I only studied his face and eyes. His eyes were teary, yet different in appearance from the last time we met. I required more time to determine his emotional status, and I did not need to say anything right now.

"I became an observer to the absurdities of daily life. I realized that money meant very little, material things in the end, they will mean zero, zilch, to all of us. I settled with my wife for an enormous amount, sold properties, the business, well, I worked out the settlement with my partner, and my wife and children grabbed parts of it too. I do not care, because, in my heart, I did finally find my religion."

He now leaned forward in the chair and smiled widely as he waved his arms and hands around the room, as if to show where he found his religion.

"It is, just as you said, in the beauty of a sunset, in the wind in a meadow of willows, in the cries of a newborn baby. It is in the joy of that baby's cries answered by a new mother nursing her baby. It is in the laughter of an old man who has lived a long life, and it lies in the glory of a pristine field of untouched snow on a cold winter morning. I am going to make it my religion to document it all. To glorify God as he has glorified my soul."

Mr. Henning paused. He wiped his eyes of the spent tears and I could not help but to smile at his inner glory. I went to speak, but I stopped when he held his hand up to indicate that he wanted to explain some more.

I honored his request.

He leaned in even closer to me, put his hands on his knees to support his weight, and looked into my eyes.

He gently spoke again, "It is all contained within the absurdities of daily religious life. I think the religious of this flawed world are merely fooling themselves. I apologize in advance for my harsh words and for my strong opinions. You nailed it when you explained to me that religion and God were very different. If the religious of this world think that it is important to God that churches with tall steeples, occupied by perfectly dressed choirs, all decked out in perfect robes, while they are all singing, perfectly sung songs of praise, are significant, then they are fools. It is wonderful to praise God. Wonderful, yes, but significant, I do not think so. You know, pompous people, pretending that all will be well, if they make sure that the collection plates are overflowing with dollar bills, all the time, they are burning candles and incense to appease God. Religion is big business. Most people go to worship services to be entertained. How silly it all is. They are under the misconception that all of that nonsense matters more to God, than does, say, a mother singing her first lullaby to her newborn babe that she holds in her arms, while the tears of joy roll down the mother's cheeks. I can only imagine how Heaven rejoices at a mother's joy of holding her newborn babe. Can you imagine that joy? It is unimaginable. A little baby, born, while a mother holds her baby close to her heart. Pastor Paul, that is the bloody, awful trouble with this entire thing that I call, please forgive me, religious bullshit."

Mr. Henning finished speaking, and he leaned back in the guest chair. He studied my reaction to his harsh words, but I had none. He had his opinion and remained entitled to it.

When I did not speak, nor react, Mr. Henning spoke again, "We make ourselves way too important in God's eyes. When we do so, we miss all the simple things, of which God actually created and we should continually praise. God and all the saints and spirits are all so far above all of the daily nonsense that we can never even comprehend it all. In God's eyes, we are single drops of rain in the midst of thunderstorms. We are the solitary edge of a single snowflake amongst a blizzard of flakes. In a hundred years, we all will be dust. Not even a memory. Therefore, with that in mind, I went to work to document it all. All the simple things that we miss. I documented God's creation and the joy of the creation's majesty. I have to tell you that your poignant words awakened my spirit to do so. I painted, took photos, published books, and happiness filled my soul."

I leaned back and watched as he reached for the gifts that he had previously set down. He handed them to me, one at a time. I took them and set them down next to my chair. I sensed that opening them right now was not his intent.

"Please, Pastor Paul. Take these. I cannot ever repay you for your wisdom, but I want you and the church to have these as a testimony. The smaller one is for the church library. The larger one, I hope you will want to grace your office wall with my gift, someday."

"Thank you. It is very kind of you, Mr. Henning. Thank you."

He nodded and without pause, continued his testimony, "I met a woman, Pastor Paul. A wonderful, captivating, kind and gentle woman. She filled my heart with desire and my soul with joy. I have felt happiness in my life, but now I have joy. There is a great difference in the two emotions, Pastor Paul. Happiness resides in the mind, yet, it is usually very short-lived. Joy resides in the soul, and it remains forever. Lost pieces of me. They actually returned. My spirit returned, and I actually felt as if I had a soul. We met about nine months ago. She assisted me with one of my photo books, and we connected. I fell deeply in love with her and her with me too. She is gorgeous, both inside and outside, her beauty is radiant, a window to her soul. She is much younger than I am. She has a young son from another relationship. You know, past mistakes, which produced a wonderful child. Who am I to judge? I love her dearly, and we married a few weeks ago. I will adopt the young man. I love him too and his biological father is now out of the picture. I now have three white ducks on my wall again and I am happier than I could ever have imagined."

I finally had a chance to speak, Mr. Henning's eyes were bright and clear and his smile went ear-to-ear. I now knew the status of his soul.

"I am so happy for you. In fact, I am thrilled. What a wonderful testimony to God's guidance and to sending you the compassion that you were missing within your life."

When I spoke the word "compassion," it was as if I hit a powerful nerve. Mr. Henning jumped out of his seat and stood straight up.

He clapped his hands together and said loudly, "Exactly! Pastor Paul, you just hit upon it so perfectly. You see, our tradition, it 'tis all wrong!"

"Wrong? You mean the white ducks?"

He nodded, and I asked, "Why is it all wrong, Mr. Henning?" I was somewhat puzzled as to the meaning of his statement.

He sat back down and reached over for me to hold his hands.

I reached out and grasped them tightly.

With tears forming in the corners of his eyes, he spoke just above a whisper, "Because there 'tis never just one bloody white duck left on the bloomin' wall, Pastor Paul. Those empty hooks hanging below are never really empty. If they are empty of ducks, then God hangs compassion on each one of them. Remember, Pastor Paul. Jesus wept."

I smiled at his insight.

He was correct.

We conducted a bit more of some small talk, and the conversation turned from intense to light in nature. I welcomed his strong opinions, but more so, I rejoiced at the remarkable healing of his spirit.

After we concluded our conversation, I wished him well; I thanked him again, and he was on his way.

After Mr. Henning left, I opened the gifts. One was a magical book of his artwork, his photos, and other creative work, all captured in full color and all of them documented as to what they meant to him and where he took them. In his written explanations, he included background information on them all. He had selected an appropriate title for the book, "To the Glory of God's Creation." It was indeed a wonderful addition to the church library.

The larger package turned out to be a fabulously framed reprint of the sunset photograph that I had admired during my visit to Mr. Henning's home. I did hang the framed, magical testimony to God's glory on a wall in my office. It was a remarkable photograph.

Sunsets in my life mean so much, they provided me such profound comfort, sometimes, when I needed it most of all. For as long as I could remember, I loved the colors, the beauty and the natural comfort of a sunset.

Sunsets were always very special to me, and I suspected that they would always remain so.

I never spoke to, heard from, or even saw Mr. Henning ever again after that meeting in my office. I did not need to, in order to know that he had finally found his religion and his way, his direction, his connection to God's plan. Whenever I glanced over and admired that photograph, I was reminded of his happiness and how he managed to overcome, as he said, "Absurdities of daily religious life" and to discover God's plan for him, as well as his inner glory.

Forever more, I knew that no matter what, there could never be just one white duck left on the wall.

Nope, no way, in New Jersey speak, "Ain't gonna evah happin.'"

Not only because of Mr. Henning's transformation and his profound testimony, but also because, today while in church, right after my sermon and just before the perfectly dressed and immaculately robed choir began the first notes of a hymn, I heard a newborn baby cry out.

You see, I know how Heaven rejoices. . ..

THE END

No Boiler Required

181 Belmont Avenue in Haledon, New Jersey. That was the address of what was a very old apartment building. Old; built in and around 1910 or thereabouts, constructed of red brick by artisans of a bygone era; sprawling, six floors, stacked side-by-side with long hallways, which echoed footsteps and whispers of the past and of the present.

A typical, inner-city building.

There was no elevator here. Shoe leather and stairs took you to where you needed to land. The building had a brick porch and a bluestone entrance stairway, which faced the busy city street, and it boasted concrete fresh air wells on each side of the building in order to ventilate the common areas of the building. The building had the typical metal fire escapes crisscrossing along the brick walls of each side of the building. Upon many of the landings of the metal fire escapes were folding chairs, charcoal grilles, hammocks tied between metal risers and even a few small tables. The metal monsters provided an escape route in the event of an emergency, but also a porch to sit upon, when the summer nights grew much too warm for comfort. At least sitting upon the fire escape brought some type of breeze.

The fire escapes rather strangely became places of solace, a lofty perch to look down upon the urban world, even a place to sleep when the heat inside of the apartment became unbearable.

An old boiler puffed steam from within a hidden lair in the basement and it sent heat up through the old building, spitting and steaming inside of old cast-iron pipes. Occasionally, where the old pipes joined into each other, steam popped, spit, and drooled, a mixture of steam and condensed water out of the joints. The maintenance man packed the leaking joints of the old pipes with steel wool and coated them with a compound in an effort to minimize the steam's escape. The apartments were stifling in the summer and for the most part, despite the boiler and maintenance man's best efforts, freezing in the winter.

The superintendent, who was also the maintenance person and the boiler operator, did what he could, but old is old.

In the building's heyday, it was quite a handsome building.

The original owners of the apartment building were an Italian family, a husband and wife, and a daughter team. They lived in the first-floor apartment in the front of the building. The building's maintenance and appearance, as well as the comfort of their tenants, were paramount to the family. The pride that the family had in owning such a fine building was easily apparent. Never, in their wildest dreams, coming from the old country, would they have thought they could ever own such a grand building. Yet, years ago, hard work and dedication brought many golden rewards.

The family constructed an arbor on the side of the apartment building and planted grapes that sprawled and clung to the arbor. From those same grapes, they made homemade wine in the cellar of the apartment. A wine, they bottled in clear jugs and on summer afternoons and early evenings, the family, along with some local Italian tradesmen, such as stonemasons, and gardeners, would gather under the arbor and enjoy the fruits of their labor. The mother of the family planted rows of glorious rose shrubs along the sidewalk next to the apartment, and even though the shrubs faced a busy urban street, they presented a grand appearance. The fragrance of the rose shrubs enhanced the air between the smoke and exhaust of the many vehicles running up and down Belmont Avenue.

For many years, it was a showplace, a wonderful place to live. Then the Italian family grew older and when her parents passed away, the daughter decided to sell the apartment and move out of the old city. Off to the suburbs, where the noise of the busy city street did not reach their ears and the smoke of the exhausts of the many vehicles did not drift into your windows.

The new owner did not have much pride in the building, and as a result, he did not take as good a care of the old building as the Italian family did. Eventually, a lack of maintenance, combined with time and age, and it all caught up with the old building. It began to look worn, gritty, and old. No longer was it a showplace. Now it was humdrum, not rundown, but certainly no longer a showplace. Many things changed because nothing ever stays the same. In this life, the one thing that you can always count on is change. The new owners removed the grape vines and the arbor, in order to make more room for additional parking, and the rose shrubs were in the way of an entrance to the new driveway. No longer did the glorious scents of the roses mix in the summer breezes along the busy city street.

The scents passed away in time, as so many other things do. Yet, certain aspects of this world, and of our lives, linger forever.

Mr. Kent Lambert needed to reorganize his entire life. He needed a fresh start. The last few years had been difficult for him. To say the least. Very difficult. Kent was still very young, only forty, and he now felt as if he held on tightly to his dreams. Kent was not going to allow his dreams to escape. Now was the time to take control and redirect. Kent was sure that he was correct. On the heels of a short-lived, failed marriage, and then a bitter divorce, combined with two or three career changes, Kent felt as if his life crumbled beneath his feet. Yet, his parents taught him perseverance, and it was that lesson which carried him through the difficult times.

Kent was quiet, conservative, introverted, unassuming, and very much a man who kept to himself, and when he ventured out in the world, it was within a small circle of friends. Kent had a best boyhood friend, who he vaguely stayed in touch with, a friend who had married and moved from New Jersey a long time ago. Now, he just kept within a few friends at work. He had one friend from work that he would hang out with more than the others, but mostly, he was a loner. He was not the adventurous type and that fact might have helped to contribute to the failure of his marriage. His ex-wife sought adventure. She was extroverted, and she thought she could transform the handsome Kent Lambert into someone that he was not. Eventually, her sense of adventure caused her to look for adventures of a different type within the arms of another man.

Therefore, here Kent Lambert was regrouping and muddling through. Working a full-time job for a local supermarket as a manager in the produce department was not his idea of the ideal career. Yet, after trying his luck at sales and then a short-lived stint as an assistant manager of a restaurant, this new job had predictable hours, good healthcare benefits and while the pay was lower than his previous wages were, the work was steady. However, the major benefit of the supermarket position was that it allowed Kent some free time to attend a local community college to study what he felt as if was his true passion, which was writing. Yes, Kent Lambert was the oldest student in the class, but he did not mind.

It had some side benefits.

Kent did not look anywhere near forty years of age and since he was single and available, as well as a tall, handsome, well-spoken man, and once he opened up and became comfortable with a person, he had quite an engaging personality. Moving crates of heavy produce all day long, unloading trucks and performing physical labor, provided Kent with employment and a side benefit of an exercise program and his muscles were lean, strong, and powerful from the heavy lifting and physical labor. Despite his efforts at remaining unassuming, his classic good looks afforded Kent quite a gathering of young women, all giving him some attention and seeking his company. Kent had an occasional date or two, but right now, money was a huge issue for him, and he had little extra cash for wining and dining a young woman out on the town. Right now, he had to pay tuition, make rent, and pay his car note as well as a host of other expenses. Besides, a romantic relationship might get in the way of his plans while he pursued his passion and buckled down in his life. After all, forty is still very young, but so many things pass so quickly from us in this life.

Kent was ecstatic to find an apartment with a reasonable rent that was centrally located to both his school and his job. In fact, the supermarket where he worked was just up the avenue a few city blocks. While the location of the apartment might be perfect, it was not located in the greatest of neighborhoods. Kent did not mind because he grew up in the city and knew all too well the evils that existed here. This neighborhood was a rougher one than the neighborhood of his youth was, but Kent knew the ways of the city. He kept a low profile, remained very aware of his surroundings, and steered clear of all the trouble. For Kent Lambert, the apartment was perfect for a crash pad. He only had a small kitchen table, with one chair, his bed, and a small dresser, and in the bedroom, he set a black and white television upon an upturned cardboard box. He also had an old radio and his most prized possession, which was his typewriter. Kent bought it used for twenty dollars. It was a good one, and he felt lucky to have it for a reasonable price, even if his ex-wife scolded him for spending so much on what she deemed, "The pursuit of silly dreams."

That was all he took from his failed marriage and all he wanted. He did not want anything else; the bad memories and nightmares were enough.

The apartment house was an old building, and the apartment was stifling in the summer and freezing in the winter, but it had some advantages. It was on the main bus route for the city buses and from just a few steps away from the front door, you could find the bus stop, and above all, apartment number 602 had this wonderful fire escape.

One might question Kent as to why a fire escape in an old apartment building was so important to him. It seemed as if that would be an unusual item for a focal point for Kent.

Yet, the aspiring writer found the landing of the fire escape outside his apartment window to be the perfect, well, for lack of any other description, "escape." He found a small table in a local thrift store for five dollars and a folding chair, and armed with a piece of plywood to bridge the metal rails, he found the perfect writer's nook. A place to escape the heat of the apartment, yet a place to retreat to and a place of solitude to write in. For Kent, it was the perfect place to write. He set his typewriter up on the table and from six stories above the yakking of the busy city street; Kent Lambert recreated the world below him into his own fictional paradise.

Originally, Kent would write in his preferred genre of science fiction, or fantasy, and then as he typed away, he changed and grew bored with the tales of fantasy worlds. Instead, he began to write of the harsh realities of life, the ebbs and flows of ordinary human emotions, and gradually, stories of unrequited love crept into the pages of his work. In retrospect, Kent could say that the change in his genre was a direct result of the experiences of his own life, the breakup of his marriage, the shifts in his career and other realities. All of those factors might be true, but above all, Kent found that his writing of fantasy worlds provided him with entertainment, but it left him empty of emotional satisfaction. The best writing requires emotion and Kent ultimately found where he could uncover where his emotions were. The emotions came wrapped up in waves of reality and within the words of love, gone wrong.

At first, his professor at college judged his writing to be at a novice level, rudimentary, and then slowly, as the emotions infiltrated his words and Kent abandoned the tales of fantasy, his writing became more polished, and classic in nature.

Suddenly, his professor took notice, and he praised Kent's transformation and talents. All too soon, the semesters of school were over and Kent had more time to write, to be alone, and to be lost in his words.

On one of the first heat waves of summer, on a stifling night, after a hard day at work, Kent grabbed a cold beer out of his small refrigerator, slipped his typewriter out the kitchen window, set the writing machine upon the table on the metal deck and shortly thereafter, Kent took up his writing post on the fire escape. There he typed away, on his first actual attempt at composing a novel. At first, it was daunting, and then as he moved from the first words, to the first sentences, to finished paragraphs, Kent found it all quite easy to become lost in the world of words and most of all, lost in the waves of human emotions.

Julie Granatelli was, in her mind, just starting out. But in reality, this was a restart of sorts. Julie had just ended a long-term relationship with what she thought was the man of her dreams.

Actually, he broke off the relationship and shattered the dream.

A dream that ended abruptly and suddenly and it came to a grinding halt with what was for Julie's heart a less than ideal result. It all seemed, as it was a dream come true, they were high-school sweethearts; he had grown into such a handsome man, successful, from a solid family, and it looked as if they would cruise to a marriage proposal and a grand life together.

Many babies and a glorious family life. A dream.

Then, instead of a marriage proposal, came the dreaded speech, "I love you, but I am not sure that I am in love with you enough to spend my entire life with you. . .."

Recently, Julie heard he had a new love. He picked his life up very quickly, and now flaunted about town with some big-breasted, fancy woman from a wealthy family on his arm.

It all seemed as if it was one big lie.

Endless lies.

Julie grew weary of it all. Recently, Julie had lost her full-time job as a data entry clerk in a large pharmaceutical corporation, due to a work slowdown and what the corporate executives label, "reorganization." It was mindless work, but for Julie, it got her through until she could decide what her future was going to be. After all, she thought she would marry and live a happy life, perhaps two incomes, a small house, and a few children. That dream failed.

Now she was brokenhearted, unemployed and in need of a new direction in her life. Above all, in her heart, Julie sought a new life. A restart. While working full time, Julie attended school for a few evenings during the week and on Saturdays. Now, after a long grind of two years, some student loans, Julie graduated from a secretarial college, specializing in legal practices and legal administrative work. Julie's mailings of her resume, combined with placement experts at her school, finally caught the eye of a lawyer in downtown Paterson, New Jersey. A lawyer just beginning his practice and seeking an administrative assistant with which he could grow his practice, perhaps, even a person who would someday become a paralegal. It was a stretch for Julie. A small and inconspicuous town located in southern New Jersey was the town where she was born, and until now, was the only place that she had ever lived. Now, to venture up north to the Metro-New York City area, high crime, high prices, and all the things, which her family told Julie she needed to stay away from in her life.

"Oh my! Paterson! It is on the news all the time. Robberies, shootings, murders, on every street corner. It is full of gangsters and organized crime."

It was all so foreboding.

Yet, the lure was too great. In Julie's heart, it was exactly the restart that she was seeking. After all, a torn heart required some type of repair.

After an intimidating journey to the city, a sit-down interview and much discussion, Julie accepted the attorney's generous offer, and she made the fateful decision to relocate to northern New Jersey. The salary was very generous, and it was much more than she could ever imagine earning in the limited opportunities of southern New Jersey, where the large pharmaceutical corporation was the only major employer in town. A corporation where they did not rehire, they only reorganized.

Julie felt as if she had found it all. The lost city of El Dorado, the Isle of Avalon! A golden sunset on the horizon of despair.

Julie packed a single suitcase with her belongings, along with her tears, mixed with some painful memories; she caught a bus in Atlantic City and headed north. Despite her joy at a restart, her leaving town and her family still caused her a great deal of pain. The goodbyes left a rainstorm of tears behind her. Julie tried to remain positive, but she also realized there were no rainbows on the end of this rain of tears, only a lonely trail of pain. Pain over lost love can make you flee to the farthest ends of the Earth in order to escape the hurt and the tears. Julie hoped the other end of this journey was where she would find the rainbow.

Julie was the only child from a mixed-family of sorts. Her mom was Jewish and her father was Italian. Taught from when she was a young child, both the Catholic and Jewish faiths, Julie felt as if she had a unique and interesting family life, and while the family was not overly religious, Julie and her parents had their moments. With her mixed heritage, Julie had dark features and captivating dark black eyes. Julie was very cute, petite, a nice, slim figure, yet now she was full of self-doubts. She always felt her teeth were too crooked and a little brown along the edges; her hair was thin and unmanageable, her nose was too long, her breasts were too small and as of late, her mind wandered with self-doubts that her abilities at making love to please a man were lacking and inadequate. Maybe that is why he left her? Perhaps she was a terrible lover. She only had ever intimately been with one man, and he left her. It all came together to fill the young woman with self-doubts and thoughts at her own inadequacies.

When she reached the big city, reality set in and there was the stark, cold cost of rent and other expenses.

Suddenly, that high salary and all the lofty aspirations of such evaporated right in front of her eyes. It was very expensive to live here. Pounding the pavement in search of an affordable apartment eventually led her to the front porch of 181 Belmont Avenue in Haledon, New Jersey. To the place where the rose shrubs once provided fragrance and to the place where the grape arbor once stood. Now, all that remained of the past glory of the fragrance and the joy of the grape arbor was a parking lot.

If you listened very closely, you could hear the ghosts of the past. Perhaps some remnants of spoken Italian language filled the air and mixed with laughter where the arbor once stood?

Perhaps.

Every place within God's great creation has a story to tell. Some are sad, some are glorious, but there are always stories to tell.

All of this was a world away from where she came from. The whispers of the high crime and a bad neighborhood lingered, yet it was on the bus line and it was the best deal in town. Besides, the superintendent and his wife, who lived in the first-floor apartment, both seemed so pleasant. How bad could it be? They watched everything, and she had triple deadbolts on her door. In her mind, it was the perfect place for a restart.

Yes indeed, every place has a story to tell.

Mrs. and Mrs. Aviv Finkelstein lived in the first-floor apartment of 181 Belmont Avenue. Mr. Finkelstein worked as the superintendent of the apartment building. In his role as the "super," he served in many capacities. He was the gardener, the security officer, boiler operator and maintenance man. In many ways, his wife told him he also was the rabbi to the residents. His wife laughed and enjoyed when her husband would provide life advice and coaching on issues to all the tenants of the apartment. No doubt, he was a very wise man, and he willingly shared his wisdom with everyone. For the most part, Mr. Finkelstein enjoyed the job; he fought the battles that old buildings can wage upon a maintenance man, with an assortment of leaky pipes, roof drips, clogged waste lines, and electrical issues. There was not too much the wily Mr. Finkelstein could not fix. He was a very handy man and his diverse skills were an asset, because the building was not exactly new. But overall, other than kick-starting the temperamental boiler on bitter cold nights when the fire eye gave out, prying the rent out of Mr. Lansford on the third floor, chasing away street thugs and hoodlums, and dealing with the incredibly cheap owner of the building, who was also his boss, it was not a bad job.

He also could do without the Friday night celebrations of Zale McAlister and his visiting hippie friends. Their music selections wore a little thin on Aviv's nerves. Aviv loved all kinds of music, mostly big band music that the Finkelsteins would play on an old record player and dance in their living room occasionally. Yes, music was grand, but blaring rock-and-roll mixed with the pungent scents of cannabis, and complaints from all the other tenants, just did not make for fun nights. Zale was a deliveryman by day and an aspiring musician by night, and in the big picture of the apartment house tapestry, Zale and his friends were harmless. He rather enjoyed them and surprisingly, the two of them shared many interesting discussions. It was just those Friday night gatherings, combined with their music, were a pain in the ass.

The neighborhood was a bit rough, and as of late, it seemed to be turning for the worse, but the location was ideal. Mr. Finkelstein grew up in the old city, knew the evil ways of the streets and he kept a baseball bat handy, right inside his front door. In his day, the little man played a mean third base and he could really swing a baseball bat. He wanted to believe that if he had to that he could still do it.

The Finkelsteins could easily walk to the temple for Jewish worship services and other events. It was on the main bus line to downtown, and the rent was next to nothing in exchange for his services. Mrs. Finkelstein still worked as a seamstress in a garment shop in downtown Paterson. Therefore, there were additional monies earned in the household. Besides, Aviv had retired after working for over thirty years, as the head maintenance man for a production garment factory in the city, and he had a small pension to collect upon as a reward for his many years in the factory. The Finkelsteins were by no means wealthy, but they were comfortable as far as finances go and that meant a great deal to them. He was from an era when Paterson, New Jersey, was the kingpin in the silk and lace trades. Now, that was a bygone time. All the factories closed and moved production overseas. The couple raised one daughter, a daughter who married a successful real estate developer and who now lives in Florida. Recently, the family blessed them with a grandson.

Eventually, when retirement finally came along, they could collect his pension, obtain a little monthly trickle from the government and live off some savings they banked a few years ago, from the sale of their home. Yes, every job has its ups and downs, but for now, this was the perfect job to cruise with for a few more years until they both retired. Florida would be the final landing spot for the couple. Somewhere near their daughter and her family. Somewhere near Tampa.

"So, Miss Granatelli, you have a new job? With an attorney. Downtown?"

"Yes, to all three of your questions, Mr. Finkelstein. It is a new practice, just starting up. Mostly real estate law. Irving Schecter E.S.Q. Mr. Schecter is very young."

Aviv smiled, and he turned the key in the lock to apartment number 402. While the door creaked open, Aviv commented, "Please call me, Ave. Everyone does. Schecter, huh? Sounds like a good Jewish boy. Very nice."

"Yes, I do think he is Jewish. I am half-Jewish, Mr. Finkelstein . . . I mean, sorry, Ave."

The little man smiled once again, this time widely, and he handed the apartment keys to Julie while pointing at the front door with his other hand.

"I need to oil those hinges. Give me a few minutes to get the oilcan from my workshop in the cellar and I will be back. I knew that I liked you and that you were beautiful for a reason. Half-Jewish is quite good! Whole is better . . . but half works too. Let me guess, your mother is Jewish."

Julie took the keys from Aviv and laughed at his correct guess.

"Why yes, you are correct. My mother is Jewish. My father is Italian. How did you know?"

"Partly because of your last name, but mostly, because you are beautiful, and all Jewish women are beautiful. Inside and outside, too. Therefore, your mother must be beautiful. Fathers, not so much. Look at me, but Mrs. Ave . . . she is gorgeous and so is our daughter!"

"You are very kind, but I am not so beautiful."

"You are, and let's not argue the point. I can see some sadness in your heart. Mrs. Ave tells me that I am the rabbi of this building. Maybe I am, but whatever you ran away from, it was not to be. Your future would not allow it. Better things lie ahead. I know these things. I have lived a long life and seen much. Most likely, it was a young man that you left behind you. A foolish man, who does not understand the prize he lost. Someday he will. So be it. You need an older man, you are too mature for the folly of young men who cannot see past their, well, you know where I mean. Listen to your rabbi."

The little man quickly changed the subject, and he pointed to the outside wall and explained, "You are going to need some fans in here. It is the middle of June and the apartment faces into the west. The brick holds the heat like an oven does. So, listen to your rabbi and buy some fans." Mr. Finkelstein was quite demonstrative in his instructions and while he spoke, he waved his hands in the air to display the motions of many fans.

"Okay, you get it. So much for that, now you really need to listen to Ave here. Always flip the deadbolts, my dear Julie. Always. I run a tight ship here. You are a young, single, very attractive woman in the midst of a neighborhood in which you do not know yet what it can be. The tenants are for the most part, good. We do have the hippies but they are harmless. Just fun guys who smoke too much weed and drink too much beer while strumming their guitars. We also have the Lopez family on the third floor, who drink a little too much Sangria wine and dance the salsa to loud Spanish music. All of them are fun. Loud and annoying, but fun. Friday nights around here can be loud and wild."

The little man smiled as his mind must have flickered with the thoughts of Friday nights in the old building. It was plain to see that he enjoyed them.

Off he went, explaining more, "You soon will know

what everyone's favorite foods are. The hallways are samples of cuisines. Across the street, in the big green house, is the Henson family. Exceptionally, good people. They have been here forever, icons of the neighborhood. I assure you that no one dares to mess with the Hensons. If you ever are in trouble, remember they are friends. The street people, not so good. Remember, Ave always knocks three times, waits, then two knocks. I also announce that it is Ave. Always. Remember the code. If it is ever different, do not open the door, even if you look through the peeper glass and it is me in the hallway."

Julie nodded and smiled while thanking Aviv. The superintendent waved, promised to be back with the oilcan and left. Julie closed the door behind him and flipped the deadbolts.

All three of them.

When Aviv returned to oil the door hinges, he used the code. Julie quickly came to realize that Aviv Finkelstein was very true to his word. The superintendent ran a tight ship; he looked after Julie very carefully and became quite protective of the young woman. Aviv Finkelstein was a very kind man and Mrs. Finkelstein was correct. He was many things, but one of his jobs was to be the rabbi of 181 Belmont Avenue.

That job might be the most important one of them all.

It was a Friday night in June. Kent Lambert just finished a long shift at the Foodworld supermarket on the corner of Belmont Avenue and John Street. Kent did his boss a favor and covered two shifts for him, and as a result, his boss tossed him some freebies. He received a gallon of milk, some canned goods from the dent shelf and a large pack of chop meat. Usually, Kent worked Saturdays to Wednesdays, and he had off Thursdays and Fridays. In Kent's mind, the extra day was no big deal. Kent did not mind the extra work; the free items were a nice touch. He did not eat much, was a very poor cook, but he could make a meatloaf and it would last him for three meals. Kent stopped off at Trio Liquors on the corner of Cook and Belmont, bought a six-pack of cold Big Boulder beer and headed off for what he felt was going to be a productive and amazing weekend of writing bliss.

When you could allow your soul to venture into a world of words, entertainment was cheap, and it was very easy. From your own mind to your fingertips, everything is available to you. Endless romance and boundless love with gorgeous women, adventures in far-off lands, being a Wild West hero riding the range and saving towns from the bad guys, and even riding to the moon in a spaceship.

Voyages of the soul.

It was all so easy. When Kent arrived at the front entrance of 181 Belmont Avenue, he waved to the young Henson teenager, who was sitting upon the front steps of the big green house across the street. The young man appeared to be an avid reader. He sat there very often, reading what seemed to be an endless array of books.

Kent made a note that someday he needed to stop and

compare notes with the young man.

With the heat of the day, the windows were all open in the apartments and even with some road noises from the busy street; you could hear the big band music playing from the Finkelstein's apartment, a quick glance through the windows and you could see them dancing together in their living room. Even after many years of marriage, the couple was still very much in love.

High above his head, Kent could hear Spanish horns and guitars from the Spanish music playing from the Lopez's apartment. Upon hearing the telltale taps of their feet upon the apartment's floor, he knew they were dancing the salsa. Kent glanced at his watch. It was still a little early, but soon, the jam session of rock-and-roll would begin from Zale and his band mates.

The apartment house was a cornucopia of different music and cultures. It was as if you tuned across a radio dial.

Up the front steps, down the main hallway, and up the staircase, all the way to the very top. Kent always kept his eyes open and was aware of the stairways.

Sometimes evil lurked there.

A quick spin of the key; he placed the food into the refrigerator, and the beer into a bucket filled with ice. It was stifling hot in apartment number 602. Kent's apartment faced west and the sun beat upon the old brick sides of the building for a large part of the day. These apartments were, for the most part, all the same. Plaster walls with spider web cracks running in many directions, woodwork with too many coats of paint to count, old cast iron radiators tucked against walls as if they were silent soldiers of heat, wooden windows with glass that was anything but clear. No amount of cleaning and washing would restore the view. A white porcelain, claw-footed bathtub stood proudly in the bathroom, paired with an old brass faucet that spit out the water as if it were an uncontrolled roof and gutter downspout in the aftermath of a thunderstorm. The apartments had a small kitchen, an open living room and dining room combination, a bathroom off the hallway, and one small bedroom. If there were six hundred square feet here, then that would be an exaggeration and a roundup figure of the actual footprint. Kent heard that the super's apartment was larger; in fact, he heard that it even had two bathrooms.

Yet, Kent knew that the fire escape off the bedroom window provided just what he needed.

A breeze.

A breeze that would lift him off on a voyage of the soul. Six stories up in the air, on a metal fire escape, there was a glorious breeze. Yes, it mixed with some smoke, haze and exhaust from the city street below, but it also had a marvelous view of a hot summer's day sunset. A sun sinking low over the old mills and factories and the edges of the Preakness Mountains, which peaked off to the west on the outskirts of the city limits. It was not all grit and crime; even here, within the midst of a maze of buildings and congestion, there was some beauty. Kent stripped his work uniform off. He pulled on a pair of shorts, and his chest remained bare. When it was this hot, it was not worth it and since he was six-stories up in the air; no one would see him, anyway. He opened the bedroom window; he took his precious typewriter and set it out on the small table on his fire escape. Next, he took the bucket filled with ice and beer and set that out on the metal deck of the fire escape. Soon, he was at his writing post, while a hot, yet somehow glorious, summer breeze blew across his skin.

There, he typed,

"Chapter One, Put Your Hand in Mine. The snow was deep, and it was wet enough to build a fantastic snowman. Early in the morning, before anyone rose, while the snow still lay undisturbed and unblemished, he went to work. Right outside her apartment window, he rolled the first balls of the body of the snowman. Then another, and another, and finally, he rolled a snowman's head. A quick dash into the apartment for a hat, a trip to the cellar to the coal burner for the boiler, yielded some pieces of coal for the eyes and then the finishing touches, some sticks cut from the remnants of old rose shrubs for the snowman's arms. He even picked strategic sticks, which resembled hands at the end of the arms. Then, he worked hard and built a duplicate snow woman right next to his snowman. The same stacked snowballs again, but this time, he placed a woman's scarf around the snow woman's neck and a woman's hat on the head. Strategic sticks allowed the two, snow people to hold hands.

Now, the ultimate romantic touch, he pulled from his coat pocket, the red paper heart that last evening, he cut out of red construction paper, and now, he carefully pressed it into the snow of the snowman, right in the spot where his heart would be. When he returned to the apartment, he gently and silently slipped the note under her apartment's door, a note which asked her when she woke up to look out her bedroom window. Actually, he phrased and laced the instructions with some additional love."

Two floors down, in apartment number 402, Julie Granatelli tried in vain to cool her apartment down. She thought, goodness gracious. The heat of the city lingers. By now, along the Jersey shoreline, the ocean breezes would be cooling the air down and a glorious sunset would mean relief from the heat of the day was now on the way. Now, well, Julie was a long way from her hometown.

Window fans and floor fans all felt as if all they did was to move some hot air around. They pushed hot air all over the rooms, but did little more than just push hot air. Until the sunset arrived and the outside air cooled down a little, the fans were futile. Mr. Finkelstein was correct; the western exposure was just as if it were a brick oven.

Julie thought that she would move the window fan from the living room window into the bedroom and that way, when the night air did cool, she could circulate the cooler air in her bedroom in hopes that she could sleep a little. Julie made her way into the bedroom and, while opening the window to place her window fan in the frame, she heard the rattle and tap of what she thought to be a typewriter. Leaving the fan on the floor of the bedroom, Julie pushed the wooden frame of the window open a little more, lifted the window screen, and studied the fire escape. She stuck her head out and looked the metal monster up and down. Sure enough, when she looked up, she noticed a man sitting on a stool, on a piece of wood, that was bridging the metal landing of the grates, and he appeared to be typing away on a typewriter sitting on a table.

"How strange," Julie thought aloud.

Although, it was difficult to tell from two stories below, and while looking up, it appeared as if the man was in a pair of shorts and was bare-chested. Julie also noticed how there was such a gentle breeze out on the landing, and the view of the sunset was quite spectacular. It seemed as if the man working above her head had made a fine choice to escape the heat of the apartment and to enjoy the view. She also could not help but notice, albeit briefly, and from an upside-down point of view that the man on the fire escape two floors above her had a nice build and appeared to be quite handsome. From her very quick glimpse and observation, Julie noticed that there was not an ounce of fat on his lean and trim body. With a large and spontaneous smile on her face, Julie tucked back into the bedroom and stood there, thinking. Thinking, within a very hot bedroom. She put her hands upon her hips, thought about how she disliked heights and then leaned back out the window and gazed down.

With a thought and a vision of her brief glimpse of the bare-chested man sitting on the fire escape above her, she spoke a thought aloud, "It is not too high, and this apartment is hotter than twenty-seven Hells are."

Off Julie ran to the kitchen. She pulled a bottle of wine out of the refrigerator, took a wine glass, poured a tall glass of wine and off she returned to the bedroom window. On the way, she grabbed a handful of magazines, a small battery-powered transistor radio, and made her way to the window. First, she set the magazines and radio out on the metal deck of the escape, then she carefully placed the wine atop the magazines. Julie took a deep breath, ran in her mind with a few further attempts at convincing thoughts that the fire escape was not too high, and with the courage of curiosity, Julie climbed out on the deck of the fire escape. Once she cleared the window, Julie sat down as quickly as she could, with a death grip on the metal rails surrounding her. Once Julie garnered some strength over the fear of being four stories in the air, she managed to look around . . . not down . . . but around.

A gentle summer breeze drifted across her skin and the air seemed suddenly to be somewhat refreshing as the heat of the day slowly drifted away. The sunset was glorious, fabulous beauty set within a cityscape of old mills and factories as the sun licked the horizon of the mountains on the outskirts of the city.

Julie's travels and now living in the northern section of her home state provided her with a new sense of how distinctive New Jersey was. Until now, Julie had no idea of what New Jersey was actually like. It was quite amazing that northern New Jersey was so diverse, old cities, worn-out streets, yet mountains, green fields, gardens, rivers, pristine lakes, and just a little farther south from here, are endless miles of gorgeous beaches and coastline. New Jersey was certainly a unique and marvelous place. It was not only the winding asphalt of the turnpike and parkway. The serene sunset helped Julie's fear and spirit to calm, and while she admired the breathtaking colors that the heat of the day created within the rays of the sun, Julie relaxed her death grip and reached for her wine. First, a long sip of the wine and then armed with a relaxed spirit, Julie managed to lift her eyes up above her and she tried to catch a covert glimpse of the man sitting two stories above her.

Julie could easily hear the rattle and the tap of the typewriter keys, even above the noise of the city streets clamoring below her. Whatever it was that he was typing, he did so very intently!

The angles were not the best for her line of sight. It appeared as if the man sat upon a piece of wood, which he used to bridge the metal grates of the deck of the fire escape, and he placed his table with the typewriter and his chair upon the wood. If Julie tilted her head a bit and leaned her body out just a little, she could see that a metal pail with the necks of beer bottles sticking out of it sat next to the man. Julie leaned back on the metal rail and took a sip of her wine. She did not want to risk the man looking down and catching her looking up, but she did so with a coy smile. It seemed so cute to see the man sitting out on the deck, a pail of cold refreshment at his feet, enjoying the sunset and the breeze while working on something quite intently.

How had she not seen him before this? He did not ride the bus in the morning, Julie never passed him in the hallways, nor did she ever see him on the streets or even in the most frequent meeting place for all the residents of the apartment building, which is in front of the trash chutes. Did he just move in? Julie now was intrigued.

A few more sips of liquid courage brought some more relaxation to Julie, and she gathered some courage to lean out and steal another glimpse of the scene above her head. He was indeed quite handsome, dark features, thick black hair that he wore a little on the longish side, which, despite the breeze at six stories in the air, remained well groomed. He tapped away on the keys of the typewriter, not lifting his eyes, but pausing on occasion in order to reach down and take a sip of beer from one of the bottles stuck in the ice bucket. When he did so, Julie admired how his arms and chest muscles moved and rippled a little. Even sitting down, Julie could tell that he was tall, his legs were long and his chest and arms were lean and strong, and with a deep breath, Julie thought, very sexy too.

On the horizon, the sun dipped even lower, and the night stole the remaining light away. But for Julie, the scenery remained captivating. Whenever the man moved from his work post, Julie moved too. She did not want to be seen staring at him, so when he leaned in for a sip of beer, Julie sat back on the railing of the fire escape. The young woman smiled as she realized that she did not need the magazines, or the radio for entertainment, Julie instead, sipped the wine and thought how she loved her new job, and despite the grit of the neighborhood and the atrocious heat, she loved her little apartment and now, well, her horizon brightened considerably.

As darkness started to fall, Kent knew that he had precious little light remaining. At six stories in the air, the summer breeze still felt glorious, but despite the atmosphere, and a little inspiration from the beer running through his veins, Kent felt as if the storyline he had just worked on for the last hour or so, went nowhere. He leaned back on the railing, studied the words and the paragraphs he wrote and after rereading his words, he angrily tore the paper out of the typewriter, crumbled it up in his hands, and tossed it unceremoniously upon the deck of the fire escape.

He took a fresh piece of paper and loaded it into the typewriter, while mumbling, "Too quaint. Too romantic and very stupid. If someone loves a person, they should just tell 'em so. Building snow people to send a message. I need something more direct, a little edgier. Everything that I just wrote. It really sucks."

And off he started to type once again,

"There was a knock at the door and he glanced at his watch to take note of the lateness of the hour. He was not expecting anyone, and he was puzzled as to who could be visiting him. He pushed the off button on the remote control to shut off the television. It had to be his best friend, Roy stopping by. No one else would do so, and besides, it was not as if he had many friends. If it was his best friend that was stopping by for an unannounced late-night visit, he did not want to have to explain the bouquet of roses sitting on the kitchen table. While a slightly harder and more forceful knock sounded at the door, Kent pondered what he would tell Roy of his failed plan of courtship. After all, the stupid planning failed, and she virtually ignored him. Being slightly embarrassed at buying the roses and failing in his plan of asking her for a date, and not even having the courage to give the roses to her, he scrambled off to the kitchen, picked them off the kitchen table and slipped the bouquet into a cupboard."

Kent finished typing. Once more, he leaned back and read very carefully what he just composed, and once again, his frustration at his composition induced a similar reaction.

"Too contrite. More of this nonsensical drivel. I guess tonight is just not my night for creativity. Why not just give her the flowers?"

Once more, another crumbled paper ended up on the metal deck of the fire escape.

Magical things float within the summer's breezes.

Unbeknownst to Kent, the crumbled papers at his feet lifted in the gentle breeze and carried in the air. A twist of the breeze and turn of the wind currents carried the papers along until they floated in the air toward the fire escape outside the bedroom window of apartment number 402. There, they drifted and landed onto the metal deck where Julie sipped her wine and admired the last fading glimpse of the sunset. It was as if the papers were silent messengers of a magical allure.

Is fate real? Does it actually exist? Is everything predetermined and was the twist of the wind that caused the crumbled papers to float upon Julie's lap a breeze sent from another place? The wind could have moved in another direction and blown the papers away forever, to be lost in the maze of the city. Instead, fate intervened.

Julie reached out and captured the wayward papers in her hands and immediately she realized from where they came. She knew they were failed efforts of literary ventures from the handsome man who worked above her. The papers afforded Julie a propitious glimpse into what it was that he was working on up there. Rather anxiously, she opened the crumbled papers to read them. Her heart pounded, and her mind raced with thoughts. Perhaps they were technical papers or reports required for his job, or maybe he wrote a sports column, or travel brochures, or something else?

A million different ideas.

In the fading light, Julie anxiously read the few heartfelt paragraphs about the snow people and about the demonstration of love, which the character created. The handsome young man was writing fiction, and he was writing about romance! He was a writer! Furthermore, Julie could not understand why he rejected these thoughts. There were no typographical errors, and the compositions were, in her opinion, wonderful. What caused the rejection of what was in her mind, two wonderfully romantic scenes? Flowers, hearts, and a touching display of love and romance. Why did the character want to hide the bouquet of flowers from his friend? Is this character shy, insecure, introverted? Julie tried hard to piece together the two sections of the story and to figure out what it was that the handsome writer was working on in his unusual, but exclusive, writing nook.

As the sun finally dipped and disappeared below the horizon and Julie finished reading the papers, she could not help but to smile. Fate had delivered love, which escaped while on a voyage from a soul.

It floated and danced gracefully in the air and miraculously landed in her lap.

As the summer waned, Julie would often sit out on the fire escape, covertly watch, and listen as the handsome writer feverishly worked above her head. Fate did not allow any additional glimpses of what it was that he was working on up there, yet Julie had a pretty good idea.

Julie approached the superintendent one early autumn afternoon as Aviv swept down the sidewalk in front of the apartment building. Julie had finished work, and she just stepped off the bus. Despite her best efforts to cross paths with the man in apartment in number 602, he remained elusive.

Julie asked, "Ave, I must ask, there is a man. He lives on the sixth floor, two apartments above me and well, I was wondering. . .."

Aviv smiled, stopped sweeping, and before Julie could even finish her question, the superintendent answered, "Kent Lambert. He works in the Foodworld supermarket on the corner up the road here and he attends a junior college at night. Studying writing. He writes books or tries to write books. He is single. I think he mentioned that he is divorced. Regardless, he is a very nice young man. Quiet, very much keeps to himself. Pays his rent two days ahead of time. Here and there a friend of his from work comes by, some guy named Roy. They drink beer and play card games together. He is older than you are, but he will be a perfect catch for you. Love knows no silly boundaries such as age. It means nothing. He is not Jewish, half or otherwise, but my dear Julie, as you know, we cannot all be perfect."

Julie laughed and smiled, and now, in a bit of posturing, she stood with her hands on her hips.

After sharing a good laugh with the superintendent, Julie playfully reprimanded Aviv, "That is not what I wanted to know. I thank you for the information and the attempt at matchmaking, but you jumped to conclusions before I could even ask my question."

Aviv returned to his sweeping and gently shook his head while commenting, "So, what else is there for a gorgeous young woman to know about a handsome young man?"

"If you would allow me to ask, then this would be so much easier."

"Then, speak and ask."

Julie felt the superintendent had indeed missed his calling and he should have officially become a rabbi.

In a roundabout confession of sorts, Julie asked the question that she fully intended originally to ask as a covert cover-up for her ulterior motives. In her heart, because of his wisdom, she knew that Aviv knew of her attraction already, but at this point Julie chose to stay with her original plan.

"He sits on the fire escape outside his bedroom window and types his books. I guess that you allow it. That is what I wanted to know. If it is allowed or not? You know, sitting on the fire escape. I think that you would have stopped it by now if it was not allowed."

Aviv stopped sweeping again, and this time he propped the broom up under his shoulder and rested upon it. The superintendent very much tended to his flock of tenants in such a caring manner.

He gently smiled and spoke in a soft and caring voice, "Technically, no, it is not allowed. Neither is cooking out on the metal monsters, nor sleeping out there when the apartments are sweltering steam baths, or sitting on the deck, sipping wine and carefully watching a handsome man working on his literary masterpiece without being caught staring."

Julie could not help herself. She rushed in and gave Aviv a warm hug and embrace as the two of them laughed.

"I love you, Ave. You are my second father away from home and you *are* my rabbi."

"Oh my, do not let Mrs. Ave see us making whoopee out here! She will be jealous, but I do love you too and if you want to catch him, be out here early, say, around five in the morning. He leaves for work very early and returns early in the afternoon. That is why you do not ever pass by him. He has to be at work very early to unload the early produce trucks. Set your alarm, be out here early and I assure you that you will catch him."

The embrace ended and Aviv picked his sweeping back up, and then suddenly stopped. He tucked his broom under his arm and made a muscle with his one arm while playfully smiling and joking. For a brief second, Julie was puzzled as to Aviv's actions, and then when she realized what he was doing, she smiled in slight embarrassment.

"You have admired Mr. Lambert's muscles and sexiness. I will tell you that, when I retire and relax in Florida every day, instead of sweeping this dirty sidewalk, I hope to read one of his books. Something tells me the young man is brilliant, and he is constructing a great pile of material that will one day make him very famous. Until then, he unloads trucks and works very hard. I also will tell you what you already know—that the unloading of those trucks gives the young man those big muscles."

That evening, before retiring for the night, Julie set her alarm clock for three in the morning.

The morning was cold and crisp, and while there was just a slight sense of apprehension at venturing out on the city streets in the front of the apartment at such an early hour, Julie spotted the light glowing in the first-floor apartment of Aviv Finkelstein. She could also see in the driveway of the home across the street that Mr. Henson was already warming up his old car in the driveway to prepare to go off to work. Even at this hour, there were people around. In her heart, she knew the rabbi of 181 Belmont Avenue was up early watching and anticipating that his information would come into play today. Julie was in luck and she had timed her early rising perfectly. The front door to the apartment opened while Julie fiddled with her purse, searching for her bus tokens. Her plan was to go into the office and take advantage of the extra early start to catch up on work.

Early rising had some extra benefits. Even if they were carefully planned ahead of time.

Julie turned around when she heard the door open and finally, there he stood in front of her. Tall, lean, and yes, close up, he was even more handsome than she ever imagined. How could they live so close to each other for so long and not meet until now? It was worth the wait. His dark eyes glowed in the city streetlights and his smile immediately melted her heart.

"Hello. Good morning," Julie squeaked as he smiled at her and passed by. He was wearing a light jacket to offset a bit of the autumn morning's chill, so admiring his build was not to be. She wore a dress covered with a heavy sweater. She almost wished that she had opened the sweater to display just a bit of her figure, but she had buttoned it up to break the chill. In her mind, Julie thought, her breasts were not much, but right for now, they were all she had to go with. That and her smile. Since her smile and her gentle breasts were what she had, Julie went with them. She casually unbuttoned her sweater just a bit.

"Hello. Yes, good morning," Kent Lambert greeted Julie and then he stopped and stood in front of her. He seemed to be searching for words beyond the simple greeting. Words that would not come, spoken words that did not arrive easily for the fledgling writer. Within written words was where he comfortably hid. On top of his outward shyness and struggle with words, it was as if he was a bit startled to meet someone at this early of an hour on the front stoop of 181 Belmont Avenue.

In actuality, in Kent's mind, he thought, 'What a meeting that it was!'

Julie stopped fiddling with her purse. He seemed so shy and slightly introverted, yet strong, vulnerable and so very sexy, too.

Julie reached out her hand and took full advantage of the covertly planned meeting by introducing herself, "Hi, I am Julie Granatelli. I live in apartment 402. Have to go to work a little earlier than usual today. I work downtown."

Julie carefully watched while his eyes wandered, first off to the city street and then to the street lights, and finally over to the Henson's driveway, where Mr. Henson's old car stood as if it were a silent warrior waiting to go into battle, while it was warming up.

She thought about how making eye contact was not his strong point. For some reason, for such a handsome man, he decidedly lacked confidence in his own presence.

"Oh yes, downtown."

While he spoke, his wandering eyes finally locked on her face. Julie never allowed her eyes to leave his. This was her chance.

"Kent Lambert." His gentle grasp felt very warm, especially so on a cold morning as he gently held her hand and melted her heart.

Kent explained, "Well, I am lucky. Only have to walk two blocks up Belmont Avenue here to go to work at the supermarket. I work at the Foodworld as a produce manager. It is not my dream choice of careers, but it pays the bills while I go to school. Say, it was my pleasure to meet you, Julie. I have to be off. Cannot be late. There are trucks waiting to be unloaded. By the way, I live in apartment number 602. How funny, I live two floors above you and we never met until now. I will see you around. Maybe soon. I hope we can meet soon. Please, have a nice day."

Now, it was Julie's turn to become lost in words, as she fumbled and stumbled and managed to eke out a weak, "You too. It has been my pleasure to meet you, too. I too, hope to see you around."

He waved, and he was off into the early morning light. Julie sighed, and her heart melted while she admired the view as he walked away. Tight fitting dungarees and oh my, his walk did not lack the confidence that his mind, and to a certain extent, that his words did too. How she wished that she would have revealed more of what it was that she knew and that she was aware of what he was working on, but in her mind, she knew that it was not the appropriate time to do so.

Recalling the papers that she held in her purse and she kept close to her at all times, Julie had another idea.

A better idea. Julie could write a little too. She did rather well in English Literature, creative writing, and in compositions in high school and in college, and felt as if writing a little was not out of her circle of talents. She could finish a few paragraphs of a story.

She turned, bounded down the front steps with an extra spring in her step, and made her way to the corner bus stop. The number fourteen bus was due any minute now.

After peeking at the first meeting on the front porch of Kent Lambert and Julie Granatelli, while hiding covertly from behind the curtain of their first-floor apartment window, Mr. and Mrs. Finkelstein warmly embraced, and they kissed for a very long time.

When you have found your soulmate, and you have been in love forever, you often kiss and embrace for a very long time.

Julie took advantage of the extra early time in the office. The bus rolled right on schedule and she arrived hours early for work. At that early hour of the day, there were very few riders and very few stops to make along the line. When Julie arrived at her desk, she took Kent's formerly crumbled papers out of her purse and carefully flattened them out in order to remove some more of the wrinkles. Being an expert typist, Julie quickly retyped the paragraph about the snow people on a fresh piece of paper. Once she finished typing Kent's original material, Julie began to compose additional paragraphs. While contemplating her writing, Kent's dark eyes and handsome face flashed in her mind, and Julie had to admit she was feeling a little bold. It had been a long time since she faced the rejection of her longtime boyfriend and had a man in her life. Julie also had a vivid picture in her mind of Kent sitting bare-chested on his fire escape.

A very vivid picture of him.

Julie studied the words that Kent wrote and with her fingers poised upon the keys of the typewriter, she thought while she read them.

"Chapter One, Put Your Hand in Mine. The snow was deep, and it was wet enough to build a fantastic snowman. Early in the morning, before anyone rose, while the snow still lay undisturbed and unblemished, he went to work. Right outside her apartment window, he rolled the first balls of the body of the snowman. Then another, and another, and finally, he rolled a snowman's head. A quick dash into the apartment for a hat, a trip to the cellar to the coal burner for the boiler, yielded some pieces of coal for the eyes and then the finishing touches, some sticks cut from the remnants of old rose shrubs for the snowman's arms. He even picked strategic sticks, which resembled hands at the end of the arms. Then, he worked hard and built a duplicate snow woman right next to his snowman. The same stacked snowballs again, but this time, he placed a woman's scarf around the snow woman's neck and a woman's hat on the head. Strategic sticks allowed the two, snow people to hold hands.

Now, the ultimate romantic touch, he pulled from his coat pocket, the red paper heart that last evening, he cut out of red construction paper, and now, he carefully pressed it into the snow of the snowman, right in the spot where his heart would be. When he returned to the apartment, he gently and silently slipped the note under her apartment's door, a note which asked her when she woke up to look out her bedroom window. Actually, he phrased and laced the instructions with some additional love."

Julie's fingers typed as the next few lines came into her mind. With a giggle and a coy smile on her face, she inserted her namesake into the storyline.

Why not? Indeed, Julie was feeling quite bold.

Away, Julie went on a voyage of her soul. That is what happens to you when you write with emotion. You allow your own soul to go on an unknown voyage, a journey far beyond where you can actually venture. However, in your own mind, with your own words, you can venture to wherever it is that your heart desires, beyond boundaries, and fulfill your wildest dreams.

Her fingers pounded the keys.

"When the licks of the early morning light danced between the shades covering the windows in her bedroom, Julie rose, she wiped the sleep out of her eyes and the curiosity over the amount of the snowfall that the storm brought overnight, was overcome by the need for a hot cup of coffee. She tucked her feet into her slippers, shivered a bit at the cold of her apartment, wrapped her body in her robe and paddled off to the kitchen. When she crossed the front hallway of her apartment, she stopped at the sight of a piece of paper, slipped under her door, and a piece of paper that now sat on the hardwood floors of her apartment's hallway. Julie tried hard to focus, realized that she would do better with her eyeglasses, but she was too anxious to see what this strange paper was about to stop and find them.

Julie bent down, picked it up and read it aloud to the walls and her soul, "When you awaken from what I hope was a night of rest, filled with visions of joy and happiness, when you lift your gorgeous head off your pillow, please look out your bedroom window."

With the note in her hand, Julie dashed off to her bedroom. She stopped off to pick her eyeglasses off the end table and with a burst of energy; she tugged at the handle of the window shade and it rattled toward the heavens. At the sight of two snow people with their hands joined in love, the snowman wearing a red heart, Julie's eyes filled with tears of joy and her heart melted in love. He did love her! How gloriously romantic of him to announce it in such a manner. Julie sat there for what seemed as if it were forever and wondered what her next move would be. Should she rush off to his apartment, knock on the door, and fall into his arms? Should she slip a note under his door, professing her love for him? A million different scenarios raced through her head.

She prepared a cup of coffee, sat in front of the window and studied the two snow people in love outside her window. Julie needed to shower, dress and put her coat and hat on and visit the snow people in person. She could see them rather clearly from four stories up, but on the ground in the snow would be the best view.

Yet, if Kent saw her studying them, what would be the next move? He was so shy, so introverted, and he lacked confidence. Here, he had made such a bold move to proclaim his love. Now, Julie needed to do so too, and do so, in such a manner to boost his fragile ego and gently tell him how amazing and wonderful that he was. With a sip of coffee rimmed with a perfect smile, she knew what her plan was going to be.

Julie waited until ten o'clock that evening. She then dressed in her best dress, a black cocktail dress, slightly tight fitting, very low-cut, and amazingly sexy. She decorated her ears with her best earrings that were glowing white pearls in each ear and she framed her long neck with a white pearl necklace. A splash of perfume, and adjustment of her cleavage, and while she looked in the mirror, in her opinion, she would knock the shyness right out of this man. Until now, she had not reacted to the snow people, nor acknowledged his efforts at romance at all. She was sure that his fragile ego was now suffering.

Julie had the magic cure.

Their love would echo to the moon and back again. After dressing, she grabbed the bottle of wine, two wine glasses and left her apartment, locking the door behind her. She walked the stairs to the sixth floor, walked over to his apartment door and knocked rather gently upon his door. Behind the door, Julie could hear some noises, some reaction, and when the door did not open within a few minutes, Julie knocked once more. This time, she knocked a little harder and louder. When she heard the locks spinning and the deadbolt unlatching, she was sure he now knew it was her.

The door had a security peeper.

When Kent threw the door open, she smiled, posed, held the wine and the glasses in the air and in a rather husky voice, she asked, "If you are not planning on venturing outside and building more romantic snow people, will you join me? After all, since those two amazing snow people are holding hands and enjoying love on a cold, winter's night, then I think that we should do the same."

Kent gently took the wine bottle and glasses from her, reached out his hand, took Julie by the hand, and led her into the apartment. When he set the wine and glasses on a table in the hallway, he closed the door behind Julie, flipped all the locks, slid the deadbolt, and took her in his arms. A long kiss led to a glorious evening. Their love and lovemaking indeed, did echo all the way to the moon and back again."

Julie sat back, studied what she just wrote, and dreamed in her heart that it would be a reality. Yes, she wrote in a rather bold manner. It was worth a shot. Was this love at first sight? Maybe. No, not maybe . . . yes. She continued to type and construct pieces of the story, pieces, which when put together went through a budding romance, to a serious involvement, to a romantic proposal, all the way to a glorious wedding and then some babies. . ..

Over the next few weeks, while additional rejected pieces of his thoughts mysteriously drifted to her fire escape post and the wayward pieces of paper allowed Julie a venture into Kent's expressions within his mind, Julie took them and relished them. She knew that with the change of the seasons, her opportunities at obtaining insight into Kent's mind were escaping. Even now, Kent only worked on the fire escape on weekends, and when he did so, Julie quickly dashed out on her metal monster and hoped that fate and the wind would bring her more pieces of the puzzle. Why this man rejected such an amazing story was a mystery to her. Perhaps he was afraid of his own dreams and the pain of sharing them. On her lunch break, or when it was slow in the office or her attorney was in court, Julie worked on the story. Julie knew that she constructed what in her heart; she hoped would become a reality.

On his walk home from work on a Friday evening, Kent Lambert bought a six-pack of Big Boulder beer at Trio Liquors on the corner of Cook Street and Belmont Avenue. He just finished working another double shift at the Foodworld supermarket and it was time to relax. This had been a long week, and aside from his labors at his full-time job, his novel just would not come together. There was something missing, a vital piece of the puzzle, and despite his best efforts, for some reason, the writing just would not flow.

It was now early November and while the year waned; the darkness came rather quickly. Kent still sat on the fire escape, not to escape the heat of the apartment, but for the pleasure of enjoying the view and the wonderful, crisp air. He was very happy that the endless and unrelenting heat of this past summer was now a memory. Autumn heralded in a welcome change in the weather. It felt wonderful when the chill of the evening settled in and the sun decided to fade away and give way to the night.

When Kent approached the front steps of 181 Belmont Avenue, he turned and waved to young Mr. Henson. The young man, who looked very much as if he was simply a wayward hippie, but nothing could be farther from the truth, was in his usual post on the front steps of the house across the street. Above all, the young man was consistent. A number of times, on his way home from work; Kent had stopped and spoken to the young man. They had shared some conversations about books, writing, and reading. It turns out that Mr. Henson was a fascinating young man. He was pursuing what he dreamed would turn out to be a career in professional hockey. Kent thought that it was very unusual to run into a man playing such an unusual sport in the midst of this urban grit. Mr. Henson also dabbled in a little writing of his own, and Kent found out that he was an interesting young man. The budding hockey player possessed a charming personality, a sharp and brilliant mind and a peaceful soul. Kent was currently stuck on the novel's storyline and he bounced some ideas for the novel's plot off Mr. Henson. It seemed as if the novel was stuck in the mud. He started and stopped it more times than he wanted to count. The young man had some solid suggestions for Kent to overcome his writer's block. It was easy to see that he had a great talent for writing, and he hoped someday to be able to exchange more ideas and materials with him. No doubt Kent enjoyed his company.

After the exchanges of waves, Kent turned to walk up the steps of 181 Belmont Avenue, when he noticed Julie Granatelli sitting on the front steps of the apartment house. When she looked up and saw Kent approaching, she smiled widely. Her smile lit up the cold evening and honestly, it sent shivers up and down the spine of Kent Lambert.

She was gorgeous.

Ever since they had met in the early morning hours in the midsummer, they had run into each other quite often. Kent had to admit that he staged and planned some of his random meetings. He did so after he tapped Mr. Finkelstein for some more information about Julie's schedule and patterns. Other times, the meetings seemed as if they were random meetings. On the other hand, could it be that Julie planned them? Kent wanted to believe that Julie did so, and that she planned some meetings. As usual, Kent's usual shyness prevented him from engaging in anything other than some general conversation and exchanges on neutral subjects. The weather, the bus routes, where to shop downtown, goings on within the apartment building, the blaring rock-and-roll from the hippies. Kent wanted to ask her for a date, but he was not sure that Julie was interested in him. His past romantic adventures still stung and lingered within his soul and heart. His confidence waned too much to risk another rejection, and this young woman was too special for him to deal with a rejection from her! No, he was better off lying low and waiting for some more signs.

They were about to arrive.

"Hi, Kent!" Julie almost shouted and she was obviously very enthusiastic at the sight of him; she even stood up from the steps and waved.

Kent waved back, and as he approached, he set the paper bag filled with the six-pack of beer down on the steps.

"Hey, Julie. How are you? Been some time since I have seen you. Have you been working long hours?"

"I have been, and I just stepped off the bus and was walking up when I saw you heading down the street. I thought that I would wait for you and we could catch up a little. Nice evening . . . it sure is a far cry from those sweltering days of summer. A little chilly, actually."

After finishing pronouncing the air temperature as chilly, Julie pulled her sweater around her and hugged it tightly in a testimony of her opinion. It was a wool sweater but it might have been just a little light in fabric for the temperature on this autumn evening.

Kent sensed her chill and commented, "Maybe you need a little heavier outwear, perhaps a jacket." This was his chance. He thought how this time, Julie obviously waited for him, and so he had better not blow it. Time to make a move and shelve the shyness. This is a special woman.

He reached in the paper bag, pulled out two bottles of beer, and held them up in the air while saying, "It would be nice to chat a little. It was a long day, a long week. You want to sit out here and share a few cold ones? Do you like beer?"

Julie smiled; she sat on a step, waved her hand in the air and patted the step next to her.

Here was the chance that Julie had been waiting for,

"Sure, a beer would be great. Ave might have a rule about it, but he will yell at us and chase us away if we are breaking any of his many rules. But the beer might make me a bit colder, I might need to run and pick out a jacket from my apartment or . . . you might need to sit very close to me and keep me warm."

"I can do that and a little more, too. Here. Please, take my jacket. I have a heavy sweater on and I actually enjoy the cold."

Kent graciously removed his jacket, and while Julie sat on the steps, he gently placed it over her shoulders. Julie smiled and hugged it while noticing that the jacket had a glorious scent. It was his smell, and it was intoxicating to her soul. Kent spun the tops off the bottles, handed Julie one of the bottles of beer, sat next to her, and held his bottle in the air for a toast.

"Deal. Cheers."

It was a magical evening and the conversation and connection were magnetic. It was as if they had known each other for all of their lives. This evening, only reinforced what the two of them already knew. It had been love at first sight.

Overhead, in the November sky, a glorious full moon randomly took turns hiding behind clouds, shining brightly upon their love. The moon cast a captivating spell on the night sky and the setting.

A few times, the combination of cold beer mixed with the chilly air and Kent did slide in close to Julie, and even hugged her once to ward off her shivers. In Julie's heart, she hoped that he would stay close to her and keep snuggling with her. But Kent always drifted away after a quick hug.

The six-pack of beer slowly expired. They shared a walk to the corner to Trio Liquors for another one, and while they walked, Julie gently took Kent's hand while they crossed the busy street. His touch was warm and gentle on a chilly evening, but much to Julie's dismay, the clasp gradually faded after a few steps along the sidewalk.

Julie sensed his shyness, but she also sensed his attraction to her. A few more beers polished off, and before they even realized the time, it was very early on Saturday morning. When they finally decided to call it an evening and gathered up the empty bottles and bag, and together, while wearing a bit of a beer buzz, they walked down the hallway and up the stairs of the old apartment. There was little doubt that both of them hoped how this evening would end. However, inside of Kent Lambert, the courage to do so faded, and instead of the rest of the evening reinforcing their new love, it ended with a gentle hug, an exchange of telephone numbers and a promise to speak sometime tomorrow. Kent even mentioned something about having drinks and then some dinner. It was a rather anticlimactic end to the evening, especially so after such a magical beginning. When Julie bid good evening to Kent, smiled and closed the door to her apartment, she stood inside the door and the smile remained on her face. Yet, in her heart, she sighed. While flipping the locks and sliding the deadbolt, she knew she had fallen deeply in love, but did not exactly know how to help Kent overcome his lack of confidence and shyness.

Kent walked slowly through the hallway and then he climbed up the long flights of stairs to apartment number 602, thinking during the entire walk as to how, despite his best efforts, he messed up what was a wonderful evening. Kent simply could not make the moves that he wanted to do toward Julie. In reality, he felt as if he had fallen deeply in love with her, and that fact frightened him. Romance did not turn out too well for Kent Lambert.

Right now, the pain remains. In his heart, he never wanted to be hurt as he was with his first marriage and feel so wretched ever again.

Ever.

December brought an early winter and Julie prayed and wished and hoped that it brought with it some early snowfall. She now had a plan. A perfect plan. Finally, to let Kent Lambert know how much she cared, how much she loved him and to show him how special he really is to her. All she needed now was some snow.

A special snow, a snow that packs tightly, a snow that often arrives in the earlier parts of December and in the early part of March.

Despite Julie doing everything she could do in order to coax Kent onward, the romance between Julie and Kent progressed slowly. In defense of Kent, there were some extenuating circumstances, aside from his obviously cautious approach. Kent was very busy these days. Kent had some challenges at work, he was covering a few extra shifts while the store was short-handed, and he was still attending school, so fitting dates and romance between their schedules was not always easy. Yet they did fit in dates laced with vague hints of romance with some shopping trips, and many bus rides to downtown Paterson to catch movies and to enjoy some pizza afterwards. However, most of all, they enjoyed romantic dinners at Gabby's Cabin, which was an old restaurant right across the street from the apartment. It was next to the Henson's house, the interior darkly decorated with oak and pine wood trim. It had dim lighting and quiet music piped in for a backdrop to their romance. Gabby's Cabin served good tasting food. Nothing here was overwhelming or particularly memorable, but it was perfect for Julie and Kent and they found a quiet booth to call their own.

They even had their favorite server, who was a kind and

a gentle older woman named Mary, who understood what it was like to be falling in love. Mary left them alone to enjoy the moments. Mary had been there once, too.

A long time ago, but Mary held those memories in her heart forever. Now, Mary enjoyed watching the romance develop from her own point of view, and she could relive her own special days of her life.

In reality, Gabby's Cabin was nothing extraordinarily special, but with their limited budgets, it was very special to Julie and Kent.

Within the old neighborhoods such as this one in North Paterson, New Jersey, there are a million special stories tucked into a million special places. All we need is someone to tell us about them.

Gradually, gentle hugs turned to kisses on the cheek and then finally, one evening, a passionate lover's kiss, but it ended right there.

Julie understood there was such intense and lingering pain within Kent's soul. Kent told his story, and Julie shared her story, too. Since she loved this man with all of her heart and soul, Julie was very willing to wait. She understood his pain remained deep and to rush Kent would be a mistake. This man needed to heal his heart before his soul could voyage onward. Somehow, Julie had to convince Kent that a new love would heal his broken heart.

"A winter storm warning is in effect for northern New Jersey tonight. A fast moving, early winter, or actually, a late autumn storm will dump as much as eight inches of wet snow upon the city and outlying areas tonight. Luckily, it is arriving Friday night and will be out of the area by midmorning on Saturday, and with the weekend, storm crews will have plenty of time to clean up to prepare for Monday morning's rush."

The radio sitting upon Julie's kitchen counter spouted the weather forecast and Julie knew that it also broadcasted the answer to her prayers. Julie ran out of her apartment. She rushed to the front porch of the building and looked out upon the city. Tilting her head to the heavens, Julie could smell the snow in the air.

It smelled so glorious to her.

Leaving the front porch, she returned inside and gently tapped on Mr. Finkelstein's apartment door. The old superintendent answered the knock and smiled when he saw that it was his favorite young woman stopping by for a visit.

"Ave, so sorry to bother you. Do you have a minute? I need a favor and I will need your help. I will not be able to lift something and will need your strong back and muscles to help me. Early tomorrow morning, maybe very early. This has little to do with apartment business, but you are my rabbi. You will need to read this little story that I have co-written."

"Of course, of course. Please come inside, dear Julie. We have to read a story? Oh, my, yes, okay, Mrs. Finkelstein will make us tea. Do you want tea or maybe some red wine? We have kosher red wine. Come in and tell me what it is that you need."

After filling in Ave and working out the details later on while alone in her apartment, Julie cut out a giant heart from some red construction paper.

That evening, a very special snow fell upon north Paterson, New Jersey. It was a snow filled with dreams. Each snowflake contained parts and pieces of dreams, and when they fell individually and mixed in with the rest of the flakes, the dreams all interlocked and became one.

Aviv Finkelstein waved to Mr. Henson and his son, who were across the street working and clearing the snow from their driveway. The old car sat in the driveway warming up; even from across the street you could see the warm smoke puffing from the tailpipe into the cold air. It was five o'clock in the morning and Aviv commented to Julie,

"How nothing stopped that man from going to work."

Even Saturday snowfalls.

"We must make the snow woman have a grand smile, gentle curves and glorious breasts." Ave smiled at Julie and he continued to convey his reasoning, "It needs to be realistic."

Julie shook her head and laughed at Aviv's suggestions. They continued to work in the snow, and as they lifted the final pieces into place, and Aviv helped Julie lift the giant snowballs needed to construct the snow people, both of their hearts filled with joy. Pieces of coal from the basement coal bin, which usually fed the old boiler, now made glorious smiles and sticks pruned from the remnants of the old rose shrubs, made arms and interlocked hands. Then there was a red heart stuck into the snow of the snow woman, right near those glorious breasts, packed out of snow filled with love. Aviv hugged Julie. They kissed each other's cheeks, and Mrs. Finkelstein came out into the snow and did the same. In fact, tears ran down the cheeks of the old woman, because she too could feel the love contained in the snow.

A tap on the car horn, some quick thumbs up and a wave, and Mr. Henson and his old car rolled up the snowy streets as the previously steady snowfall gradually slowed. It was quite apparent that Mr. Henson approved of the snow people too! Young Mr. Henson finished shoveling the sidewalk, waved his shovel in the air in approval of the snow people, and the young man smiled warmly at the sight of their work.

Early morning light filtered down and the darkness slowly waned. Julie and Aviv's grand creations were finished. There, the two snow people sat in the side yard of the apartment, directly below Julie and Kent's windows. A testimony to their love. The old number fourteen bus rumbled by them, the snow chains on the tires slapping time on the snowy streets and the city snowplows followed along, carving away the snow and making cavernous paths in the streets. The bus driver waved at the sight of the snow people, and the snowplow driver gently tapped his horn in approval.

With the conveying of many warm thanks, a few final hugs, and wishes of good luck, Mrs. and Mrs. Finkelstein left Julie with just the touch needed for the final part of her plan. They handed Julie a bottle of their finest kosher red wine and bid her a final farewell. They knew Julie needed to work quickly before Kent might awaken. Julie took the envelope with the carefully constructed story lines neatly tucked inside and with joy and love in her heart; she silently slipped it under the door of apartment number 602.

Now, if her plan worked, all she needed to do was to wait until ten o'clock this evening.

This would be a very long day.

Gradually, the snow ended, and the sun peeked out from behind some clouds. Passers-by admired the amazing snow people sitting in the side yard of 181 Belmont Avenue. The old city bus chugged up and down with the glorious sounds of the tire chains still slapping time upon the asphalt. In addition, the city snowplow made a few more final passes on Belmont Avenue, with the driver now smiling at the thought of the testimony of love he saw in the side yard of the old apartment building. The driver also smiled at the thoughts of how much overtime he just packed into his paycheck.

In celebration, the driver of the snowplow lit a cigar.

In the basement of the old apartment building, the old boiler puffed steam in the basement and sent heat up through the old building, spitting and steaming inside of old cast-iron pipes. Occasionally, where the old pipes joined into each other, steam popped, spit, and drooled, a mixture of steam and condensed water out of the joints. Mr. Finkelstein did the best he could, while he fought another battle with his basement nemesis. He packed the leaking joints of the old pipes with steel wool and coated them with a compound in an effort to minimize the steam's escape.

Not too much changed here. The apartments were stifling in the summer and for the most part, despite Mr. Finkelstein's best efforts, freezing in the winter.

Old is old, but on the sixth-floor of the old apartment building, there was a change and something new was born. Inside of apartment number 602, a man's heart glowed with love, and outside, what was once a dark and snowy sky now filled with a glorious sun. The day warmed, and snow and ice dripped from the ledges and bricks of the old apartment house, and the snow people sagged in the sun, but it did not matter too much. Even when the snow people sadly melted into a spent pile of coal, along with some trimmed sticks from rose shrubs, the red heart will remain.

Snow filled with love turns into water that feeds your soul and cleanses away the pain.

Kent Lambert slipped out the side door of 181 Belmont Avenue. His plan was to work his way to the bus stop on Burhans and Belmont Avenue. There, out of sight, of the front door of the apartment building, he would catch a ride on the number fourteen bus and head for the florist. He needed to purchase a bouquet of red roses. His plan included using the side door to return to his apartment because this needed to remain a surprise and even if he wanted to knock on the door of apartment number 402, grab Julie and hold her in his arms for now and forever that plan just would not work.

In the basement of the old apartment building, from his well-worn boiler battle post, Mr. Finkelstein heard the side door open and then slam. While peeking out of the smutty window, the old superintendent smiled at the sight of Kent Lambert making his way across the snowy side yards.

Julie waited until around nine thirty or thereabouts. She then dressed in her best dress, a black cocktail dress, slightly tight fitting, very low-cut and amazingly sexy. She decorated her ears with her best earrings with glowing white pearls in each ear and she framed her long neck with a white pearl necklace. A splash of perfume, and adjustment of her cleavage, and while she looked in the mirror, in her opinion, she would knock the shyness right out of this man.

Julie had the magic cure.

Their love would echo to the moon and back again. After dressing, she grabbed the bottle of kosher red wine, two wine glasses, and left her apartment, locking the door behind her. She walked the stairs to the sixth floor, walked to his apartment door and knocked rather gently upon his door. Behind the door, Julie could hear some noises, some reaction, and when the door did not open within a few minutes, Julie knocked once more. This time, she knocked a little harder and louder. When she heard the locks spinning and the deadbolt unlatching, she was sure he now knew it was her.

The door had a security peeper.

The plan was sealed and their love was now forever.

When Kent threw the door open, she smiled, posed, held the wine and the glasses in the air and in a rather husky voice, she asked, "Since it stopped snowing and we cannot go outside and build romantic snow people, I thought that I might have a better plan. A plan for now and maybe forever? So, Kent Lambert, if we are not planning venturing outside and building more romantic snow people, will you join me? After all, since those two amazing snow people are holding hands and enjoying love on a cold, winter's night, then I think that we should do the same."

Kent gently took the wine bottle and glasses from her, reached out his hand, took Julie by the hand, and led her into the apartment. From behind his back, he handed her the glorious bouquet of red roses and after they admired them together; he set the wine and the glasses and the roses on a table in the hallway; he closed the door behind Julie, flipped all the locks, slid the deadbolt and took her in his arms. A long kiss led to a glorious evening. Their love and lovemaking indeed did echo all the way to the moon and back again.

With the arrival of the cold of the evening came the celebrations of life. On the first floor of 181 Belmont Avenue, you could hear the big band music playing from the Finkelstein's apartment. Inside, between sips of kosher red wine, the old couple danced the night away in the living room, while their love and romantic magic filled the air. Even after all of these years of marriage, they were still very much in love.

From the Lopez's apartment, the sounds of dancing feet whipping around on hardwood floors during a salsa dance echoed into the old hallways. It was just a little too early but, shortly between the echo of Spanish horns and guitars from the Spanish music playing from the Lopez's apartment, the jam session of rock-and-roll would begin with Zale and his bandmates.

On the sixth floor, in apartment number 602, well, it was a much different type of celebration. Suddenly, the old boiler chugging along in the basement was not required to generate any heat. It was certainly hot enough in apartment number 602.

No boiler required.

Within the old neighborhoods such as this one in North Paterson, New Jersey, and old apartment buildings such as 181 Belmont Avenue, there are a million special stories tucked into a million special places.

All we need is someone to tell us about them.

"Ave, it looks as if the mail brought you some kind of gift of some sort. Or a package of something, it looks as if it is a book."

"Close the door, honey. The heat is crazy today. I don't want to have to fix that air conditioner today. Not today, too hot out there. Want to relax here in my chair and drink red wine so that we can dance later. Sometimes, I miss that old sidewalk and the snow too. Not too often, but some days I do. Florida is so hot. We can't even walk to temple without sweating terribly."

Mrs. Finkelstein smiled at her husband's remarks. She closed the door and walked over to his easy chair and handed him the package. Mrs. Finkelstein knew that he loved living here in Florida and spending time with their family, but she had to admit that she missed certain parts of New Jersey too.

It did get very hot here in Florida.

One good thing was that there was no boiler required.

"A gift? A book? I have no idea what it can be," Aviv said while opening the cardboard flaps of the package with his pocket knife. With Mrs. Finkelstein watching intently with waves of curiosity overcoming both of them, Aviv peeled away the cardboard and from the inside, he removed what was indeed a book. A hardcover, with a glorious picture of two snow people sitting in a bed of snow. The snow people had sticks for arms and their sticks interlocked as if they were holding hands. One of the snow people was a snow woman and, on her chest, right near her snowy breasts, was a large, red heart. He fingered the book, opened it, and flipped through the pages. The back cover of the book had a picture of the two coauthors holding what appeared to be twin baby girls in their arms.

"Well, I'll be," Aviv Finkelstein immediately started to wipe away his tears, as his wife wrapped her arms around his neck and his wife began to cry. Between tears of joy, Aviv read the cover aloud, "Love on a Fire Escape, by Julie and Kent Lambert."

Later, on the same day, back in the old neighborhood of north Paterson, New Jersey, Mr. Paul John Henson, walked into the old kitchen at 182 Belmont Avenue. He banged and bumped his equipment bags filled with hockey gear along the way and made his way into his bedroom of the old house. The young man just returned from a road trip. Playing professional hockey and living his dream.

"Hi, Mum. I am home. We won!" He called out to his mother, while announcing his arrival home.

"Oh, good! I am in the bedroom folding laundry on my bed. Nice to have you home, Paulie. Come in here and tell me about the trip and the game. I am sure that you brought me some disgusting, sweat-filled laundry of a hockey mess. I can do a load right now. Oh, yes, you received a package in the mail today. I set it on your bed. It looks as if it is a book."

"Thanks, dear Mum. Yes, I got it. I do have laundry, and yes, it is a disgusting hockey-related mess. I am sorry, but you know how it is." Paul John called out as he picked the package up and carefully studied it.

The young man remained puzzled as to the contents. As far as he could recall, he had not ordered anything. He flipped open the cardboard flaps of the box and pulled out a book. It was a hardcover book, with a glorious picture of two snow people sitting in a bed of snow. The snow people had sticks for arms and their sticks interlocked as if they were holding hands. One of the snow people was a snow woman and, on her chest, right near her snowy breasts, was a large, red heart.

The young man smiled widely at the sight of the cover

and he read the front cover aloud, "Love on a Fire Escape, by Julie and Kent Lambert. Very cool."

He fingered the book, opened it, flipped through the pages, and studied the picture on the back cover of the book with the two coauthors and their lovely twin girls.

Many babies and a glorious family life.

Once again, he spoke aloud his thoughts, "Geez, amazing, dreams fulfilled. Good for them. He is living his dream out too and writing for a living. Writing with Julie. Can't wait to read it. What a fantastic end to their story. Good for him, he must have married her. Lucky guy, she is a stunner. I remember when they built the snow people there in the side yard."

Across the street from the Henson's home, in the basement of the old apartment building located at 181 Belmont Avenue, Mr. Jose Lopez worked in the basement of the building, fighting the old boiler, trying hard to convince it to puff out just a little of steam. He read the notes that Mr. Finkelstein gave him, he needed to understand what to do when the fire eye decided not to see the flame.

Now, Mr. Lopez danced the salsa with the old boiler.

On the front steps, Miss Rosa Lopez slowly walked up the steps while she studied the basement lights of the building. She just stepped off the number fourteen bus and by seeing the glow of the basement lights, Rosa realized that her father was working once again on the troublesome boiler. Rosa grew up in this old building and from the age of seven, she knew of the temperament of the silent monster lurking in the basement. Not too much changed here. The apartments were stifling in the summer and for the most part, despite her father's best efforts, freezing in the winter.

Now, Rosa was in her early twenties and her plan was someday to escape the confines of 181 Belmont Avenue, if she could only meet the right man.

Before she could make it to the front door and open it, it suddenly swung open and a man . . . a lean, tall, and very handsome Latino man swung the door open in front of her. Rosa jumped back to avoid the door and the young man jumped, too.

"I am so sorry! I hope that I did not scare you or that the door hit you?" The young man reached out and gently held Rosa's arm to prevent her from tumbling backwards.

She carefully studied him. He was stunning and her heart immediately melted. He might be a bit older than she was, but love knows little in the way of boundaries. Yes, indeed, the heat was on inside of her heart.

No boiler required.

Rosa gently spoke in Spanish, "Estoy bien. Gracias."

Then she smiled and gently clasped his hand.

Within the old neighborhoods such as this one in north Paterson, New Jersey, and old apartment buildings such as 181 Belmont Avenue, there are a million special stories tucked into a million special places.

All we need is someone to tell us about them.

THE END

I Write

I write to occupy the empty house that I live in.
To chase away the ghosts who dwell in all the corners.
The ghosts who float everywhere I look.
That is why I write.

I write to perpetuate the memories.
Never to forget the joy of our passion in the night or the afterglow that we shared.
To remember the laughter, to remember the good times, and to forget the sorrow.

I write to pass the nighttime and to enlighten the day.
To extend the hope, to fall inside past dreams.
To share in the times when we were all happy, before the defeat of our souls, or the crush of our spirits.
That is why I write.

I write to hide behind all the characters that I have created.
To have them say the things that I cannot say.
To experience all that I have experienced, and maybe just a little more.
To laugh when I cried.
To cry when I laughed.
To stay when I ran.
To run when I stayed.
That is why I write.

I write to recall all the people that I met along the way.
To remember their faces, to share once again in the sound of their voices.

To thank them all for what they have done for me.
To thank them for their love.
To share with them some joy they all brought to me.
That is why I write.

I write to forget.
I write to remember.
The smell of your hair and the feel of your body on a long night together.
The sound of your voice in the morning.
The sound of your whisper in the night.
The joy of my heart.
That is why I write.

I write to remember our love.
To try to chase away the pain of this loneliness.
The emptiness that will not leave me alone.
Since the joy of my memories can only bring me so far.
Then it dies.
It leaves me empty and on my own.
I cannot go any further without you and your touch.
I cannot exist to think of only our long, lost love.
That is why I write.

When my mind finally rests, I come to realize.
I write for you and for me, and for all that we have shared and all that we have.
That is really why I write.
I write for you.
That is why I write.
Only for you.

Until the End of All Time

The train ride was a long one.

It was about four hundred-miles or thereabouts. Seemingly endless steel rails, which rolled from the city where he lived, to his final destination. He did not care; all he hoped for was that it was far enough away from here.

As he sat and thought about it, on the other hand, to be accurate, it was about a four-hundred-mile train ride to the next destination. You see, in his mind, he actually did not have a final destination planned.

He only had plotted for an escape, a way out, a way to forget. Far beyond the mountains, which separated the place that he lived from the rest of the world, far beyond the top of the ridge where he would often sit on his front porch staring at the golden sunsets dipping below the rugged ridges of the mountaintops. Staring far beyond the river valley, where the winding river that fed the valley began in the icy mountains of an unknown place.

He was off seeking an unknown place. He did not actually care where the train stopped, as long as it was far, far away.

Yes, indeed, he sought an unknown location.

An undefined future, no plans, and no commitments. He sought only an escape. An escape from many things, including life, pressure, but mostly, it was an escape from the memory of her. She haunted his days, and she especially haunted his nights. When he closed his eyes, she was there. When sleep did finally come to his weary mind, when he woke, she was there again. Right in front of him, smiling, laughing, the smell of her skin, her hair falling all around her, he could even feel the touch of her hand upon his arm.

Now, escape was his only hope.

A train of around ten very lonely Pullman cars, chugged alongside a snow-covered landscape, struggling up the side of a mountainside, the steam billowing from the stacks of the locomotives, cascading down the side of the mountain and drifting down into the valley below.

Boilers, all in high fire.

He sat next to the frosty window, in the third Pullman car from the front of the train. He pressed his hand against the glass and left an imprint into the frost. The feeble efforts of the heat vent above the glass failed to warm the glass very much. He took his finger and carefully wrote in the frost gathered on the glass, "YOU ARE MY ONE TRUE LOVE." He did not know why he wrote that sentence, but it provided him with some relief to read it.

Slowly, the heat from the vent melted the words away. He sat, while sadly watching the steam billow out of the locomotive stacks and the puffs of steam drift down into the valley. When he turned, and strained his neck, to follow the clouds of steam, he thought how it was so strange that the valley seemed as if it shone like gold in the early morning sunlight.

Funny how it never looked that way to him, and he lived there for most of his life. The other side of this mountain was where the golden sunsets always were.

When the weight of life starts to crush your spirit, the golden sunsets are always on the other side of the mountain.

He did not care; he was heading in the direction of the golden sunsets, to a place where no one knows him, where he can start over. All he had was one piece of luggage, his six-string and twelve-string guitars, and a few measly dollars to his name, but it did not matter.

She would not be there.

Only her ghost would follow him.

He sat, still staring out the window, mindlessly recalling all that had happened.

"So, you can play a little guitar and sing too, eh?" The owner of the tavern asked him, while he was looking the young man up and down and sizing him up. "You only have to keep them entertained between periods of the hockey game, once the game starts back up, ya need to pack it away and shut the hell up."

The musician nodded and went to say something, but the owner cut him off before he was able to speak.

"Oh yes, my expectations are that you help clean up the joint at the end of the night, too. Think of this as a grassroots job. Ya sing a little, ya sweep a little, and I pay ya twenty dollars for the night. On Saturday night, aftah closin' we lift all the chairs off the floor, put them up on the tables and mop the floor. That will take ya a little longer, so I will pay ya twenty-five dollars for Saturday night."

"I am in. I would love to help you clean up. "

"Ha! Ya full of shit. You just want to have a chance to play and sing, eh? Ain't no one who likes to clean and mop dirty ass, beer and whiskey-soaked floors, but your honesty got ya this far, so let's hear ya play that thing and sing. What kinda music ya play, eh? My buddy heard you and said ya were good. So, watcha play?"

"Folk rock. Well, sorta folk with a rock twist. It is mostly my own stuff, but I also do some covers too."

"Folk rock, that sounds boring. Ya better stick with covers, because this is a rough crowd, full of beer-drinking, hockey lovin' guys and hard-core chicks lookin' for hockey lovin' men. Ya might not last long with some weepy-eyed, boring ass folkie tunes."

The owner looked the musician up and down as if he was suddenly reconsidering the potential of even offering the job to him.

He blurted out rather impatiently, "Well, ya gonna play something or what?"

The young man eagerly nodded. He reached down for his guitar cases and with his hands poised upon both of them, he asked the owner, "Twelve-string or my six?"

"Oh shit, I don't really give a damn. I would not know the difference! I guess I could count the strings. Just play ya best."

"Okay, I have to go with the twelve-string then. It is a beauty. I put a capo on the second fret, kind of locked into that now since I started writing songs with it during the folk era."

"Geez, I really don't have a clue whatcha talkin' bout. Just play the damn thing, will ya. I got me a beer delivery comin' any minute now. If ya stall anymore, then your ass is hired to unload the truck!"

The owner had very little patience for the technical explanations, and the musician was awkwardly fumbling and stumbling, obviously nervous at his precarious and anything but sublime audition. The young musician fumbled a bit more, adjusted the capo on the fretboard and fiddled a bit with the tuning. He then finally sat on the edge of a table, ran his fingers along the strings, and immediately, the impatience of the owner of the gin joint faded away.

The sound of the twelve-string guitar invoked such a stir within the owner's heart that it shook him to his inner soul. It calmed the owner's impatience in a manner of which he had never experienced from music before. It was beautiful, almost magical in the resonance of sound.

The owner stuck his bar towel in his back pocket; he

tugged at a chair and sat listening. When the musician broke into a song and his acoustical magic echoed around the old tavern, the owner smiled.

He closed his eyes and listened.

His friend had been correct, this young musician was pure dynamite and his voice and guitar calmed your soul. His voice was captivating, and his guitar playing was delightful.

When the musician finished playing, the only thing that the owner could manage to do was to stand up, shake his hand and say very softly and gently, "You're hired. Ya can start tonight. Whatcha name?"

"Jack Cardin."

"That's ya real name, eh? You a Canuck?"

"Yes, my real name. I am from Ontario, but far north of here. In fact, way far north. My family is originally from Wales, but we have been in Canada for three generations. Mostly, we are or were, coal miners."

The owner nodded, smiled, shook Jack's hand and gently told the musician, "Well, let's get to work, eh?"

And, start he did, a thirty-five-year-old struggling musician, rambling on the road, going from gig-to-gig, gin mill-to-gin mill, trying hard to make a name in the music world.

It was a familiar story, which everyone has heard a few million times before. He was looking for the big break, that one magical moment. Jack Cardin was from a small town in north Ontario Province, and he left home at a young age to strum his guitar along with a group of his boyhood friends.

Despite their best efforts, they were not quite good enough for professional hockey and these days, it was either play hockey, work in the coal mines, or local lace mills, or find a poor-paying position in some retail store. The most romantic story for those musical people such as Jack was, came from those musicians, who would strike out on their own, and head for Toronto or even Edmonton and give it a whirl in the music business. They heard just enough of the random success stories to keep Jack and his little group of fellow musicians inspired and dreaming. They did not have very much, but they played some mean instruments. The little band they formed played some folk-rock covers and mixed in some of their own compositions. They called their little group, "No Need to Repent."

And they lived up to their name.

The band featured an acoustic string bass and an electric bass, an electric rhythm guitarist, a light percussionist, and Mr. Jack Cardin on lead vocals, playing lead on his acoustic guitars, and featuring both six and twelve-string guitars.

Eventually, the road wore them out; the money grew lean, the empty stomach syndrome grew wearisome and their spirits collapsed. Boiling pots of beans and sleeping in the park in Toronto were acceptable in the summer, but those long, long winters were some different stories.

You see, No Need to Repent, was in fact a very good folk-rock band, however, so it seemed as if there were a few thousand other bands.

Gradually, they grew apart. First, they lost the percussionist, then the electric guitarist, and finally the bass player returned home to a life of dreary living, while working a dusty life in the coal mines.

Now only Jack remained, and he still had no need to repent. There were many lovers along the way. He was an attractive man and musicians always seemed to attract the young women.

Attracting them was not the trouble; keeping them was always the issue.

He wandered here and there, and managed to find some work in coffeehouses, taverns, pubs, and an occasional nightclub gig or two. First in Toronto, then Quebec City, then off west to Vancouver, always finding something, but never hitting the big time.

Critics and the occasional reviewer praised his voice, his songwriting, his guitar skills, but the big contract or opportunity never arrived. In between, he worked day jobs in food stores, where he grew quite proficient at stocking shelves, and unloading trucks, and he lived in cheap flats, in shady neighborhoods that all had leaky roofs and musty hallways.

In the quiet of the flats, by candlelight to save electricity, he strummed his guitar; he wrote songs and continued to dream.

By-and-by, in this little tavern, tucked just off Yonge Street in Toronto, he grew to have a loyal following. It was not an easy place to play or to make a living as a musician. This was a hockey bar, and you had to slip a quick set in while the game was between periods, calm them down, and pick the correct song for the tempo and mood of the night. You know, read the crowd correctly and by now, Jack was an expert at doing just that.

Hockey season was busy, and in the summer, the activities centered on the outdoor seating, where the burly and rough and tumble crowds of beer and whiskey drinking men, could watch the young women walk by and dream of the possibilities of spending even one night with one of these gorgeous women. When the hockey games were a memory, and the Stanley Cup awarded, when the nights were warm and the breeze was gentle, he sat on a quiet stool set off in the corner of the outdoor seating area; he strummed his guitars and tried very hard to make a name for himself.

Every night was the same, a one-man band, and it seemed as if every night could be his last gig. He never really knew when it would end. Yet, the crowd loved him; they filled a little glass jar with tips; they slapped him on his back and some of the rough and tumble types even shed a tear at his sentimental songs. Especially the ones about lost loves.

Even the rough and tumble types knew the pain of love lost.

One late August night, when the evening breezes had shifted from the states, to the wilds of Alberta, and a tinge and whisper of the autumn to come was in the air, he spotted her. He was on his stool, under the canopy, in the corner of the outdoor seating, and she caught his eye.

She hung on his every word, his every note, and the first thing that he thought of was that he had never seen such sparkling and magnificent green eyes. The gorgeous woman had long brown hair, which hung straight and framed her long neck and perfect facial features in a manner which captivated you. She was gorgeous, and even that word did not sum it up properly; in fact, there were no words. He had seen many gorgeous women hanging upon his words with stars in their eyes, dreaming of spending a night with the handsome musician, and some had actually achieved their dreams, but this woman was different.

It was a classic case of love at first sight; it just had a twist to it, because she had a male companion with her on this night and he was one of the rough and tumble types. In addition, there was this little thing about a wedding ring upon her finger. When his set was through, she came over; her husband stayed at the table sucking down beer after beer. It appeared as if beer was his primary mission and music was not his thing.

Her voice was soft and gentle, and her smile ignited his soul, "I must say, and it might just sound a bit cliché, but what is a handsome and talented musician such as you are, doing by playing a stale, beer joint like this?"

"Thank you. I do what I have to do, in order to make rent. Well, sometimes I make rent, other times, the landlord either fronts me or throws me. Hiya, I am Jack Cardin." He extended his hand and set his twelve-string down.

"Nice to meet you, Jack, but I knew that already. It says so on the sign out front." She smiled again. It was obvious that she sensed his attraction to her.

It was impossible to hide.

"Hello, I am Leigh DuPont. Mrs. Leigh DuPont and I think that I just became your biggest fan."

She turned and pointed to the table where she sat with the beer-sucking chap.

"My husband, he does not appreciate music as much as I do, but even he said that you had a nice voice. Believe me, coming from my husband, that is quite the compliment. He does not appreciate much," Leigh said while she smiled a forced grin; that was almost a shameful smirk.

Jack knew right away that her statement had a hidden meaning. If her husband was unable to recognize this rare and precious gem of a woman, of which he was fortunate enough to have for his wife, then he was a very sad example of a man. If that was indeed the case, then it was more than just tragic—it was confounding to Jack.

They began a thoughtful conversation, first about music, then about some general subjects. The connection was immediate, and powerful, and the entire time that they spoke to each other, Leigh's husband did not even glance their way. Jack did catch him checking out some of the young barmaid's backsides, while they wiggled about, serving drinks and food.

Yes, it was confounding.

Leigh DuPont was true to her word; she became Jack's biggest fan and a lot more. After set lists, on the nights when her husband did not accompany her, she would sit at a table with him and they would talk about everything, and when they ran out of subjects to speak about, they somehow would talk some more. She made him laugh and at times, he made her laugh and his songs made her cry.

She told him about her woes, not for sympathy, but for a friendly ear.

When her husband did come along, Leigh would visit quickly, and do her best to say hello, while her husband drank down beer after beer, and was lost in his nightly haze, and flirted openly with the barmaids. It turned out that her husband mostly ignored her. He was a long-distance trucker, and he did earn a very good living. However, Leigh was sure that he made a number of "unscheduled stops" along his many roads. He was seldom home, and when he was home, he was lost in a haze of beer and a drunken stupor.

Autumn arrived, a long winter set in, and the musical activity moved inside. Once more, Jack played his music in-between periods of the hockey games. Leigh came to visit, and there was more time to chat in the winter.

Hockey was paramount, beer was second, and Jack and his music lagged far behind.

It was obvious that Leigh and Jack had fallen deeply in love. It was a forbidden love, love with no future, no hope, no right or wrong, just in love. After all, her husband, despite his faults, kept Leigh fed, warm, safe, and with a roof over her head.

Jack had nothing to offer and all the roofs over his head generally leaked.

Then one night, while her husband was away, they crossed the line, and now the magic really erupted. They were not only friends but also now they were lovers, and their love set the world on fire. Now, there was no return, no way to go back, and no way to deny what they felt in their hearts.

Jack's songs and performances became more poignant, more mystifying, more captivating. Leigh's love had transformed him into a minstrel of the night and a weaver of songs filled with depth and emotion.

Her love was the missing piece of the puzzle.

What he had searched for to bring his career to the next level. Until now, he always played his music, but now he felt each line that he sang and would write.

The crowd sensed it; they felt his transformation and his

musical and emotional peak. A solid review in a local newspaper of one of his performances brought even larger crowds. His following grew larger, and for just a few short weeks, it seemed as if they would have a future together.

He dreamed of the day when he could offer Leigh something more than broken guitar strings and smoky beer halls. In reality, he could not, he would always be a road musician. Deep down he knew it, and Leigh knew it too.

When the fog of love lifted, and the dreams became just a pile of spent wonder, the fateful night finally arrived for the two lovers to have the discussion. A discussion, of which they both knew would someday come and they would have to admit they had to have.

The painful discussion would have nothing at all to do with love. There was no question as to the depth of their love and connection, but this discussion had all to do with reality.

After a long night, together, one last night of passion, it was much to his own surprise, Jack, who first brought up his yearning to leave Toronto for Leigh's own welfare. He had become a poison to her; he was going to cause trouble; he was going to cause her to lose everything, and he was just not worth it.

In his heart, he knew his temporary success would fade; his dream, however, would never fade.

When it all shook out and reality set in, the painful truth was he had nothing to offer her. Nothing except his love. Love would not pay the bills, nor feed little children, nor keep a roof over their heads that did not leak.

Jack broke the news to her gently; lovingly, and it did not go over too well.

"No, I will leave him," Leigh pleaded, "we will find a cabin in the woods, you will write some hit songs, and I can find a job. Maybe in Winnipeg. Yes, we can go to Manitoba!"

Jack held her head gently in his hands and kissed her

hair as he pushed away the tears with his fingers. He was well grounded, and his intense love for her drove him to make the correct choice.

"I would not allow you to give your life up for a road musician without any actual future. You cannot give it all up. I would leave before I allowed that to happen. I would leave and you would never find me. I would lie and tell you all that I cared about was sharing your body!"

Leigh shook her head gently; she knew that Jack was much too kind ever to say such a thing.

She tried in vain to convince him that the hit song was right around the corner, "Jack, you will write that one special song. I know you will!"

"No, Leigh. I have yet to write that hit song. All of these years and still, I cannot write it. Fanciful dreams will only bring us despair. Here you are safe, warm and perhaps, someday, children will fill your life and help to make you whole again. They will fill the voids in your soul that your husband vacates."

She looked up at him through shipwrecked eyes and asked, "And how do I fill the void in my heart that you will leave?"

"I will always love you more than life itself. We will always be together. In some way, there will always be Leigh and Jack. Our love is more than just physical between us. It is deep within our souls. We could never solely predicate our relationship upon our bodies touching as one. That act just validated and honored our love, but it is much more than that. I know in my heart, just before I take my last breath, the vision in my mind and in my soul, will be of you. Our connection is deep, it is profound, and even if we are apart, we will always be together, in each other's heart. Until the end of all time."

There, the romance ended in a shower of tears.

Jack felt the car rock a bit as the train rolled along a steep incline. He kicked at the guitar cases under his feet. He needed to confirm that they were still there. It provided Jack with some sort of comfort, knowing that the only tools of his trade that remained, or in fact, that he ever had, were still nearby.

After what seemed as if it were ten lifetimes, the train pulled into the final destination.

Jack felt a bit foolish while listening closely when the train conductor announced loudly, "Last stop. Winnipeg, Manitoba Province!"

At least now he knew where he was.

Then again, he always knew that it was the place where those golden sunsets were always slipping behind the mountains.

He wandered about, boiled a few pots of beans in the local park, and eventually found a job stocking shelves in a food market in downtown Winnipeg.

He tried hard to crack the bar scene, auditioned hard, but it seemed as if his "Toronto label" worked against him here in Winnipeg. He was surprised when the locals called him "a flatlander from the big city scene" in the smaller city out west. It was obvious that he had crossed the line between east and west. At least his job in the food market kept him out of the park.

Leigh never left his dreams, but sadly, she entered his nightmares. She was in all of his thoughts, and she never left his heart, not for one second and not for one instant. She haunted him day and night and one night alone in a cold, dark and terribly dank flat; he wrote a song. At first, it came along slowly, and the twelve pack of beer, which he consumed, made the notes and lyrics a little clearer to him. They resonated through his twelve strings and forced tears upon his cheeks.

He entitled it, "Until the End of All Time."

Two weeks later, he answered an advertisement in the

local paper, which was advertising for a musician to entertain a bar scene between periods of the hockey game. It was a position of which Jack felt that he was well suited for, considering his experience.

When Jack finished playing, "Until the End of All Time," the only thing that the owner of the tavern could manage to do was to stand up, shake his hand and say very softly and gently, "You're hired. Ya can start tonight. Whatcha name?"

"Jack Cardin."

"That's ya real name, eh? You a Canuck?"

"Yes, my real name. I am from Ontario. From southeast of here, in fact, way southeast. My family is originally from Wales, but we have been in Canada for three generations. Mostly we are or were, coal miners."

"How old are ya? I think I see some grey creeping in on the edges of that jet-black hair, eh?"

"Forty-one. I think."

"I might need ya to hang around here and help me clean up every night. Ya know, sweep and mop. Ya sing a little, ya clean a little too. You okay with that?"

"I am. I have done it before."

The owner nodded, smiled, shook Jack's hand again and gently told Jack, "Good, good. Ya sing very nicely and that guitar has quite a sound. That is a beautiful song. Sounds as if ya lost a special gal along the way, eh? She still lives in ya heart. I know, 'bout that too. Sometimes, I think we all have. I hope mine finally found her rainbow's end."

"I think you are correct. I agree. It seems as if we all have. The rainbow's end and golden sunsets, for sure, that is my dream for her."

The owner patted Jack on the back as if to provide some type of comfort. He smiled and said, "Well, let's get to work then, eh?"

It seemed as if this were a scene, which Jack had been a participant in a few times before in his life.

In the wintertime, during the hockey season, he played in between the periods of the game, but in the summer, he moved outside to a familiar stool under a canopy in the corner of an outdoor seating area. It all reminded him of a time that now seemed as if it were so long ago.

It was late on an August night, and it was a night when autumn loomed so close that you could smell it. The gentle summer breezes had changed from the south to the north and no longer blew over Minnesota and Michigan, but instead, the breeze came down out of the Yukon and out of Alberta.

On this special night, Jack Cardin sat on his familiar stool and he played, "Until the End of All time." For some reason, this evening, he played it extra well.

When he finished, the crowd politely clapped, and some cheered. Most of the crowd tonight was regulars. They had heard the song before and it was familiar to them. For some patrons, it was the first time they had heard it, it was a new song, and it seemed as if overall, they appreciated it.

That was the final song of his set and while Jack bent over his guitar case and carefully packed his twelve-string guitar away, a gentle tap came upon his shoulder. Jack looked up, and he saw a short, round, and balding man staring at him.

The man smiled, handed Jack a business card, and he spoke, "Say, Mr. Cardin, pardon me, but I would like to speak with you for a few minutes. Please, first, I need to introduce myself. My name is John Castile. I am a music and talent agent as well as a music executive with a publishing company. That last song was amazing. Is it your own composition?"

Jack stood up, shook Mr. Castile's hand, and answered, "It is. I call it, 'Until the End of All Time.' I wrote it about three years ago."

Mr. Castile smiled again, and he explained, "Well, it is fabulous. The woman who tipped me off to your talent was not exaggerating at all. This was certainly worth the long trip to listen to your entire set. That one song is spectacular, but you have an entire list of great stuff. All your own too. No covers. Impressive body of work, for sure. I would like to speak to you about coming down to New York and maybe we can discuss a recording contract and lay a few tracks down in a studio or two."

Jack's heart skipped a few beats when he realized that this might finally be his big break.

Finally, his chance.

His euphoria over what Mr. Castile was telling him suddenly became overshadowed, because over Mr. Castile's shoulder, he saw her. . ..

At first, he thought it was his mind playing tricks on him. Then, he felt weak in his knees, but strengthened in his spirit. There she stood. Once more, she returned to his life, only this time it was different. Very different. She stood with her green eyes sparkling, her smile, and her long hair hanging down all around her. His heart melted, and he had to think that hers did, too.

Between what Mr. Castile was saying and offering him, as well as once again seeing her golden smile and magnificent green eyes, Jack knew that this time, she would never leave him and he would never leave her.

Not now, not ever, not until the end of all time.

The young couple slipped into the seat on the Pullman car. They sat close together, shared a kiss or two and they smiled. It was very exciting to be leaving on an adventure to visit Toronto. They were very much in love and when you are young and in love, the world is full of rays of golden joy. While the train slowly chugged out of the station, the young man noticed how the sunlight reflected onto the glass of the window of the car.

There in the glass, he could read the words, "YOU ARE MY ONE TRUE LOVE" written on the dusty window, and now the remnants of the words reflected in golden sunlight. He reached over, pulled his lover in tightly, and pointed to the words.

Upon seeing them, she laughed and smiled, then kissed the young man very deeply.

After kissing, she gently whispered to her lover, "I guess that someone else feels the same as I do! I wonder how long ago they wrote those words on the glass?"

The young man smiled and said, "I think they have always been there and always will. Now, and until the end of all time."

THE END

Epilogue

I steal a quick glance at the clock on my smartphone. Ditched the watch a few hours earlier. Actually, I ditched the watch a long time ago. Sometime, yesterday. When it was still Saturday. No more wristwatches when I write because they put boundaries and rules on my writing edge. I am on the edge of memories and that is all that need. Time means nothing when I am rolling in the flow with ideas. Time means nothing when I am rolling in the flow with an idea.

Okay, it is 3:30 A.M. and I am just about to finish this draft. It feels good. Everything about the story feels good. Perfect. No chats, emails, or text messages on the phone. Everything is quiet and calm because normal people are sound asleep at this time on Sunday morning.

I am not normal.

Man, oh, man, Hausleben. Another all-nighter and a long weekend. A bloody marathon of writing. You really need to change your lifestyle. You really do, Paul John.

It is long past due now.

Here we go, just one big finish and this one is in the draft stage.

I type it out:

"Within the old neighborhoods such as this one in north Paterson, New Jersey, and old apartment buildings such as 181 Belmont Avenue, there are a million special stories tucked into a million special places.

All we need is someone to tell us about them.

THE END"

Done deal. I tuck my arms across my chest, lean back in my chair, study the words, and feel the flow.

Save the file. Eject, and then pull the USB drive out of my writing laptop. Plug the USB drive into the other laptop, wait for the files to sense, then open the story. Okay, now where the hell are my earbuds?

On the radio desk.

Got 'em.

Plug the earbuds in, highlight the text and push the talk button.

A golden, robotic female voice reads it to me. I listen once, then twice, and it sounds good.

Add a comma. Needed to pause there. Nice. Big ending and I love the flow. Save the files. Double check the save and move the file onto the hard drive and then onto another USB drive. I cannot take any chances with all this effort and work.

It is now four o'clock in the morning.

I swig the last drop of beer, shut off the lights, and make my way upstairs to take a shower. Another collection is complete, and it feels pretty good. I will catch a few hours of sleep and be back at it early tomorrow for the first scrub on the material. Time for a nice shower and a little rest.

Yet, as the first trickles of water hit my body, I feel the doubts creep in. They always creep in. The ghosts are always all around me.

Despite my efforts to shut down my mind, I cannot help but think, "I wonder if Julie would have really reacted that way? Geez!"

Shut down the water, towel off. Pull on my sweat pants over my bare ass. No shirt. No underwear. Sorry, a bit too much information for an epilogue. Honestly, when the flow returns, there is no time to dress. I have to get this out of my head. It is autumn and a cold night. The writing command center is 60 degrees and I am happy as I can be with that temperature. It is a good thing that I keep the shades pulled down. I climb back down the stairs and head for the laptop.

What the hell, sleep is overrated. Hausleben, write it correctly this time. You will be back tomorrow, anyway.

On the other hand, maybe you will just stay here and continue to write.

Maybe.

As I said, time means nothing when you are in the flow.

Nothing at all.

"I write to recall all of the people that I met along the way.
To remember their faces, to share once again in the sound of their voices.
To thank them all for what they have done for me.
To thank them for their love.
To share with them some of the joy they all brought to me.
That is why I write."

ABOUT THE AUTHOR

If you ask Paul John Hausleben, he will tell you that he is not an author, he is just a storyteller. His mission is to continue to write and tell stories to warm your heart, make you laugh, and sometimes make you cry, just a little. Most of all, he deals in memories, and helps you to remember the good times of your own life, and the special people who touched you along the way. Paul was born and raised in Paterson, and then nearby Haledon, New Jersey, and began writing at an early age. He revisited a writing career later in his life, and he now is the author of a number of novels, compilations, short stories and audio and video works. Most of his work touches upon nostalgic remembrances of simpler times, and tells the stories of heartfelt, humorous, and special human relationships. Other than writing, among many careers both paid and unpaid, he is a former semi-professional hockey goaltender, a music fan and music reviewer, an avid sports fan, photographer and amateur radio operator. He now resides in Somewhere, U.S.A., but his heart always remains along Belmont Avenue in good old Paterson, and Haledon, New Jersey.

Other Work by Mr. Paul John Hausleben

The Time Bomb in The Cupboard and Other Adventures of Harry and Paul

The Night Always Comes, Another story from the Adventures of Harry and Paul

Reunion, A sequel to the Night Always Comes and Another story from the Adventures of Harry and Paul

The Autumn Collection

The Christmas Tree and Other Christmas Stories. Tales for a Christmas Evening

Crows on a High Wire

The Miracle Tree, Another story from the Adventures of Harry and Paul

The Summer Collection

Special Edition: The Time Bomb in The Cupboard and Other Adventures of Harry and Paul

Tales of the Quiet Stranger in the Black Hat

Geyer Street Gardens
Beneath the Mask of a Hockey Goaltender
Another story from the Adventures of Harry and Paul

And a few others too!

You may write to the author at ctte27@gmail.com

Published by God Bless the Keg Publishing
Somewhere, U.S.A.

You may write to the publisher at
Godblessthekegpublishing@gmail.com

"Life's simple pleasures are so often the best ones!"

www.ingramcontent.com/pod-product-compliance
Lightning Source LLC
LaVergne TN
LVHW020705110826
845149LV00012B/2112
9780990697992